T0268717

THE CONTINENTAL AFFAIR

ALSO BY CHRISTINE MANGAN

Tangerine

Palace of the Drowned

THE CONTINENTAL AFFAIR

CHRISTINE MANGAN

FLATIRON
BOOKS
NEW YORK

THE CONTINENTAL AFFAIR. Copyright © 2023 by Christine Mangan. All rights reserved. Printed in the United States of America. For information, address Flatiron Books, 120 Broadway, New York, NY 10271.

www.flatironbooks.com

Designed by Donna Sinisgalli Noetzel

Library of Congress Cataloging-in-Publication Data

Names: Mangan, Christine (Christine Rose), author.
Title: The continental affair / Christine Mangan.
Description: First edition. | New York : Flatiron Books, 2023.
Identifiers: LCCN 2022055168 | ISBN 9781250788481 (hardcover) |
    ISBN 9781250788467 (ebook)
Classification: LCC PS3613.A53685 C66 2023 | DDC 813/.6—dc23
LC record available at https://lccn.loc.gov/2022055168

Our books may be purchased in bulk for promotional, educational, or business use. Please contact your local bookseller or the Macmillan Corporate and Premium Sales Department at 1-800-221-7945, extension 5442, or by email at MacmillanSpecialMarkets@macmillan.com.

First Edition: 2023

10 9 8 7 6 5 4 3 2 1

To Ron, for always reading the first and last draft—
and all the ones in between.

And to the memory of *Shadow*, whose travels took
him many places throughout his lifetime—and even
once to the shores of Oran.

THE CONTINENTAL AFFAIR

ONE

HENRI

Pardon me, but I think you're in my seat."

Henri looks up at the other passenger, a young woman of twenty-five or so, a single leather satchel held between her hands and an expression of something like suspicion on her face. She has spoken in English, and for a moment he cannot think of the correct response, the words vanishing before they have an opportunity to arrive. It's a ridiculous reaction, he speaks the language as well as his own. Still, he is taken aback, unprepared. He wishes, suddenly, that it were still early morning, that he were back in the Hotel Metropol, that he had more time.

Henri takes out his own ticket, pretends to study it.

"You see, you're supposed to be in the one just there," the young woman says, pointing with a gloved hand to the seat opposite him. She is smartly dressed in black trousers and a blouse. Her thin frame is partially obscured by her wool coat, on which hang several large gold buttons that clang together as she leans forward. He has yet to grow accustomed to the sight of women in trousers, but he thinks it suits her, somehow.

"Of course," he responds, conscious that he has yet to reply. "My apologies."

"Oh good," she says, sounding relieved. "You speak English." Her smile is small and tight, and he notices her left eyetooth is turned, curved in a way that no doubt drove some parent mad when she was a child. This, too, suits her.

He stands, indicates to her leather satchel. "May I?"

"No, thank you, I think I'll keep it close for now." Her hand, he is certain, imperceptibly tightens.

He nods. *"Bien sûr."*

They sit, then, one across from the other. The air in the compartment is stale. He thinks, watching as she sets her satchel onto the seat beside her, that he can detect the odor of those who came before them. For while standards on such trains had once been revered, all crisp napkins and polished brass, now he can see smudges on the light fixtures, slight tears in the fabric seats. He wonders when the windows were last washed.

Another passenger approaches their compartment, looks in, and turns away.

"I wonder whether we'll have it all to ourselves," she says, watching the stranger disappear down the corridor.

He thinks she sounds hopeful. "If so, I might reclaim my previous seat," he replies, then hurries to explain, stumbling over the translated words as he does so. "Sitting backward on a train makes me feel strange—not like myself."

"Unwell, do you mean?" she suggests, pushing a strand of hair behind her ear. "There's a saying about that, I think. Something about not dwelling in the past, but looking toward the future."

"An English saying?" he asks. When she only shrugs in response, he presses, "But you are from England, *n'est-ce pas?*"

She nods. "London. South of the Thames." She pauses, lets her gaze linger. "France, I presume?"

"French," he confirms, then after a brief hesitation, he adds, "Algeria."

He sees something then, reflected in her face. He wonders if he is only imagining it, tells himself he must be, for how much can this young woman know about the country he was born in and its internal strife, about Algeria and its fight for independence. She murmurs an affirmation—but no, he realizes he has misunderstood, that she has said something else entirely—*Oran*. His childhood home, whispered on her lips. He thinks back to a moment, nearly two weeks past.

She must read something on his face then, for she smiles tightly and says, "Lucky guess." Turning to the window, her breath causing the glass to fog, she continues, "Someone told me once that I should visit."

He finds his voice. *"Vraiment?"*

For a moment—longer than that—he is uncertain whether she will say anything further. There is no indication that she intends to, and he is prepared to sit back and turn away—in disappointment, he thinks—when she looks to him and says: "Yes. There's a particular view, I'm told, from an arched window in the north wall of the Santa Cruz Fort, the best in the entire city. I would have to rent a motorcar—I couldn't take the people mover, I can't bear the thought of heights. But I should like to see it, one day. That vast, never-ending blue." She pauses, takes a breath. "Afterward, I would drive the motorcar out of town, find a café that overlooks the mountains and the sea, and order *creponne.*"

He can taste it—the sharpness of the lemon, the sweetness of the sugar. It is the taste of his childhood, the smell that still haunts him, even in exile.

She turns to him. "It sounds almost too good to be true, *n'est-ce pas?*"

He is slow to answer. "*Oui.* Particularly in this weather." They both turn to the window, where the sun is lost behind the fog and cold of the early morning.

"I'm Louise, by the way. Louise Barnard." She leans across the aisle, closing the distance between them, and holds out her hand. "You can call me Lou—everyone does."

"Do they?" he asks, thinking it doesn't suit her.

She holds his gaze. "Yes."

"Henri," he responds, mirroring her lean, accepting her hand. "A pleasure to meet you."

A moment passes, and eventually they release their grip.

"Do you mind?" she asks, indicating the closed window. From her coat pocket, she withdraws a packet of Gitanes. He thinks her hands are trembling, just slightly.

"No, of course not. Allow me." He stands, opens the window, notices she still has not removed her coat. "Were you long in Belgrade?" he asks, sitting down again.

She tilts her head back, blowing the smoke from her cigarette into the air above them.

"Only a night or two."

The train conductor interrupts them then. Henri retrieves his ticket and passport from his coat pocket. The conductor looks it over, nods. He turns to the young woman, who in turn opens her small leather satchel, retrieves her ticket and passport, and hands them over. The conductor looks from the passport to the woman, then nods, apparently satisfied. "*Hvala vam,*" he says and closes the door to the compartment.

They sit back into their seats. The engines rumble and a blast of steam fills the air with its whistle. Neither of them turns to the window, toward the platform, nor do they glance toward the hall-way, toward the occasional traveler and passing attendant, luggage in tow.

Instead, they sit and stare at each other.

In the silence that follows, as they wait for the train to depart, Henri does not bring up the last fortnight, does not mention Granada or Paris and the moments they shared there, however small. In turn, she does not speak about what happened in Belgrade. There seems to be an understanding, an unspoken agreement between them, in which they will pretend—at least for now—that the past does not exist. That this particular moment, here, on this particular train, is their first encounter. He does, however, think, as he settles back into his seat, feeling the initial lurch of the train beneath him, that it is a pity—a damn shame, really—that everything about her is a lie.

BEFORE

It was the smell of *creponne* that he dreamt of most often.

That familiar scent of sugar, caramelizing in the air around him, so strong that he could almost feel the promise of the sharp lemon on his tongue, he could almost believe, in those moments before his mind had fully awoken, that he was back home. That he had only to open his eyes and he would be greeted by a pair of French windows leading out to a filigreed balcony, the strong North African sun filtering through, depending on which way the wind blew, depending on the time of day and the sway of the bougainvillea.

Henri opened his eyes.

Now in another country, another continent, he lingered in bed, allowing himself a moment more to remember. And he did, he remembered it all—motor trips to the beach, to Tipasa, to walk among the Roman ruins, to contemplate what had come before. The smell of diesel, of the sun and sand and olive trees, burned into his senses so that one could not exist without the other. He remembered going to the cinema with friends, was it the *Balzac* or the *Escurial*, he could never recall, and the image of the carpet, a deep rouge with a pattern of flowers, forever imprinted on his mind, along with the kernels of popcorn left behind in the wake of the concessions girl. He recalled the place just outside of town, where his father would take them if he was in a particularly good mood. The restaurant perched on a cliff, its whitewashed walls set against the blue of the Mediterranean, which stretched out endlessly, and all around them, and throughout it all, the smell of pine in the air. And the sun, always the sun, shining brightly—

Only it was no longer a sun before him, but an orb of light that burned and blinded, and he was no longer outside, but in a small room, cramped and dirty, entirely dark, save for that one light. He could feel the sweat pooling, dripping down his temples, sliding down his back. The sound of the shouting, screaming— protestors, he knew—just beyond the room, rose and fell, along with something else. Gunshots, he thought, though it was hard to tell, hard to translate anything through the thickness of the walls. And there was a scratching sound, though he couldn't place exactly where it was coming from. He could hear it, louder than all the other noises, as though whatever it was must be pressed right up against his ear, but when he brushed the side of his face, he felt nothing but air. He looked up, squinting against the bright light.

Two eyes, wide and accusing, stared back at him.

Henri jolted awake, his body drenched in sweat. He opened his eyes and saw the room before him, stark and barren. He must have fallen asleep. It had only been a dream, then, or a nightmare. Oran was hundreds of miles away, and his memories, the time between then and now, over a year already, and growing more still with each passing day.

The dreams, the nightmares—they were all he had left.

Sleep unattainable, Henri pushed the covers aside and decided to begin his walk to the Alhambra, where he was scheduled to be in several hours' time to collect the money.

He bathed quickly in the tiny sink that sat in the corner of his room. As he wiped away the sweat that had settled, he looked into the mirror, at the reflection staring back, and he thought of those eyes in his nightmare. He had grown used to them—the nightmares, not the haunting eyes—as much as it was possible to grow used to something so uncertain. At least he knew what to expect. A replay of that day, the one that had convinced him, finally, to leave. To uproot his life, once and for all, because the life he had been living was suddenly unrecognizable to him. Sometimes he wondered when it had happened, had known that it was gradual, day by day, month by month, so that he had been able to bend and adapt, to close his eyes to the truth around him. It had been so easy to continue, to pretend—until it was impossible.

It was still early as he left his flat, the sun would not rise for another hour or so, but he decided there was no point in putting it off. He would go to the thirteenth-century palace, and there he would do the job he had been hired to do, by people he could not say no to. Not out of threats or coercion or anything so expected, but because they were blood, which meant a certain responsibility, a certain loyalty that could not be ignored, and because he had been unable to think of a reason to say no when they first asked.

The streets were empty at this hour. Henri crossed the River Darro, the border that flowed around the fortress, without encountering a single other person. The silence suited him. Granada always seemed to be so full of people, so full of life, that he found himself desperate as of late for quiet, for space. He continued on, up the steep path, past houses, his breath becoming hard and labored.

He caught the scent of the cypress trees around him. Near the top, he paused. He had never seen the fortress up close before, his only view having been from down below. It felt strange, now, to be on the other side of it. In the meager light of the morning, peering down at the houses, he could almost understand how people fell in love with the city.

In Oran, his mother had spoken little of this place, the city of her birth. But then, she had spoken little of her past in Oran either, including her time spent living with her family in the Jewish enclave of town—*it was good for a time, and then the French came and it was better and then it was much worse*—or how she met his father—*in town*—or their ensuing courtship—*we married and I moved into your father's flat in the French town.*

Of her own home country she remembered little, only the faintest trace of orange blossoms in the air—she was little more than a baby when her family had fled Spain—though sometimes, particularly when they sat in the warmth of the kitchen together, she spoke to her son in Spanish, so that he learned enough to understand and speak it on his own. It was there that Henri had learned he had an aunt, his mother's sister, that they had grown up alongside each other in Oran, but that she had married a Spaniard who had taken her back to their home country. He was not told the man's name, and when he asked, his mother had only frowned and shaken her head, until eventually he learned not to mention that branch of the family.

When asked of the past, his mother had spoken of France, of his father's hometown. All her memories outside of Oran set exclusively in Marseille, where they had gone for their honeymoon and spent a week eating bouillabaisse and *moules marinière* and drinking pastis in bars by the Mediterranean. His father, who was born in the port city, decried it all as filthy and depressing, but his mother described it as others might describe Paris, boasting to neighbors that her family was from Marseille, never noticing the confused expressions that such an admission elicited. *What's wrong with the port here?* his father would demand, to which she would cry, *It's not the sea, is it,* and from which would always ensue a lively debate on what body of water exactly—Mediterranean or otherwise—the port of Oran overlooked and whether it wasn't all one and the same.

This, Henri soon understood, was how they spoke of things that were important—by speaking of things that were not.

The only part of her past his mother seemed to carry with her was the making of *dafina* for Sabbath. All the other religious observations she ignored, but each Friday night she would prepare the potatoes and meat and chickpeas and take it to the local baker, her name etched into the pan so that there would be no mistaking it as anything but her own. Though there was no need, really, as she was among only a few other women baking such dishes in that part of town. In the morning, every Saturday, Henri would walk with her to the baker to fetch the finished dish, which had been baked overnight on low heat, per his mother's very specific instructions. Despite this, she was never satisfied. The dish was too dry, too cold, the oven must not be working properly, so perhaps they should find another baker.

Henri thought he understood why the perfection of this one dish mattered so greatly to his mother, thought he understood what she was saying in the words she spoke instead.

Henri stopped and looked up at the Alhambra, wondering whether his mother had ever done the same. She had never mentioned it before, this magical, mythical place. Though her silence did not surprise him. It seemed a trait particular to his mother—her innate ability to leave the past behind.

Henri only wished that he had managed to inherit it from her.

The job, the collection of money no doubt earned by illegal means—and that he was now making his way, slowly, but inevitably toward—had come about in the way most things of that nature came about. That is to say, gradually and without any real intent.

Upon arriving in Granada, Henri had rented an apartment near the aunt whom he had never intended to contact—the one his mother had mentioned to him once as a boy and never again—and whom he had sought out in the end, hoping to find something familiar, something that made sense, wanting his days to take on the same shape as they had before in Oran. And it had felt nice to be brought into a family, to be part of something. To not be entirely alone. His aunt had introduced him to the others. His uncle had long since passed, but before he did, there had been children from their union, so that every time Henri went to his aunt's place it seemed he was introduced to a new son, a new son of a son, or some distantly related relative far removed. Used to the small unit he and his parents had made, Henri found it difficult to remember their names, to know who it was that he was speaking to and where they would fit on a genealogical map.

Soon Sunday lunches at his aunt's became a common affair, as did visits to the bar around the corner with his cousins, where the *cana* was cheap and he didn't feel too guilty about spending what money he had left, hidden under the floorboards in an apartment that depressed him. It had taken some time before his cousins relaxed around him. He had felt it the first time he had gone to his aunt's—a tightening of the shoulders, a narrowing of the eyes. Henri had sat down at her table and nodded before one of his cousins had raised his eyebrows and asked, *"Policía?"* It had been a collective question, and so Henri had shaken his head, had raised his voice for anyone interested, and answered, in Spanish, *"Ya no,* not anymore." He hadn't explained further, had let them fill in the rest on their own. Whatever they came up with among themselves, no doubt sprinkled with whatever tidbits his aunt had learned over the years, he was certain there would be an element of truth in it.

Soon, his cousins seemed to relax. A nod here, a *buenas noches* there. And then eventually, they began to talk with him, about the past, about money, about jobs. About the future. Henri offered little, but it was enough. They understood what he did not tell them—a man had a right to his past, after all—understood what it meant to be a man in a country that was not his own, the idea of returning to where he came from impossible. Eventually, when they mentioned the possibility of a job—nothing too important, just a package to be picked up, taken to another location—he hadn't hesitated. After all, he was fit for taking orders, his previous life had made certain of that, and so when someone gave him those once again—and not just someone, but family—he accepted.

The jobs were simple and the money easy. And Henri was always in groups of two, sometimes three or four, so it was never down to him entirely. His cousins seemed appreciative of the simplicity with which he conducted each task, the way he did not try to insinuate himself further into their world, though sometimes they tried to insinuate themselves further into his. "Come out with us tonight, celebrate," he would often hear, after they had retreated from his aunt's into the local bar.

Henri always thanked his cousin—it was never the same one—telling him that this, gesturing to the bar around him, was all the celebration he could handle, that he would see him next week, at his aunt's, for lunch. The cousin would laugh, placing his hand on Henri's shoulder. Once, one of his cousins had said, "I like you, you're smart." Henri had assured him that he was not. The man had insisted: "That's how I know you are. Only a smart man would deny such a thing." Henri didn't agree, but he didn't argue either. Instead, he signaled to the bartender and ordered them another round.

It did not matter to him that these men, cousins and nephews alike, were criminals. After all, the things he had done in Oran were criminal, though sanctioned by law, which made it worse—much worse, he decided—in the end. At least the men he surrounded himself with now were honest about their deceptions. And they were smart as well, so he hadn't worried at first about being caught, about ending up in some Spanish jail, at which point he was certain they would be quick to forget their association, bloodlines be damned.

But then—something had happened.

There were eyes on them that had not been there before, they said. Two of their own had been arrested in Tarifa, so it was obvious that someone, somewhere was talking. Henri had listened to their new plan: the money left somewhere around the Alhambra, under a bench, in a darkened hallway, just off one of the gardens. The Alhambra was popular among locals and tourists, and Henri had thought it sounded like a bad idea—ridiculous, even—like something out of a hackneyed spy novel. He told his cousins as much, but they had only laughed, had said, "Yes, like a spy novel." They spoke Spanish, in which Henri pretended to be only moderately proficient, hesitant to let them know just how much he actually understood.

A part of him felt guilty for the pretense, especially where his aunt was concerned. And yet, even before the jobs, on that very first day he had met his mother's sister, he had remembered the look on his own mother's face, the deep frown that had settled between her eyebrows at the mention of the woman before him, and he felt himself hold something back, told himself that he was only being smart. Some days he worried that his aunt knew—that she saw the glimmer of understanding in his eyes when he sat around her table for their weekly meal. Henri had taken to looking down at his food instead of at her face, which seemed too close to his mother's anyhow. He did not know how much she knew of her sons' business, but when he remembered the way his mother's face had darkened at the mention of her sister's new husband, Henri suspected that she knew enough.

The man's tone that day had indicated there would be no more questions, but Henri had shaken his head in disbelief, ignored the warning, and asked what would happen if someone else came along and took the money before he could get it. He laughed, said it was Spain and nobody rose that early, particularly on a weekend—not even to go to the Alhambra. The man had bought him another *cana* then and paid Henri half the amount owed, with the other half to be paid upon completion.

"This one you will do alone," his cousin informed him, nodding as he spoke, as if he were still in the process of deciding. "Let's see how this goes, and then we'll talk."

"About?" Henri asked.

His cousin mentioned the idea of Henri becoming more involved now that he had impressed them. After all, he was family. Henri had smiled and nodded, though his stomach churned. He pushed the money into his pocket and continued to focus on belonging, on becoming a man who had adopted a new country as his own.

A man who fit in, who was built staunchly of the present, who did not live in the past.

Henri had been told to wait on a balcony overlooking the open courtyard.

It would give him the advantage of knowing when the person with the money had arrived, without being seen himself. Once they departed, he would make his way down the stairs and toward the bench where the money would be left. The whole thing would be over in a matter of minutes. Glancing at his watch, he saw that he still had another ten minutes before the money was set to arrive. He bent down and peered out. It was difficult to get a clear view of the space without doing so. The curved windows that ran the length of the balcony all featured low ledges, no doubt built for one to sit rather than stand, as was tradition in Islamic culture. Henri debated, decided he had time, and then lowered himself to the floor.

So this was it, he thought: the oldest garden in the world. He gazed out at the roses and orange trees, at the water fountain, and the canal that ran the length of the garden. An irrigation system, he guessed. The sun had risen by then, casting its golden light across it all. It was beautiful, he knew, and he could appreciate what it was meant to elicit from an onlooker, but all the same, he could not feel it, not in any way that mattered.

It had been this way ever since he first stepped off that boat—before that even, if he were being honest. Now, he spent his days roaming the city for hours at a time, retiring to his room only after the sun had set. In between, he ate and drank, tasting neither. He slept with women but felt empty afterward, crawling out of their beds and leaving before the sun had risen. He was a shadow, he often thought, or a reflection of someone who had once existed. On some nights, he climbed to the roof, looked out at the Alhambra, at the shadow she cast across the city, and waited for it to hit him, that experience he had heard others describe in songs and poems in tribute to the impressive fortress—but there was nothing, just the absence of what should have been.

Still, he did not give up hope. Every day he waited for the forgetting to begin, for his new life to take shape before him and the feeling of being adrift to leave him at last. He woke, he wandered, he slept. He tilted his head to the sun, felt the warmth on his face, but still, he could not smell the orange blossoms on the tree.

It was not that he minded the solitude. He had always been a solitary person, even in childhood, had played mostly with another boy at school, Aadir, the two of them a spitting image of each other until one day they were not, until politics became more important—or, at least, the politics of their parents. They had been friends through *sixième*, and though chances were they would have drifted away naturally, sometimes Henri wondered. After, it had been his first love, Marianne, around whom he had rearranged his world. Marianne, who had been his friend and then something more, so that her eventual departure had left him shaken, left him rearranging once again, but this time only to allow acquaintances and colleagues, never anything that bordered on real intimacy. He couldn't quite explain the reason for his detachment, but he found it easier to operate within the world when it was placed at a distance.

At Université d'Alger, Henri had leaned toward history and linguistics, had even considered life as a professor. His parents had been proud of his degree, his mother especially so, but when she turned to him after graduation and said how wonderful it was that he could always read Voltaire in his spare time, he had understood. Afterward, Henri joined the gendarmerie, just as his father had, knowing that it would make his parents proud, which would, in turn, make him content. And it had worked. He had shaped his days around making them happy, had molded his life on being what his mother wanted—which was another version of his father, what she considered to be a good man. A man who came home each night, who drank little, argued less, and did not spend his money on games and drink and women. It pained him, sometimes, to realize that his mother's definition was so narrow, so limited. But he did his best to do what was expected of him without questioning what he himself expected. Just as he did what the army asked of him, his role in the gendarmerie required another set of instruction, another set of rules to live by, as dictated by others.

And then his parents had died in a motor trip to Madagh Beach. A crash along the coastal road that had stopped traffic for several hours. Henri had seen the aftermath, the broken and steaming bits left behind, the stains on the road. They were gone, and after, Henri found that nothing was the same.

The next day, he had stood outside the Porte du Château-Neuf, leaning up against its façade, the heat against his back, and feeling, for the first time, the constraints of his uniform. He pulled at the collar, wondering whether he had managed to damage it in the wash. But he knew it wasn't that. It simply did not fit him anymore, if it ever had. Over the years, his occupation had become harder to endure, the *événements*—that inconsequential word they all used, as if it could hide what was actually happening—now escalating across the country. Algerians were demanding their independence from France, and it was all reaching the point of no return. The *événements*, they all said, eschewing names like attacks, bombings, riots, *war*. Even his parents, before they passed, had waved it away with their words, their shrugs, their refusal to recognize that the country they had made a home in for decades no longer wanted them.

Henri had found himself tired, then, of words that were used to avoid saying what needed to be said, that provided distance, a distorted truth, when the truth was plain to everyone. He thought he could see where the French were headed with the Algerians—though it often surprised him to be included as such, having never actually set foot in the country of his nationality—could predict exactly how it would end, and with such astounding clarity that it made him wonder whether everyone else could as well, whether they were simply too stubborn or too frightened to admit it. And then December had come, and the protests had begun, and his need to leave solidified. The things he had witnessed that day, the interrogations that he had participated in during the days after—where before he had been content to do as he was told, to not think of the consequences—they were all that occupied his thoughts. He saw exactly what it was that they were doing, what he himself was doing, and he knew that he could not continue with it any longer—not for another day, not for another hour.

He had stood, his final night, in the Santa Cruz Fort, overlooking Oran. My city, he thought, the city that he had lived in for his entire life. A city that would soon no longer belong to him, or he to it. It was a strange thing, he often mused, to be identified as a Frenchman by the world, when he himself did not. He looked out at the port, at the ocean just beyond. Here was where he belonged. He looked to the old town, where lines of laundry were strung in between the buildings, a tenuous link that held each together, a jumbled mess that made it impossible to pick out where one began and the other ended. He reveled in its chaos, breathing it all in: the smell of baking somewhere in the distance, nutmeg and cloves, fennel and anise, and for him, lemons, always the sharp, bitter scent of lemons. *This* was real. *This* was home.

And yet, it no longer was. The Oran of his childhood was now only that: a place that no longer existed, perhaps had never existed at all, anywhere other than within his own memories.

Afterward, he packed up all his things—there wasn't much, he had lived the spartan life of a soldier—procured a fake passport from one of the many contacts he had made during his time in the gendarmerie, and then boarded a ferry, looking out onto the Mediterranean as it took him away from the only place that he had ever known, a place that marked and defined him. He went to Marseille first, his father's birthplace. He spent a week in the city, feeling more foreign than a tourist. Eventually, he found himself in Spain, in Granada. In the city his mother could not remember, except for the delicate smell of orange blossoms.

When he had first arrived in the red-ochre city, Henri had walked the remaining walls, found them familiar but different enough, and decided it would do. At least for now. His mother had been Spanish, after all, even if she had not remembered what that meant. In this way, he often thought, they were similar.

He was French and didn't know what that meant either.

There was a rustle from somewhere below, the sound of pebbles underfoot.

Someone had entered the garden. At the sight of the stranger Henri hesitated, uncertain whether this was the person he was expecting. Something told him it wasn't. For one thing, the woman standing below him was carrying a suitcase—and while he supposed that could be where the money was hidden, he thought it seemed too obvious, thought that the people they usually dealt with were more clever in their techniques. There was also the way she walked—slowly, as if she were in no hurry, as if she had no real business there. Again, it could be part of the plan, but Henri thought it didn't seem right, the way she paused at the flowers, at the water fountain, as though she were a tourist, taking in the sights. He frowned, glanced at his watch. It was still early; perhaps this woman had only wandered here by chance. He paused when he saw her face. At the expression that had settled there, one of reverence and awe at her surroundings. He felt himself at once envious of this stranger, of this person he had never met.

Henri averted his gaze, tired of the emptiness that he carried inside him, tired of gazing out at this city, its splendor, and feeling nothing at all. Even these gardens—when he looked at them, he only thought of another garden, hundreds of miles away, of the sloped terraces perched atop another city, its buildings stained not red but white, its length filled with roses and geraniums, oleander and fig trees, so that even now, here, he could—

A scream ripped through the air.

Henri started, bumping his head against the arched window. He cast his eyes over the garden, over the woman, searching for the source of her pain. When his eyes fell on her, he could see that she was still alone. Bent slightly forward now, hands balled into fists, eyes squeezed shut, the scream emitting from her was raw and guttural, so that all at once, he was reminded of home, of the sound that the local women emitted to show joy or grief or rage, and he wanted nothing more than to clamp his hands over his ears, to close his own eyes at the image, at the memory. Henri had never been able to put into words what it had felt like to leave Oran—a decision that hadn't felt like a decision at all—and yet here it was, all that grief and anger and inner turmoil reflected in the face of the stranger standing below him. It was uncanny, he thought, like seeing a double of himself, the idea so strange and grotesque that he found himself unable to break his gaze.

The woman looked up toward the balcony.

Henri stepped quickly from the opening, pushing himself against the wall, hoping that she could not see him, that she had not already seen him—but she *had*, he was certain of it. She had looked up and directly at him and yet—he thought of the sun, of the shadows, and he told himself that it was impossible. She could not have seen him standing there, watching. He slowed his breath, tried to compose himself, knowing it was ridiculous to come undone by such a thing as this.

By the time he looked back, it was already too late.

Only after was he able to make sense of it. How another woman, the one he had been waiting for, must have entered the garden, must have strode down the length of the canal and toward the interior of where he now stood. By the time he returned his gaze to the scene below, the woman was all but gone, just a flash of her leg, a black heel, and the money—the money she was supposed to have placed carefully in the hallway, underneath the bench—somehow fallen to the ground, littering the garden below.

The strangeness of it caught him off guard. He knew what had to be done, knew that the moment called for him to abandon his post at the window, to turn and run down the staircase to retrieve the fallen bills before they had time to float away on the wind, or into the hands of someone else. He did none of these things. Instead, he remained still, his gaze fixed on the woman with the suitcase who had screamed. He felt his breath catch as he took in the look that appeared on her face as she noticed the fallen money—something smart and calculating—and he smiled, despite himself.

He knew that he needed to act, knew that there would be consequences—terrible, far-reaching consequences if he did not retrieve the money—and yet, Henri continued to stand hidden in the shadows of the balcony, watching as she gathered up the money, as she placed the bills into her suitcase. Until she began to walk away from the Alhambra.

He followed her out of the fortress.

From there, they continued across the city on foot, Henri following her in a halting pattern as she retraced her steps, from one street to the next, sometimes circling back on herself, and leading him to the conclusion that she was not from Granada, for even he knew the streets better than she. All the while he kept telling himself that he would take back the money: when they reached the next block, when they turned the corner, before they came to the next cathedral. He didn't, though. He only continued walking, continued following until, eventually, they passed the bullfighting stadium that sat on the outskirts of town, and from there arrived at the only place left that made any sense: the bus station.

Inside, Henri followed her, trying to remain inconspicuous, turning his head whenever a guard walked by. She went first to the toilets and then to a bank, where he saw her hand over a few of the bills. He cursed. Now would be the time to stop her, before she could spend any more of the money that he would no doubt be responsible for replacing. He didn't think a familial connection would earn him much special treatment where matters of money were concerned. From there, he watched as she found a café and ordered a coffee. Henri perched on a stool on the opposite end of the bar, in a position where he could see her, but she could not see him—not that she would have noticed. She seemed unaware of anyone at that moment, her eyes focused intently on the cup she held between her hands.

All this he observed, and yet he did none of the things that he knew he should do, that common sense, that years as a gendarme had conditioned him to—instead, Henri waited until she purchased her ticket, then went to the counter and told the agent that he wanted the same fare as the woman before. The man behind the counter frowned but didn't question him.

Henri looked down at the bundle of tickets he was handed, at a series of tedious connections that would eventually end in Paris. He didn't give himself time to think—he headed toward the platform.

The first time the driver stopped for a break, he saw the confusion sweep over her face as she took in the changed landscape.

Prior to this, she had been asleep for several hours. Henri was seated several rows back, and even though he couldn't see her face, he could tell by the lolling of her head. He had been fighting sleep for a while now himself, the heat of the bus pushing down on him, the hours he had lain awake the night before wearing. When the bus came to a stop, she jolted in her seat, and he along with her.

He stood, stretched, listening to his body groan in protest. He was too old, he thought, for such a journey, though there were several men and women decades beyond his own age who had sat without complaint through the last few hours, who would presumably do so for the hours still ahead. Henri lingered on the bus as long as he could, until he worried he was in danger of drawing attention. He moved toward the exit, head down, though he could not stop himself from glancing as he passed by, from noticing the look that had crossed her face—panic, he thought. He pushed himself forward, told himself not to intervene.

In the café, which sat adjacent to the petrol station, he waited for her to exit the bus. When she finally did, it was with her satchel clasped between her hands with such force that it looked as though she expected someone to pry it from her at any moment. Once inside, she followed the other women to the toilets. He ordered a *café* from the bartender, dropped a sugar cube in it, and drank, trying not to blanch at the bitterness. Spanish coffee was one of the many things he had struggled to reconcile himself to while in Granada.

When she returned from the toilets, she seemed more confused than before. She moved slowly, as though still laden from her deep sleep. He wondered when she had last had anything to eat, whether she was used to the sun, to the heat of this place. Her pale skin suggested this wasn't likely the case.

She came to stand at the bar, taking the seat next to him. He inhaled, noticed a small freckle on the side of her neck. Her hand half lifted—for the bartender, he thought—and he noticed the way it trembled slightly. Henri wondered then whether she spoke Spanish, even just a small amount, and if not, whether that accounted for some of the confusion he had seen when the bus driver had stopped. He thought perhaps she had only been asleep for his announcement, but now, he wondered whether it would have mattered.

Henri ordered two *ponche* from the man behind the bar and pushed one toward her, advising her, in Spanish, to drink. She only looked at him, confused. Not Spanish, then. He tried again in French, and he saw something bloom behind her eyes—an understanding, he realized. He told her to drink, then ordered a *bocadillo*. He asked her where she was going, how far, and told her to eat as well.

"You'll feel better soon," he promised.

When she thanked him, he knew she meant it, could see the

relief written across her face. He knew, too, that he shouldn't have done it. He wasn't there to take care of her. He was there to get the money, to bring her back. He didn't think she would remember this, her eyes were too glassy for a clear recollection. Still, he knew that he was taking too much of a risk.

Henri felt something shift against him—her leather satchel, he realized. He had not noticed it before, but now he became aware that it half rested on his thigh. He looked down, saw the glare of the zipper just below him.

It would be easy, he thought, to take the satchel now, to instruct her to follow him out of the café and toward the petrol station, where surely there was a mechanic of some sort, an automobile that could be purchased for cheap. They could be back in Granada by night.

Or he could just take the money, leave her to continue on to wherever it was that she was planning to disappear. He didn't think she would protest, didn't think she would attempt to claim that he had stolen what belonged to her. It would lead to questions, to possible searches, and something told him that this was the reason she was here, on this dusty autobus, rather than in the comfort of an airplane or train berth. The anonymity was part of her plan. It was also what made her vulnerable in that moment, her mind and body addled by the heat.

There wasn't much time left to decide, he knew. He lowered one hand, inching it closer to the satchel. It wasn't too late, things hadn't gone too far. He was certain there was a telephone somewhere in this town. He could let them know back home when to expect him, that their money was safe. It would all be over before it really began. He could go back to Granada, continue with the life that he had been leading, and this, today, the moment in which he now found himself, would be only a memory, a temporary upset on the road that he found himself on.

His hand rested on the leather bag, his grip tightened—

The bus driver stood up and called out: "*Atención, pasajeros!* The bus leaves in five minutes."

Henri felt the woman next to him shift, and he withdrew his hand quickly, as though he had been burned. He felt his face flush, certain she had noticed, that she had felt the pressure of his attempt, and so he hastily translated the bus driver's warning to divert her attention. She only nodded, looking down at the sandwich she had been breaking into small pieces before placing each in her mouth. His own stomach ached, and he wished he had thought to order another.

Henri stood, carefully transferring the weight of her satchel back onto her own lap. The bar had grown too close, too stuffy, and he found himself desperate to be outside.

Back on the bus, Henri frowned when he realized that her own seat was still empty. He turned to look out the window, squinted, but they were parked too far away, the café itself too dim to be able to peer in from this distance.

The line of passengers slowed to a trickle. Even the oldest passengers had already made their way from the café to the bus now. Surely, the woman would realize that she was the sole remaining passenger still seated in the café. Unless that was her intent. Henri half rose from his seat. Perhaps she had felt his hand on her satchel after all. Perhaps she had realized what that meant and decided to alter her plan.

He was already standing when he saw her emerge from the café.

Henri sat down, patting his pockets, pretending to have located whatever missing object had caused him to stand, just in case anyone was watching. From his seat at the window, he watched as she made a brisk sort of dash, clutching her satchel as she ran.

When at last she stepped onto the bus, he felt something loosen in his chest—until he realized that she had passed her seat and was instead heading for his own. Myriad possibilities flew through his mind. They were endless, though they all seemed to conclude in the same fashion, with Henri thrown off the bus and into some makeshift jail in the middle of nowhere.

She had reached him now, was standing over him. He watched as she thrust her hand in her pocket—perhaps she had a weapon, perhaps she meant to threaten him—and produced a sandwich, wrapped in a napkin. "*Gardez votre coin*," she said, her tone brittle.

He frowned at her choice of words.

"I can buy my own lunch," she said. "*Maintenant nous sommes quittes*. Now we are even."

He barely had time to murmur *merci* before she turned and disappeared to her own seat at the front of the bus, leaving him certain of at least one thing now—she was not French. He thought of her words and smiled.

Henri still didn't know why he had followed her or for how long he would let this strange adventure continue. But he did consider then whether he wanted to follow such orders anymore. He had thought what he wanted was familiarity, that there would be a measure of comfort to be found in such directives, but somehow, he was back to where he had begun, once again being told to do something that put another in harm's way. He wasn't naïve. He knew what would happen to her if he brought her back, what they would do to her in order to get the answers they wanted. He thought of those last days in Oran and shook his head. He would be damned if he were to contribute to any more bloodshed.

Henri turned to his right, where an older woman was watching him now, smiling, looking pointedly at the sandwich he had just received. He could only imagine what she thought—what all of them thought. He tried to imagine the expression on their faces if they knew the truth. If they knew who had been on the receiving end of the telephone call that he had just placed, moments before the bus had departed from the rest stop, the owner of the petrol station granting him several minutes in exchange for several pesetas.

"Something has happened," he had said when they picked up the receiving end.

"We expected you back by now."

"Yes, I know." He considered how best to explain. "The woman who was supposed to drop the package—"

"Si?"

Henri could hear the confusion, though he could not recognize the voice. There was one man that he liked better than the rest, who seemed to him more real than the others in the way that he spoke to Henri, in the way that he listened. He tried, as he explained, to imagine that it was him on the other end of the line. "She dropped it in the garden. Maybe it was an accident, a hole in her bag, in her coat, I don't know." And he didn't. There was something strange about it, he thought, the way the money had just fallen so easily, so effortlessly. Not just a bill here or there, but everything, or so it seemed. And all without her noticing, without a single glance back. What had she done, he wondered now, when she had noticed it was missing—had she retraced her steps in an effort to discover its location, had she contacted her own people, frantic at her mistake—he didn't know, hadn't waited to find out before deciding to follow the woman who had taken the money.

"Were you able to retrieve it?" the voice questioned.

"Someone got to it first." Before the voice could interject, he explained, "I have her in my sights. I'm only waiting for a less public opportunity to take it back." He looked around. "In case there are *policía* around."

There was a pause. "When you bring the money, bring her along as well."

"Yes," he replied, trying not to hesitate.

"Where are you now?"

"A rest stop, several hours outside of Granada. She's headed to Paris," he said, regretting it, although he didn't know why, couldn't explain the reason for wanting to keep this piece of information to himself. He glanced around, as if expecting one of them to appear before him. "I'll be in touch as soon as I've retrieved it." He disconnected before they could answer, before they could tell him damn the public nature of the place, just take back the money and go. It was the only thing to do—the logical and sensible side of Henri knew this.

And yet.

He couldn't say to them what he was already telling himself—he wasn't ready. It was a moment of insanity, he knew, following this woman to Paris, a full day's journey. It was madness. But then he thought of her face when she had screamed, and he decided to ignore the rest. He could feel it, though—a sense of duty, loyalty to those he was bound by and that he had so easily cast aside for the stranger now sitting several rows away from him. He couldn't explain it, even if he wanted to, the whole thing defied everything he had ever known. But then, he thought, the current world in which he found himself was also in direct opposition to things he knew, about the world, about himself. Everything, it seemed, had been turned upside down when he left Oran, and since then, nothing had ever righted itself.

But this—Henri glanced outside, through the window that had been cracked open just an inch or two, letting in a steady stream of hot air. He wasn't certain, but he thought he could detect something, just the slightest trace in the air when the bus departed. Something floral and green.

He thought it was the smell of orange blossoms.

‡‒‡‒‡‒‡‒‡‒‡

TWO

LOUISE

Earlier, Louise had been surprised to find him sitting in the compartment—and in the wrong seat, she had noticed, glancing down at her own ticket. She wondered whether the choice had been intentional. Surprise was not the only emotion she had experienced in that moment—there was relief, she allowed, and embarrassment, too, after what had transpired in Belgrade, and anger as well. At him, for continuing to follow her, at herself, for allowing him. She was no longer afraid of him—not that she ever had been, only about what he might do—but even that threat had softened and rearranged itself after what had passed between them.

Now, she was left with an uncertainty—of how she felt, of how he felt, and what that might mean. She found herself grateful that her arrival had gone unnoticed, for she had needed that moment in the corridor to compose herself, to shake off the startled expression on her face, to decide how to proceed. Would she greet him with familiarity, speaking in French, using *tu* instead of *vous*? An acknowledgment that they had, in one way or another, been in the other's company for nearly two weeks now. No. She needed to put some distance between them, needed to rebuild the barrier that had

crumbled and fallen away with such ease. She needed, she told herself, to steel her resolve, to remind herself of what was important:
the money and everything that it meant. A new life, a new beginning. There would never again be another opportunity like this, she
knew. She would be reserved, she decided. Cold, even. The way any
traveler might be toward another stranger. After all, that was what
they were. Two strangers, traveling alone. Nothing more, she had
told herself as she pushed through the doors.

Now, she glances toward the corridor, where not a single person
has walked by, despite the passage of an hour. She tries to recall
whether there had been many boarding—surely, based on the jostling crowd in the train station that morning. But then, perhaps that
had only been for other trains that ran within the city, within the
country. She supposes most people would choose to fly, rather than
endure the tedium of a long-distance train journey.

"The age of train travel is apparently past," Louise observes
wryly.

"A train attendant once told me something similar," her traveling companion replies, turning to her. "What made you decide to
travel by rail, then?"

"I suppose I wanted to take the route while it still exists." It's not
altogether a lie. She does remember seeing the announcements in the
papers about the line cutting service, remembers feeling saddened by
the news. Though she hasn't been anywhere, not really, travel—and
trains in particular—seemed a firm part of her childhood, rooted in
all the books she had read. To finally step out in the world and find
their popularity diminished had been startling, as if the whole world
had changed while she had been stuck inside. "What about you? Not
a fan of airplanes, then?"

He seems to consider. *"Non,* I don't think so."

No, she doesn't imagine so either. There's something old-fashioned about the man before her, despite his age—which she estimates to be a good decade or so more than her own—and that assures her that he was made for the golden age of travel. There is something in his posture, his carriage, she thinks with a small grin, the way he holds himself so different from others. Even his dress sets him apart—the carefully pressed suit and tie. She imagines long, arduous train journeys and even larger steamer trunks. If she didn't already know why he was here, she would wonder that he had not booked a private berth on the train.

"And where will you go, once the train reaches Istanbul?" he asks. "Back again to London?"

"Perhaps." She allows herself a small smile at the question, wondering if she said yes, whether he would follow her there—whether he would follow her around the world and back again, if that was what suited. She turns to look out the window. "Or perhaps I'll sail across the Bosphorus and disappear forever."

BEFORE

She had wanted to see the Alhambra.

That was how it had begun. Sitting at the kitchen table, only moments after the death of her father, and her first opportunity for freedom, for escape, right there before her. She had looked down at the money—near forty pounds, a vast amount, all things considered—and known that it was not the proper reaction. She was supposed to be feeling grief, shock, even. She was supposed to be planning. There were the coroners to be summoned, payments for the funeral to be made. Bills long past due that couldn't be avoided much longer. And here was near forty pounds. With that, she could do all those things—she could pay off their debts, she could hold her father a proper funeral—not that he deserved one—and she could continue in the same house that she had lived in all her life, continue in the same job at the same factory that she had worked in since she was school-age, when it became apparent that her father's disability war pension would not get them far. She could do it—nothing had to change if she did not want it to.

But of course she did.

She had always wanted it to, locked away in her father's house, imprisoned, as she had often felt, like those heroines in the books she had read as a child. She had spent too many years in the servitude of a man who had never said thank you, had never smiled, had only taken it for granted that she had nowhere else to go, no money to begin again, that she was a woman, and that meant certain things in a world dictated by men. And so she had pushed aside thoughts of duty, of honor.

Instead, she thought of Spain.

She thought of Madrid and that red-roofed Moorish city called Granada that she had once read about as a child, and she decided, in that moment, her father's cold body in the room above growing slowly colder still, that she would like to see it, that she would like to walk its marbled floors, would like to see the sweep of the Sierra Nevada from one of its many balconies.

Louise had turned twenty-eight years old the week before, and the thought of continuing on in that same vein for another twenty-eight more made her ill. It might be terrible, but then she was terrible, she knew. And that was why, sitting at the table, the lights turned off in a bid to lower that month's electric bill, she had decided: she would take the money, though it wasn't hers to spend, and she would go to Granada to see the Alhambra.

Louise made two telephone calls from the village telephone box, asking the operator to first connect her to a travel agent so that she could book a room at the Alhambra Palace Hotel, in Granada, Spain. It was an extravagance, but standing in the dimly lit country lane, it all felt a bit surreal, like something that would never happen, so that when she was finally connected, she found herself emboldened by the seeming impossibility of it, booking a room for three nights instead of just the one she had planned. When they asked for a name, she paused, thought of the book she had only just set aside.

"Virginie," she said. "Virginie Varens." It seemed silly to use an alias, particularly one that could be found within the pages of a book, but she figured it was unlikely that anyone would notice, that anyone would be bothered to check. Surely people booked into hotels all the time with false names. In fact, it seemed a thing that people most likely did in the real world, and Louise was thrilled to finally be a part of it, in however small a way.

The second call she made was to book a flight to Madrid with British European Airways for the following morning. Louise packed only a few items in a suitcase that she had never had occasion to use. Two pairs of trousers, two blouses, a skirt, as well as a pair of stockings that had been mended several times before. At the last minute she added one of the bottles she had taken from her father's room weeks earlier—a nearly full prescription for luminal tablets. It was already past its expiry date, and she didn't think they even prescribed them anymore, but she had been having trouble sleeping and had started to take a tablet here or there to help settle her down at night or soothe her nerves during the day. Sometimes she took several, reasoning that they were old and not as effective. Finally, she added her passport and the money.

The next day, Louise boarded an airplane and flew—across the English Channel, across the Bay of Biscay—all for the purpose of being able to stand within the thirteenth-century palace, to look out over the sweeping mass of the Sierra Nevada and feel something more than the drudgery of her daily life had ever allowed, weighed down as it had been by her father's illness and her mother's absence.

She did not allow herself to think about what would happen when her shillings were gone, her pence spent.

She would figure it out later, she told herself.

In Madrid, Louise ate gambas and *boquerones con anchoas,* drank *cana* and *vermut.* She wandered streets with names she could not pronounce, stumbling upon an open-air market, where she was told by one of the sellers, in halting English, that the street used to run with blood when the slaughterhouses would transport animals to the tanneries in the city. He told her the market's official name in Spanish, before translating it to English—*a trail of blood*—and Louise found herself unable to look away from the ground underneath her. At night, she favored the same tavern, one that had, in turn, once been favored by Hemingway.

It was small and dark, and she would always occupy a seat in the back, sipping sherry—the only drink they served there—poured straight from the wooden barrels displayed just behind the bar. She laughed often those nights, felt more herself than she ever had. Her third time there, she ordered a carafe of oloroso and a plate of *mojama,* took up her place in the back, avoiding eye contact, avoiding conversation, and feeding most of the dark-red strips to the cat who had settled beside her. She wore a pair of new stockings that she had purchased in Marks and Spencer before her flight for five shillings and six pence. At the end of the night, she found she didn't want to be alone anymore, allowed herself to be led through the Latin Quarter and into the bed of a man whose name she could not recall in the morning.

Afterward, she left quietly, walked to the Plaza Mayor, found a place just on its outskirts, tucked away from the more crowded restaurants, and ordered a *cana* and plate of *calamares fritos,* despite the early hour. Her lips shone with grease. She had eighteen pounds remaining in her purse.

The next day, she boarded a bus headed farther south.

She knew her decision to leave, to take the money, might have seemed strange to others—callous, perhaps—but then, even as a child, Louise couldn't bring herself to want what others wanted, to do what others expected. She couldn't manage to see the future as anything but a sentence waiting to be served. *Don't think so hard,* her mother used to tell her, before she left, abandoning her husband and daughter, before she disappeared from the country lanes of their village and into the unknown *rues* and arrondissements of Paris. *Don't think so hard, it will only make it worse.*

Louise could argue that her mother had done the exact opposite—had thought her way out of their small existence and into another life—but by the time she realized the contradiction, her mother had been gone several years already. Louise often wondered whether her mother, wherever she was, was still terribly unhappy. Most days, Louise hoped she was, but on others, she decided that she couldn't blame her. After all, she had married a man who had promised her a different type of life, but who instead had come back from the war with his body broken and aching, his mind, too, so that all at once their life became something else entirely.

Gone was any possibility of adventure, the money no longer enough to take her far away. And as for weekend breaks to London, well, her father disliked them because of the crowds, because of the filth, because of the grime. And then his injury from the war had worsened, his legs failing altogether, and he had lost his job. The money had become less and the burden more. He had trapped her in the house, just as he would eventually trap Louise. The wheelchair meaning he was dependent on her, meaning she couldn't move if he did not say so, her whole life, her whole being, wrapped up in his pain. So no, Louise didn't blame her for leaving—she only blamed her for leaving her behind.

After her mother left, Louise had lost herself in books, the only evidence of her mother's existence, the fraying spines left over from her mother's own youth. Louise would hide herself away and read—devouring the words eagerly, greedily, imagining others who had read these same words and feeling angry, somehow, at being forced to share the experience with them, wanting to keep it solely hers and hers alone. Washington Irving's *Tales of the Alhambra* had been a particular favorite. That a place could hold someone under its spell, could enrapture them, entrap them—she had never felt that way about anywhere, had spent most of her life longing to be somewhere else.

Later on, she had read Françoise Sagan and wished she could afford to be one of those waiflike creatures who spent their time mooning over the vagaries of youth. Instead of basking in the sun in southern France or meandering the charming boulevards of Paris, Louise was stuck in her small village, sneaking cigarettes out her window, her gaze sweeping over nothing but the endless foggy moors. Perhaps for these reasons she marveled at the shrewdness of Cathy, felt she understood Victoria, while hating Lilla with spitefulness, and wishing that Lady Audley had gotten away with it all. She read Jean Rhys and felt her heroines were kindred spirits—penniless and often miserable. There was a realness to the women who populated these novels, one that made Louise feel as though she knew exactly who they were, these women who would do anything to survive.

Louise decided quite early on that she had no time for blushing heroines, something she would never be herself. She wasn't beautiful—she was blond, but not the type that came from a salon or bottle and that other women strove to achieve—and while she was thin, she was also tall, taller than most of the boys she had grown up with. Instead of delicate, she was strong and sinewy, her hands calloused and blistered from helping her father in and out of his wheelchair, from scrubbing the floors, the dishes, from whatever else the house needed. And that was before her job at the factory. Her wardrobe contained none of the lacy frills and buttoned kid-skin gloves that belonged to the heroines in her novels. Her dresses were all secondhand from her mother's closet and whatever else she could manage to stitch together with needle and thread.

And her face—sometimes she would spend long hours standing in front of the mirror, holding up her hands, sectioning it off, piece by piece. If she did that, she could just about convince herself that she was beautiful, but together, there was something not quite right. Her eyes were too large in context with her mouth, her teeth had a tendency to stick into her bottom lip when she was thinking, an eye-tooth turned a bit too much. It made her look innocent, she thought, like a frightened animal, which irked her, as it wasn't at all true.

Louise would look out her window and tell herself not to think, not to make things worse, but then she smelled the sheep and the pigs and thought her heart was full of nothing—or no, it was full of something, something that burned and raged, so that she forced the windows back shut, her hands trembling. She hated the place, she hated the man who kept her there, she hated the woman who abandoned her. Her life, her childhood, was marked by this feeling, was scorched by it, so that it obliterated everything else.

And so while the world told her to despise the Becky Sharps—women who were cunning, ruthless, and, more oft than not, terribly clever—Louise found herself wanting to emulate them, to taste even just a fraction of their freedom, even if it meant the same kind of tragic fate. It would be worth it, she thought, if only to be free for one brief, shining moment. It had to be better than the alternative, locked away in a dirty house, reeking of death. She was wretched, she knew, but in the end, she found she couldn't help it— didn't want to, if it meant a different sort of life.

Her first afternoon in Granada, Louise walked through the Albacín, up and down the narrow streets of the old Arab quarter, her legs throbbing, unused to the exertion. She made the steep climb to the Church of San Nicolas, gazed out at the Alhambra, looming in the distance. It was warm, certainly much warmer than in England, despite the fact that it was already October, and she felt her cheeks burn. Down below, on the Carrera del Darro, she allowed herself to be led into a shop or two, beckoned by the enthusiastic shopkeepers, but she only smiled and nodded at the colorful rugs, at the leather poufs whose time at the tannery she could still smell, pungent and fertile, at the lanterns that hung, casting a dizzying array of light and shapes across the white walls. She did not make any purchases. Instead, she gazed up at the Alhambra, which now towered above her like a giant.

Afterward, Louise stopped in a tiny bar on Calle Navas. She ordered a *cana* and was given a small dish alongside it, something fried and golden, buttery and flakey. *Cazón,* the waiter told her when she tried to ask, in French, though he spoke only a few words and responded mostly in Spanish. She ordered a full *ración*, just for herself, and ate the whole thing standing at the bar. She licked her lips, tasting the bitterness of the beer and the salt of the fish.

On her second day, she walked to the Sacromonte neighborhood, though the concierge had looked vaguely alarmed at her intention to do so. *It's not safe for a young woman alone,* he had insisted. *The caves are filled with gitanos.* She thanked him for his advice, then asked him for directions. The climb to the caves was more arduous than her wanderings the day before. She passed few other tourists—ones who stopped to tell her it was a waste of time, who shuddered and refused to elaborate on their experience—but mainly she saw only the inhabitants of the caves, carrying buckets, walking beside donkeys, hauling wares from below. The caves, Louise could not help but think, looked more like pleasant little cottages than anything else. The road was hot and dusty, and she paused more than once to wipe the sweat from her brow.

During one of these, she noticed a woman—younger than herself—staring shyly from beside one of the cave doors. Louise raised her hand in greeting, and the woman made a beckoning motion before disappearing through a doorway. Hesitant, Louise looked around her, searching for a sign it might be a trap, but finding no evidence and wanting a respite from the sun, she decided to follow.

Inside, Louise blinked against the darkness. There were no windows, and only a few light bulbs hung from the ceiling. When her eyes adjusted, she was surprised by her surroundings. It was a cave—that much was obvious from the slope of the ceiling, the uneven texture of the walls—but it was also very much a home. There were tiled floors, pieces of furniture—scant, but sturdy—and copper pots that hung from the walls. Louise could see she was standing in someone's kitchen. The woman who had beckoned her inside was seated at a table, alongside an older woman dressed in black. Again, the woman waved Louise forward, indicating that she should sit.

The old woman reached for Louise's hand.

So this was it, she thought. A fortune-telling scam. She gave a tiny shrug, settled back into her chair. She could think of worse ways to pass the time. She only hoped the old woman wouldn't demand too much—she was likely to be disappointed with the modest amount Louise could offer her.

After only a few minutes, however, the old woman pushed her hand away, shaking her head.

Louise frowned, looking down at her palm as if some answer might really be found there.

"What is it?" she asked the younger woman.

The old woman said something, but Louise couldn't follow, could only look between the two women, trying to make sense of the words.

"*Nada*," the young woman said.

"*Nada?*" Louise repeated.

The younger woman nodded. "*Nada*, she says. She sees nothing."

"Nothing at all?" Louise asked, disappointed. She took out a few pesetas, laid them on the table, reasoning that they had to be worth something, even a glib warning or two. The old woman shook her head then, and, as if reading Louise's thoughts, pushed the money back across the table.

Louise left after that, embarrassed. Outside she found she no longer had the desire to climb any farther. Her mouth felt tacky, and she longed for a drink of something cold. The way down was easier, but felt longer. She was grateful when she found herself back in the Albacín, heading into the nearest café. As she drank her *cana*, she tried not to think of the old woman's face as she had said that word. *Nothing.* She ordered a second and then a third. She ignored the looks that a man sitting alone in the corner of the bar threw in her direction. Louise didn't feel like company that night.

The next day, Louise didn't go out. She felt tired and lonely, thought she detected the start of a cold coming on. She ordered a cognac and spent the night in the bath, which didn't have much hot water, thinking of the next day. Once the hotel bill was settled, she would be down to only two pounds, a few shillings, and a scattering of peseta. She had spent lavishly since her departure from England—had enjoyed every minute of it. She had no regrets.

Louise stood at the window, looking out at the Alhambra, at the shadow it cast over the city, and wondered if anyone else was doing the same. It seemed impossible that one could grow immune to such a scene—but then, she didn't know about other people, other lives. Only her own. And Louise knew, without a doubt, that she could spend the rest of her life gazing out at the Alhambra, content.

In the morning, she tried not to think about the money she had left, about what that meant. There would, she knew, be time for that later—but now, in this moment, she wanted only to think of what had brought her there in the first place, what had filled her mind that night of her father's death, all those hundreds of miles away. And so, Louise went to the Alhambra, which she had dreamed of for most of her life and which had always seemed beyond reach, tucked away as she had been, surrounded by sickness and poverty. She went to the Alhambra to see what had inspired Irving, the words of which she had read but never fully understood.

She went to the Alhambra—and everything changed.

Louise began her pilgrimage early, in the hours before the sun rose. She checked out of her hotel and settled the bill—estimating she had just enough peseta for a *café con leche* and a *mollete*—and began, suitcase in hand, to make her way toward the Alhambra. From the hotel, it was only a short distance, and so she made the journey on foot, stepping onto the Cuesta del Realejo, on Sabika Hill, where she paused for a moment, certain she could hear the sounds of the Albacín behind her—the strumming of guitars, the accompanying claps, the shouts of laughter. Evidence that, for some, the night had not yet ended.

Louise pushed on, into the Alhambra woods, beneath the elms and the poplars. She did not worry about the darkness, for those were not the sorts of fears she carried. It was a short climb, but steep, and she found herself winded by the time she reached the top. It had taken her longer than she expected, and the sun had already begun to rise. She set her suitcase down and stood, watching the golden pale as it cast itself across the border of the Sierra Nevada and the red, ochre-tiled rooftops of the city below. She wished that she owned a camera to capture it all, but then she knew she wouldn't have been able to afford it, let alone the price of film. And it wouldn't be the same, she thought, picking up her suitcase.

Memories never were.

At the entrance, Louise glanced down at the map that the hotel clerk had sketched for her of the sprawling compound. She had asked about the Nasrid Palaces in particular, and he had done his best to remember where they were located. She turned left, in the direction indicated in the rendering, hoping his memory was right.

She need not have worried, for within minutes she was standing at the façade of the Palacio de Comares, where she looked up in awe at the wooden eaves, at the engraved ceilings and the geometric designs. In the Patio de los Arrayanes, she lingered in the open courtyard, casting long, wistful glances at the pool, at the flashes of gold and orange and red just beneath its surface. Walking the length of it, she peered through one of the arches, caught a glimpse of the hammam and its skylights—the geometric shapes carved into the ceiling letting in rays of filtered light. It was more grand than anything she had dared to imagine. She continued around the pool and into the Sala de la Barca, the antechamber to the Salón del Trono.

In this curiously cube-shaped room, Louise stood for some time, staring up at the ceiling. It was, she knew, supposed to represent heaven. Or rather, the seven heavens, the stops before the eighth and final one, the entrance of which she knew she would never be allowed to cross because she wasn't of that faith—or any faith, for that matter—and because of the things she had done. Still, she thought it looked like what she imagined heaven might, if she believed in such a place. The complicated set of geometric wheels combined to appear as stars, so that it felt as though she could have been staring upward at the vast, unending sky. She felt something stir within her, felt it catch in her throat.

She looked for the exit.

Don't think, it will only make things worse—she heard the words echo in her mind as she hurried her footsteps, paying no real attention to where they took her now. *Don't think*. The words repeated to her as a child each time she had looked out her window and toward beyond. She glanced up, saw she had walked in the direction of the Torre de los Picos, and pushed through a door to her left. She found herself in a passageway, walls high on either side of her, trapping her, blinding her. *Don't think*. The words shaping her life for years, so that she could still hear them now; her mother's words, her mother's voice, all these many years and miles away. She pushed through another door, found herself on the periphery of the walled city, in the Generalife. She took a deep breath, felt it run through her like a shudder, and made her way forward, into the gardens, into the Patio de la Acequia. In the open courtyard, she gazed at the water canal that ran through its middle, at the gardens that flanked it on either side—and she felt it again.

It was a strange sort of pain, she thought. Realizing that the words of Irving, of other writers, had not been exaggerated. She wondered whether it would have been better not to know, whether it would have been easier to have never seen this at all. To continue with her life assuming that it was merely a fiction. To know that it was real, that she could reach out her hand and lay her palm against it, such was its tangibility—it elicited something from within her, and she found herself wanting *more*, more of whatever this was, despite knowing all the while that it wasn't possible.

And so she screamed. She screamed as though she were a child throwing a tantrum over being told what she could not have. She screamed, surprising no one more than herself with the sound of it, with the force of it, feeling, as she did so, the vibration of it throughout her body. She screamed, the rage that she had swallowed throughout the years threatening to choke her, until her voice faltered, until it grew hoarse and strangled and there was nothing left, no sound at all, nothing but her breath, hard and heavy, gasping for air. She dropped her suitcase beside her, felt her legs falter. Louise placed one hand on her chest, another on her stomach, willing herself to breathe—or no, that wasn't the problem, she knew, it was that she was breathing too much, too quickly. She inhaled slowly, willed her body to stop shaking, her hands to stop trembling.

It was then that something caught her eye—movement, in the alcove above. A shadow, she thought, belonging to someone watching her. She started to move forward—to do what, she didn't know—but was stopped by the rustle of fabric, by the distinct sound of someone else, coming from within the garden where she stood.

It was a woman, her pumps clicking against the tile, as she made her way through the open courtyard. The two women were separated by the canal—a distance of only a few yards, though it was enough to keep Louise hidden from the woman's line of sight, tucked away as she was behind the garden's lush foliage. This vantage point also afforded Louise the opportunity to see exactly what happened next, as a series of banknotes began to fall, quite inexplicably, from the woman's purse and onto the tiled floor, one bundle after another, a few breaking apart, the individual notes fluttering to the ground like leaves on an autumn day. Louise felt her breath catch in her throat. She felt as though she could not breathe, as if the air had grown too thick—it was hot, the humidity causing her hair to stick to the back of her neck.

At first, Louise was certain that the woman would turn back, that she would realize her mistake. But she didn't—didn't turn, didn't slow her steps, didn't do anything at all but continue walking, her fast and hurried gait taking her from one end of the garden to the other, and then into the adjacent building until she was gone, swallowed up by the darkness of its interior. A hush seemed to fall over the gardens, as if everything had been paused for this one, singular moment.

Louise moved slowly at first. Down the length of the wall, toward the Acequia Real, the platform in the center that connected both sides of the garden. She stood, looking down at the fallen banknotes. These were not the pesetas that she had become accustomed to—no, these were pound sterling and printed in large denominations. Tens and twenties, even a few fifty-pound notes. Far larger than anything Louise had ever held, familiar as she was with shillings and pence. Her breath caught in her throat. Louise bent over, sweeping the bundles together with her hands, the tiles underneath warm to the touch.

She had wanted to see the Alhambra. That was how it had begun, and now, she stood—in Spain, in Granada, in the Alhambra and the Palacio del Generalife, water from the fountain running softly in the background, the smell of roses thick in the arid summer climate of Andalusia—clasping a stack of banknotes between her fingers, the total of which amounted to more than she dared to imagine.

Louise paused then to rub her thumb against one of the notes, to assure herself that it was real, that this moment, and her place within it, was real. She should return the money, she knew, either to the woman or the nearby *policía*. It wasn't hers to keep—but then, she knew that she couldn't. That she wouldn't. That she would take the money, damn right or wrong. She didn't need to count the pile to realize what it meant: years without worry. More, if she was smart—and Louise knew she was nothing if not smart.

And besides, she couldn't go back—not after what she had done.

And so she didn't allow herself to think—about who the money belonged to or why it was dropped there, in that particular manner, by that particular person. She was frightened, could feel her heart pounding, a warning sign, perhaps, but she only brushed it aside, steeled her nerves, and pushed ahead.

She crossed the Acequia Real once more and placed the banknotes into her suitcase. As she did, she thought she could hear her mother's voice, but this time she pushed it aside. She was done with not thinking, she told herself, done with not wanting—for they were the same in the end. *Don't think*, her mother had said, because she knew the danger in wanting what was impossible. But now—

Louise closed the suitcase, took one step forward, and began to think.

At the bus station, she found a public toilet, locked herself inside, and counted the money. Five thousand pounds. It was a fortune. Louise felt her heart begin to race, felt a lightness in her head, a ringing in her ears. Five thousand pounds. She thought about what that could buy, about what she could do, with that amount of money. A house back home might cost her two thousand, not that she would go back, not that she could. Still, it was a comfort, one that she had never experienced, knowing that such things were possible. That she could buy a house, a motorcar, that she could have a telephone— hell, she could have two if she wanted—and even rent a television as well. And at the end of all that, there would still be money left. Quite a bit. Enough to allow her time to think, to plan, to decide how it was that she wanted to spend the rest of her life.

But she would not go back—she couldn't. There would be too many questions, too many accusations—and besides, she didn't want to go back, had already made the decision that she was done with the place she had been miserable in for so long. No, the only thing to do now was push ahead, to get herself out of Spain and disappear further into Europe—before anyone came looking for her, for the money. Five thousand pounds. With that amount, she could go anywhere she wanted, could start over in an entirely new place, with an entirely new identity. And the farther she went, she knew, the farther the money would go. Hands shaking, Louise placed the money back into her suitcase, unlocked the door, and decided to go buy herself a drink to steady her nerves. Then she would be able to decide what to do, where to go. Five thousand pounds. It was too much for someone not to come looking. She would have to get out, unnoticed, before they did.

She needed to change some of the money into pesetas.

The amount she had left from her own money wouldn't be enough to buy much, let alone a ticket to somewhere else. And besides, the pesetas would be good to have on hand for the hours she still had left in Spain. She wouldn't change the fifties—not here, that would arouse too much suspicion. But a ten-pound banknote, that shouldn't raise any eyebrows, and it would be enough, more than enough, to buy something to drink, something to eat, as well as a bus ticket or two, or however many connections were needed to make her way out of the country.

Louise had already decided that the bus would be her safest option. It was also the longest and the most uncomfortable, but on a bus the chances were greater that no one would check her passport, no one would ask to search her bag. If she were to go to the airport, there was a strong possibility that someone would notice the money and ask her questions she couldn't answer. Even the train seemed too risky. The thing to do, she knew, was to get out of Spain, and then she could reassess her options. It would be worth the inconvenience, she told herself.

In the main hall, she found a bank. Heels clicking against the tiles—the noise of which brought to mind that other woman, made her wonder if she had noticed the absence of her money yet, and if she had, just what she might do—she approached the counter. *"Dinero, cambio?"* she asked, not knowing if the words made any real sort of sense. She withdrew the ten-pound note she had placed in her pocket while in the bathroom.

The man behind the counter reached for the note. *"Ciertamente,"* he said, glancing behind him at the board of numbers that displayed the exchange rate.

She held her breath. The whole transaction took only a few minutes, at the end of which she was handed sixteen hundred pesetas for her ten pounds, distributed to her in an array of various-size bills and coins. After, Louise nodded, murmured a quick *gracias*, and went to find a café. She could feel herself trembling. She needed to sit, to clear her mind for a moment or two, to figure out where it was that she should go next. Her mind had not stopped racing since that moment she had stood in the gardens of the Alhambra, banknotes clasped in her hands. It still seemed impossible that any of it was real, that the banknotes she had hidden in her suitcase were anything but worthless sheets of paper—but no, the teller at the bank had exchanged them, turning the pounds into pesetas without a word. He would not have done so if there was something amiss with the notes, if they were not genuine.

Louise ordered a *café carajillo* and drank, slowly, standing at the counter. She had to leave Spain, that much was clear. She took another sip of her *café*, felt the liquor warm her, and decided Paris would be the best place to begin. She also knew it was a decision that she had made long before that moment, perhaps when she had first seen the money.

Paris. She had spent years imagining it, ever since her mother had left, ever since she had received that first letter. The only letter, though there may have been more, she didn't know, only that her father had burned the first when he found it, along with the fraying books that her mother had left behind. She had watched them all go up in flames, mourned the loss of Irving perhaps the most. After, her father had taken charge of checking the post, and she figured it likely that if any more letters did follow, he had done the same to them.

In that first and only letter that Louise received, her mother had written of the city, describing the cafés she visited, the bar she stopped into every day after work, the old woman who worked there far too old to be tending bar but left on her own following the death of her husband and the debts left behind. She wrote about a bookstore on a foreign-sounding street, the address of which Louise promptly memorized, where she would spend hours browsing, though she didn't have the money to buy anything—not yet. At the bottom of the letter had been a promise—for more letters, for her intention to bring Louise there once she found her footing.

But then, despite the passport that Louise obtained in anticipation, despite the hours scouring French-language books at the local library, she had never been summoned.

Now, Louise finished her coffee, grimacing at the bitterness, and left several coins on the countertop. She would buy a ticket to France, she would see the city her mother wrote to her about all those years ago, see what it was that had pulled her away from Louise and into a new life. She would go, but she would only stay for a short time, no longer. After, she would find a place for herself, somewhere untethered to the past.

Her eyes flicked to the right, at a series of travel posters adorning the walls. She paused for a moment, taking a step closer. The advert featured a large white palace that seemingly floated atop crystalline blue water. *Istanbul.* She gave a curt nod, as if that decided things.

Before the bus departed Granada, Louise stepped outside the station and found one of the vendors she had noticed on her way in, the ones with their wares displayed on a blanket, ready to be snatched up at the first sign of police. She had seen it happen before. The rising shouts of *policía, policía,* and then, like a magic trick, the bundles pulled upward, strung tightly with ropes, the corners snapping in together, the wares disappearing from view—along with the vendors themselves. She paid too much for a leather satchel still reeking of the vats. There was no time to haggle, her bus left in ten minutes.

Inside the station's toilets, she emptied her suitcase and placed everything into her new purchase. It was lighter, easier to manage—easier to keep close, when she needed to. She left the empty suitcase by the bathroom bin.

As her steps sounded against the tiled floor of the station, she pushed all thoughts of England, of her father, from her mind. Instead, she began to plan her first day in Paris, just as she had done so many times throughout the years. She held on to the feeling of lightness it always gave her, clasped it between her fingers, as she hurried toward her platform and what she told herself was a new beginning.

The bus was more crowded than she had expected. And hot. Louise watched a pair of old women fanning themselves with cloth fans, wishing she had thought to make a similar purchase before taking her seat. She had seen the vendors selling them but had assumed it was more of a souvenir than a thing of any practical use. She regretted her decision now.

After several uncomfortable hours, Louise managed to fall asleep, lulled by the motion of the bus, by the warmth that caused her face to flush, the armpits of her dress to grow damp. She wasn't certain how much time had passed—her sleep long but disturbed, her eyes half opening, then closing again at any little sound, any little bump in the road—when she became aware that the bus had, at some time or another, come to a stop. She sat up, opening her eyes, trying to throw off the confusion of sleep. She saw that the driver had already departed the bus and that the other passengers around her were now preparing to do the same.

"What's happening?" Louise murmured, confused. She didn't really expect an answer, was only saying it to ground herself, to assure herself that she was not, in fact, still asleep. She peered out the bus window. They had stopped in what looked like a small town, nothing more than a few dirt-stained buildings, the wash formerly white, a petrol station and what appeared to be a café attached to it. The country, she supposed, although all she had ever seen of Spain were its cities. "What's happened?" Louise asked, turning to address the person behind her. "Have we broken down?" An older man, dressed much too warmly for the heat pulsing outside, frowned and shook his head. She tried again in French, but the man only shook his head.

Louise felt a sudden twinge of panic. Perhaps she should have taken the train. At least then there would be a timetable, scheduled stops—not whatever this was—and the heat, the heat would have been more bearable, she thought. She grabbed at her bag, wondering what she should do—if she should follow the others. A few of them, she could see, had left their bags behind, but Louise knew that wasn't an option—not with what it contained. She wondered whether it would look strange if she were to bring it with her, or worse, whether they would assume she had given up her seat, driving away without her.

"*Descanso*," a woman said then, pausing by Louise's seat.

Louise shook her head. "I'm sorry, I don't understand."

"*Descanso*," the woman repeated, miming something now that Louise couldn't interpret.

The woman in front of her repeated the gesture a few more times, then gave a small shrug and a tiny smile, and continued down the aisle.

Louise watched her go, watched the rest of the passengers depart the bus until she was the only one remaining. She tapped her foot, tried to calm herself with the motion. The heat on the bus was unbearable—she couldn't remain on board. Louise grabbed her satchel and hurried her steps to follow the others.

Outside, it felt as though it was approaching the heat of the day. She could feel it pulsating in the air around her. Louise raised her hand to her face in a vain effort to block out the sun. She could see that most of the other passengers had begun to make their way toward the petrol station, to the café attached. Perhaps, if anything, she could find a toilet there, she reasoned, and freshen up. Though she had known it would be a long journey, she was surprised to find herself so uncomfortable after less than a day's travel. She worried about the night ahead—though at least it would be cooler, without the sun beating down on them.

In the café, Louise followed the sign to the toilets.

The smell inside was overwhelming. Despite this, the women

stood, waiting patiently in line, the minutes stretching. Louise felt herself sway in the heat of the afternoon. When it was her turn, she pushed into the stall, locking the door behind her.

Turning to the toilet—or where a toilet should have been—she found only a rudimentary hole in the floor. And there was something else moving in the darkness. She took a tentative step forward so that she could see. Cockroaches, she realized. A gasp escaped her, and she jolted backward, colliding with the bathroom door behind her. A string of words rang out—a question, an inquiry. Louise didn't respond, didn't know how to in a language that would make sense to anyone here. She shut her eyes, breathing through her mouth. She turned, did her business as quickly as possible, then joined the other women in the queue for the basin, feeling as though the cockroaches were still there—beneath her, on her—feeling as though they were covering her skin.

At the bar, she tried to catch the bartender's attention, but found that her hand trembled when she raised it. Again, there was that strange swaying sensation, one that threatened to take hold of her. She felt a man at her side—a patron, another passenger—she didn't know, but she felt almost grateful for his presence, worried, at that moment, that she might soon need something to prop herself up against. It was the most curious sensation, but she felt sharp little pinpricks at the back of her neck, at the tips of her fingers now. Everything around her seemed to take on the sheen of a dream, as if it were not quite real, as if she were not really there, standing at that bar, in some tiny forgotten town in the middle of Spain. She tried to recall what she was doing there, how she had arrived, for she did not remember the space in between the bathroom and here. Her tongue felt thick and dry, useless in her current state.

The man next to her called out something in Spanish to the bartender, who responded swiftly, placing two small glasses in front of him and filling them with an amber-colored liquid. She watched, transfixed. He turned to her then, said something in Spanish, so that its meaning was lost to her. She shook her head, didn't bother to explain that she didn't speak Spanish—the attempt would only confuse them both further.

"*Buvez ça*," he said, after a brief hesitation. "Drink this."

She looked up, startled to hear the man speak French. Her trembling hand reached for the glass, not bothering to wonder at the advisability of drinking something from a complete stranger. He had spoken French to her, a language she understood, and in that moment, it was enough—it was everything. She sipped the liquid—a dark amber, she saw now, as she moved it nearer to her mouth. It was perfect, the bite of liquor lessened by the sweetness of oranges.

"Where are you going?" the man asked her then. "How far?"

She frowned, tried to remember. "Paris," she responded. She had decided on Paris. On the city that had enraptured her mother—no, *captured* her, so that she was never to return. Louise remembered one of the snippets that her mother had written in that first and only letter—about the studio she had rented, an eighth-floor walk-up in what used to be the maid's quarters, which meant she had shared a bathroom with the many other tenants on her floor. She wrote to Louise about the suspicious old landlady who insisted on making the monthly journey upstairs—a wheezing cough and a sheen of sweat on her forehead—to inspect the flat with a shrewd eye, always claiming that something was missing, something was moved. She had even charged Louise's mother a number of francs for the disappearance of a painting that her mother was certain had never been there.

Louise had read the letter so often that she felt as though she had experienced it all alongside her mother, instead of simply reading her words from miles and miles away. In the years between, as her memory began to fade, she invented pieces, added them to what she remembered, so that sometimes Louise could no longer recall what her mother had actually written and what she herself had imagined.

Now, in the heat of a different country, hundreds of miles away from that city she had never been to but felt she knew as well as the village in which she had been born, the man next to her pushed two pieces of crusty bread—some type of meat sandwiched between— toward her. She wondered whether it had been there all along or if he had only just ordered this as well. *"Mangez,"* he instructed.

She did, wondering as she chewed when the last time she had eaten was.

"Vous vous sentirez bientôt mieux," he assured her.

"Merci." She looked up at the man in front of her, wondering how she had not noticed him before. He had to be a passenger on the bus, for she doubted very much whether anyone in this small town would have bothered to learn a language that was not spoken there. And then there was the cut of his clothes—they didn't speak of a rural town, although they weren't particularly expensive either. They were neat, she thought, well cared for, as was the man in front of her. She felt her hands begin to steady.

"Attention au soleil," he said, pointing outside, toward the sun. "If you're not used to it, it can be a bit much at first."

"Yes," she murmured, wiping a crumb from the corner of her mouth. "I'm not used to the heat." Louise wanted to say something else, something more, looking up at him, feeling his gaze on her. She felt herself blush, hoped that he would only assume it was sunstroke, as it must be—the confusion of her thoughts, the strange feeling in her limbs. She leaned forward, meaning to thank him again, to ask for his name—when a voice rang out, louder than all the rest in the café. It was the bus driver, she could see, standing, waving his hand.

"Ah, break has ended," the man next to her translated.

Louise nodded, understanding. She watched as the bus driver set down his *café* next to an empty plate. He turned and headed toward the bus, the other passengers standing, unwinding themselves from stools and chairs, pushing aside unfinished food or wrapping it into paper napkins and placing it in their pockets. She turned back to the man to thank him, but he was already gone.

Louise frowned, looking around the shop, but found no sign of him. She wondered how long she had allowed her mind to drift as she watched the others—long enough that she had not even detected the initial absence of his presence. She wondered whether she should be insulted by his disappearing act—decided she would. She also told herself that she would need to be more careful, in the future. She paled to think what might have happened if he had been someone else. Her leather satchel, she realized then, was half dangling from her lap. She pulled it closer to her body, shifting so that it was placed firmly against her.

She glanced again toward the café's window, saw the line forming at the bus, and thought she might have caught sight of him there, at the front, but she wasn't certain. Quickly, she wrapped the rest of her sandwich in a napkin, placed it in her luggage, and signaled to the bartender. In the absence of other patrons, he responded promptly. After a series of rushed gestures, she managed to order another sandwich. Tossing a few coins on the counter, she hastily thanked him, then made her way out of the café, toward the bus, anxious not to be left behind.

THREE

HENRI

Henri sneaks a glance toward the woman sitting across from him. She is staring out the window, a somewhat steely expression on her countenance. Ever since her arrival he has felt himself placed at a distance. He suspects he knows the reason for this coldness, but it makes the moment no less difficult to endure, particularly after everything that has passed between them. "I was thinking of visiting the dining car," he says, beginning to stand. He wasn't, not really, but he is desperate to be outside the staleness of their compartment, trapped within his own thoughts. "Would you care to join me?" His words sound unbearably formal, even to his own ears, but he tells himself to follow her lead, though he wants only to lean forward, to take her hand and begin, "Louise—"

Louise looks surprised by the abruptness of the request, but still she nods and stands.

"To the back of the train," Henri instructs, as they exit their compartment. He indicates to the right, the corridor deserted. The train has a strange feel, he muses, as though they were walking in a museum, in something that had been preserved. She was right, it seemed, when she had earlier observed that train travel was no longer fashionable. The corridor seems to match the state of the cabin—the carpet trodden upon by hundreds of passengers showing its age, the lampshades stained and torn, their fabric edging toward a relic in need of retirement.

She—Louise, he reminds himself, the name new on his tongue—walks ahead of him, swaying slightly with the rhythm of the train. He watches as the sun glints off the windows in the corridor, catching her hair. He had thought her a blonde, but now, in this light, he can see traces of different hues, evidence of red, even.

The train jerks and she places her gloved hands to either side in order to steady herself. His own have gone toward her waist. It's a reflex, and, embarrassed, he removes them. For her part, she says nothing, does not even glance over her shoulder, only continues down the corridor. He can still feel where his hand touched her waist—can still feel her flinch.

They pass through two more vestibules—maybe three, he is distracted, after all—before arriving at the dining car. Henri places both hands deep into his pockets and says to the waiter, "Two, please."

The dining car is no great affair. There is more of an effort at upkeep here, perhaps because of its popularity among the guests, but there is the same feeling of disrepair. The waiter seats them in the back, away from the only other couple in the car.

"Istanbul is a long way to go by train," he says, once they are settled, starched napkins arranged in their laps. He wonders if she finds it all as unbearable as he does.

"Only a day or so," she responds. "And besides, I find travel to be relaxing."

She doesn't look relaxed, he thinks. She looks ready to bolt, to disappear at the slightest provocation. "I think most people would probably disagree with you," he says, more to be argumentative than anything else. He's injured, he admits, by this distance she has placed between them, wishes she would stop using *vous* instead of *tu* whenever the conversation veers to French, wishes she would stop behaving as if they were complete strangers. He feels an ache begin somewhere behind his eyes. "It's always such an ordeal. The packing, the moving of luggage from one place to another, porter or not. And the hours spent actually getting somewhere."

"I love those hours," she counters. "I find them incredibly soothing. It's a moment where nothing is required of you—there is nowhere to go, as you're already on your way, and there's nothing to do. You need only sit back and watch the scenery go by."

"Plenty of time to think—to worry," he says, throwing in the latter, just to see her response.

She meets his gaze. "Only if you have something to worry about."

"*Vraiment.*" He adjusts his napkin. "Still, such travel can be dull."

"Only if you have the misfortune of being placed with dull companions, or if you yourself are dull." She leans back into her chair, smiles. "You don't seem dull."

He doesn't know how to respond, and says in place of silence, "You're young to be traveling alone."

She shakes her head, as if disappointed. "Not so young." She pulls the packet of Gitanes from her coat, lights another cigarette. "I didn't ask before, but would you like one?"

He shakes his head. "Still. A woman, on your own. It's unusual."

"Oh, I don't know. That seems rather old-fashioned." She exhales. "And what about you? You're traveling alone."

"Yes."

"No wife?" She smiles. "No fiancée?"

"No, nothing like that."

"Not ever?" she teases.

"Once," he concedes, reaching for the pack of cigarettes she has laid on the table. He needs something to do with his hands, especially if they are going to speak to each other like this. He lights one, exhales. It's been ages since he's smoked, longer still since he's had a French brand.

Yes, there had been someone, once, but that had been ages ago. Marianne. It had been years since he had last seen her, at the port of Oran, on her way to university in France. It had been the conclusion of her first trip back to Algeria—for the holiday break—and they knew already that it wouldn't work. That she had been changed by her time abroad—*at home*, she had said, though, like him, she had never been to France, at least not until she left for university. She had been dismayed at his reluctance to join her there, at his insistence in attending the Université d'Alger, and then resentful, a bit angry, even. Eventually, it all disappeared—what they had in common, that spark of anger at her decision to leave. Until at last it was only the past they held between them. It was the last time she returned to Algeria. Her family had followed her to the continent a few years later.

"What was her name?" Louise asks.

"Marianne."

She appears to be studying him. "You look like you're thinking of her now."

"Yes, it just reminded me." It's difficult to explain, he thinks, the way that Marianne is bound up in his memories—of his home, of his parents, of his youth. That when he thinks of her, he is simply thinking of the past. He doesn't know, out of all these remembrances, which he misses the most.

"It must be nice to have someone to remember," she says, her tone somber. "I've never had that."

He wonders if she is telling the truth—about it sounding nice, about her never having anyone. It seems strange, hard to believe, that this young woman in front of him has never had a sweetheart.

She is attractive, though he admits that it's a beauty that might be overlooked. Hers is a face that requires more than a passing glance—that demands it, he thinks. Still, surely someone else must have noticed it over the years. He cannot be the only one.

"We're rather maudlin, aren't we?" she says, shifting her tone. It sounds forced, unnatural, even. "Besides, I don't suppose we should be talking about past affairs, not when we're strangers."

He hears the challenge in her voice, is unsure whether he should meet it, has been uncertain ever since she first stepped foot into the compartment earlier. The waiter appears just then, pulling a notebook from his pocket and saving him from having to make such a decision. They listen to the specials, to the prix fixe menu. She orders the *sole meunière*, he orders the *confit de canard*, with *pommes de terre dauphinoise*. They order a bottle of Burgundy.

When the waiter returns with their bottle of wine, Henri fills both of their glasses to the top. "What shall we toast to, Louise?"

"I told you, you can call me Lou."

He shakes his head. "No, I don't think so."

"Why not?" She frowns.

"It's a horrible name. I hear Lou and I think of some old man, short and bald."

She betrays the beginning of a smile. "With a cigar hanging from his mouth."

"Yes. He's got a nasty temper."

"That's why his wife left him ages ago." She laughs then, reaching for her wine. "All right. You can call me Louise."

"And you can call me Henri."

"Henry," she says, with an English accent.

"Henry and Louise, then," he concedes.

She nods. "Henry and Louise."

Their food arrives and they eat in silence. Or rather, he eats.

Louise only pushes the food around on her plate, her eyes occasionally darting to him, to somewhere just over his shoulder. He is about to ask, when she drops her fork, leans over, and whispers, "I haven't wanted to say anything, but I can't ignore it any longer."

For a moment, he holds his breath, wondering what it is that she is about to say, wondering if she is about to make a confession. He finds himself both delighted and frightened at the idea. "What is it?" he prompts.

"It's just that I have the strangest feeling that the man sitting in the front of the dining car is watching us."

Henri curses under his breath. He knows this already, but he had been hoping to hide it from her for at least a little bit longer. That the man following them is now sitting in the same car, openly watching, can mean only one thing. He curses again.

Time is running out.

BEFORE

In Paris, Henri waited to be disappointed.

He knew already the foolishness of what he had done—he had just spent the better part of two days reflecting upon it, as he watched the landscape shift from the wide-ranging terrain of Andalusia, golden flatland to craggy mountains, to the green valleys of Basque Country and over the Pyrenees, arriving back in the country of his nationality. Now, he prepared himself for the eventuality that the only reason the woman he was following had traveled this far was because she meant to spend the money the way most people would—on clothes, a fancy hotel, a few lavish meals in the City of Light. That what he had seen that day in the garden—a reflection of his own inner turmoil—was only a fleeting moment. He told himself that either way, it didn't matter. Disappointed or not, he had a job to do, which was, he told himself, probably for the best. The bus journey had been long and he was tired—and back in Spain, they would no doubt be growing more concerned with his extended day trip.

Henri watched as she stepped off the bus and onto the platform—and then went directly to the counter to purchase what appeared to be another ticket. He could see the exchange of money at the counter, could see the paper handed over to her. He frowned, wondering where, if not Paris, her final destination might be. He watched as she turned and made her way to the station's exit. For a moment he was torn, wanting to know what ticket she had purchased, but also realizing such knowledge would be useless if he lost her now and she disappeared. Perhaps it was only a decoy for anyone who might be watching—for him, he reminded himself. And besides, it didn't matter. He would not let this go beyond Paris.

He hailed a taxi, followed her to a hotel in the ninth arrondissement, and waited outside while she checked in. The place wasn't extravagant, but it appeared to be a decent area of town. He bought a packet of cigarettes so his presence wouldn't draw any unwanted attention. When she finally reemerged, he trailed her on foot to a café situated on the Rue des Martyrs, which curved around the corner and onto the adjoining Rue Choron. She sat on the Rue des Martyrs side, while he continued walking, eventually taking a seat on the Rue Choron. Despite the distance, he could still glimpse her through the glass windows, if he tilted slightly back in his chair, if he turned his head just so. He did his best to make the gesture look natural.

Henri had grumbled, at first, over the thought of returning to France. But sitting at the café she had chosen, ordering a *café noisette*, he felt a certain quietness, a peacefulness almost, descend upon him. It was one that he had not experienced in quite some time, and certainly not in those frantic days in Marseille. It made it difficult to remember why he was there, what he was supposed to be doing.

Though, in truth, Henri did not feel the sense of urgency that he supposed he should. Perhaps it was because the family he worked for was his own, however recently acquainted, or perhaps it was because none of it really seemed to matter, in that way that nothing had seemed to since that day in Oran. He felt, almost, like a child playing truant. Yes, he expected a stern look when he returned, a reprimand, but he could not bring himself to believe that the consequences would be so dire. He would return the money and that would be that, just a few days later than expected. Perhaps he was being naïve. A part of him knew that he was. But in that moment, the autumn air rising up to fill his nostrils so he thought he could smell the entire city—petrol from the motorcycles, yeast from the bread baking in ovens, even the espressos being poured, one after the other—with each inhalation, it was difficult to feel anything but content.

The waiter emerged from the café with his tray to deliver her coffee first, followed by his own. Henri tilted back, watching as she added a bit of sugar, noting the way she closed her eyes just slightly at the first sip. He did the same. The hot fusion of coffee and milk coated his tongue, followed by sweetness, just at the back. He was transported back home, or not home, exactly, but a type of home nonetheless, although he knew that didn't make sense. He knew, too, that he was veering into a sort of sentimentality he hadn't allowed himself much as of late, maybe not since he was a boy.

It seemed silly, to ascribe so much feeling to something as trivial as a cup of coffee—and yet, how to explain what he had missed in Spain all these months, trading the coffee his father would brew, sweetened with a pinch of cinnamon and eaten alongside the *m'shewsha* his mother would bake, for the bitter beans he had encountered in Spain. He remembered, too, the coffee that marked the warmer months in Oran—the sweetness of the sugar, the sourness of the lemon juice—and he wondered if they had something like that in this city he had never thought to visit. He could almost believe they might, almost dared to hope.

When she finished, Henri took some change from his pocket and left it on the table.

This time, he trailed her to the area just east of Abbesses Metro, where she disappeared in and out of the fabric shops that lined the street. Perhaps, he thought, leaning against the side of the building, she meant to commission a new wardrobe rather than purchase it prêt-à-porter. He watched her through the window as she pointed to different spools of fabric, waiting until the shop assistant had unfolded them before her to touch, to consider, tilting her head side to side as she came to some sort of decision. Mostly she shook her head and moved on. The whole thing should have bored him to tears, and yet, there was a comfort—in waiting, in knowing what he was supposed to do. It reminded him of those hours he had passed under the heat of the North African sun, where he had done nothing so much as observe the others around him.

That was before. Before the riots. Before the violence began to escalate. Before that day that had changed everything. He felt his breath sharpen. There was that scratching noise again, close and insistent. He closed his eyes, but all he could see were *those* eyes, watching him. He shook his head, trying to dispel the memories, the things he had seen, the things he had done.

Henri felt something then—a prickling at the back of his neck.

He turned, looked right and then left, certain that someone was watching. He knew even before he finished his search that there was no one, that the feeling was only a symptom of something greater, of his inability to forget, to let go. He turned his focus back on the woman he was following, and who was, just then, emerging from the shops empty-handed—though he was certain he had seen her buy something, that he had seen her hand over francs and take an item in return—and he was grateful for the distraction.

Later, when she sat for lunch, tucked into a corner at a restaurant in the Marais, eating a crepe and drinking a carafe of cider from a white-and-blue-swirled ceramic pitcher, he hailed a taxi and instructed the driver to take him back to the ninth arrondissement, to her lodgings, anxious to keep busy, to keep moving. To not drift backward, into the past. He was, as well, anxious not to be noticed by her, still unsure whether she would remember him from the rest stop in Spain, but hoping that her memory of that time was addled enough that she might not.

At the reception, Henri flashed his gendarme identification—not fake, exactly, but certainly no longer in use—and asked to see the most recent registration cards.

"Is there a problem, monsieur?" the man behind reception asked, looking visibly pale at the idea as he handed over the documents.

Henri did not respond right away, continued to flip through the cards, searching for her. There had been a number of recent check-ins—a family of four, a married couple, a few single businessmen—but only one single female traveler. He looked at the name. *Virginie Varens.* Occupation, secretary. Traveling from London. He didn't believe any of those to be true. He looked at the passport number, figured it was unlikely that it was real either, and didn't bother writing anything down. She had booked only the one night.

"Did you find what you were looking for?" the receptionist asked, leaning forward to see the card Henri held.

Henri looked up. He could sneak into her room, he didn't think it would be that difficult. He could tell the concierge that he was her husband, that he suspected her of having an affair, hence the secrecy, the use of his official credentials. There would be little question after that, he suspected. But then—what *then*, he wondered, after he had retrieved the money, after he had decided what to do with her.

Back to Spain, that was the only answer. Back to his makeshift life, and on to the next job, to more involvement, more possibility of danger, of violence. The prospect filled him with a sense of dread, so that Henri desired nothing more in that moment than to avoid his return to Spain, to his family, for as long as possible. He would give it time—a day or two, maybe more. He would continue to follow her for a little longer yet, continue to see the city that she had taken them to, and then he would return, eventually, when he felt he could face what would be waiting for him there.

Henri shook his head at the concierge's question. "No," he responded, shuffling the cards and returning them back to the deck before the man behind the counter could distinguish the name of the traveler who had captured his attention. "No, I found nothing." And then, because it looked like the concierge did not quite believe him, he added, "It doesn't appear that the man we're looking for has checked in yet."

The next day, there was a strike at the train station.

The area just outside was chaos. It had been difficult to find a taxi willing to take him there, let alone continue to keep his eye on her while he did so. By the time his driver managed to pull up to the curb, she had already disappeared inside the station. He instructed the taxi driver to wait for him, then turned to follow.

Henri chose a spot just outside of the station, where it would be easy to disappear into the crowds should he need to do so. From there, he watched as she approached an agent, showing him her ticket. The man shook his head and she nodded in return, before heading back outside. Pushing her way through the crowds, she hailed a taxi. He hesitated for only a moment before sprinting into the station toward the agent she had just spoken with.

"*La femme,*" he began. "The woman who was just here. Where was her ticket to?"

The man frowned. "Who are you?"

He searched for a response. A husband, a lover—no, it would

seem too threatening. An acquaintance, not enough. "Her brother," he responded. "We were supposed to meet at the station this morning, but the strike," he said, gesturing to the station.

"If you're her brother, why don't you know where she was headed?" the man questioned.

Henri could not think of a suitable response. He cursed and headed back outside and into his waiting taxi.

The next few days proceeded much the same as the one before—she led, and he followed.

To museums, to the Tuileries Garden, to a bookshop not far from the Seine. When she paused at a painting, he would pause as well, though only after she had moved on to the next one, searching for whatever it was that had taken her interest, careful that she did not notice his presence. He had even bought a bowler hat from one of the shops, which made him feel like the unnamed protagonist in a spy novel he had just read. Though he soon found it only garnered him narrowed stares and deep frowns when worn indoors. Upon entering the museum, he had been quick to tuck it under his arm.

She seemed to particularly like the statue department, while he preferred the Egyptian antiquities. Afterward, in the gardens, they sat at opposite ends of a café, and although they did not speak, did not share their thoughts on what they had seen, he felt that in a way they still shared something. That there was a conversation, even if only he was aware of it. The next day, at the bookshop, he picked up a copy of a book he had watched her purchase only moments before. It was in English, written by an American author. He thought the stories sounded vaguely ridiculous and placed it back down on the stack of books. But then, he had never been a fan of novels, preferring instead historical accounts that were real, that could be verified by research.

He was also, if he allowed himself, more interested in the young man he had seen approach her while she was browsing. He was not concerned that it had anything to do with the money—he recognized the boy's type immediately, knew he was a hustler, a grifter, but suspected his crimes were petty, the type local police would rather push aside than go through the hassle of dealing with.

Always, Henri was careful to keep his distance, to remain as hidden as possible—which was a feat given the openness of their surrounds in that particular moment.

Watching her, there were moments when Henri was nearly able to convince himself that he had got it all wrong. That this was not the same woman he had seen that morning in Granada, her fists clenched, her face wrenched into something that was entirely both painful and familiar. She looked nearly content now—serene, almost, he thought—though her face was momentarily obscured from him, her gaze, in that moment, directed at the Seine below. He began to feel a strange affinity for this woman who seemed to have no real connections. Since following her, he had waited for her to reach out to someone, somewhere, to post a letter, a telephone call. Soon, he realized that she was as alone as he was—and that thought made him feel no longer quite as lonely as before.

At some point, Henri realized he was being followed.

Later, he tried to pinpoint exactly where he was when he first became aware of it, but found that it was impossible, that the realization had been slow, like creeping bougainvillea, so that before he could answer *when*, it was already upon him, invading every part of his senses. He didn't know how to describe it exactly either, this realization, this knowing—something close to a chill at the nape of his neck. He had cast his eyes around the street, taking in all directions. There had been no one who he could see, no one who looked especially out of place, no one who seemed worthy of further scrutiny.

He told himself it was only the cold and continued to a *tabac* shop.

But the feeling persisted throughout the day. It wasn't out of the question, after all, to think that someone might be trailing him. This had been his first solo assignment—surely their trust wasn't that freely given, family member or not. And Henri had told them where he was, had given them an idea of where he was headed. Perhaps there had been someone close by, in Spain, or perhaps they had been waiting for him in Paris.

Henri decided that he needed to know for certain.

Up ahead he could see the start of one of the many covered passageways that he had taken note of while exploring the streets of Paris. He didn't recognize this one, was uncertain of where exactly it led, but decided to take a chance. The man following him had yet to make his presence known and he didn't think he was likely to reveal himself now, didn't think he was in any real danger of trapping himself. If he was, indeed, being followed. Henri was fairly sure, but he would be the first to admit that he hadn't been himself lately, that his instincts were off. He supposed there was only one way to find out.

Henri turned up the collar of his coat and stepped into the passageway.

His footsteps sounding on the tile beneath, he looked up at the ceiling of glass and wrought iron. The sun was just barely peeking through the clouds. He increased his speed, already aware that a shadow had darkened the entrance of the passageway behind him. Glancing around, he saw mostly artwork and old, leather-bound books displayed in the storefronts. Ahead, his eyes caught on one in particular—and the spiral staircase inside.

Henri paused at this shop, rummaging through the cart of books placed just outside the entrance, pretending to browse the titles. Picking up one book, he turned slightly to the left, saw that the man had paused as well, only a few feet from where Henri now stood, similarly pretending to peruse some fine art that sat in the window. Henri still couldn't see him, not properly, but he didn't recognize him either, didn't think it was anyone whom he had met before. That would make things easier—no doubt it had been part of his cousins' decision as well. Henri turned back to the books. If he was going to attempt what he was about to do, he would need to act now—and quickly.

Henri made his way into the bookshop. He didn't give the seller inside a chance to greet him. Instead, he made his way directly toward the spiral staircase, where he proceeded to give the no doubt centuries-old wrought iron a rather vigorous shake, one that made even himself grimace at the audacity of his actions.

"Monsieur," the bookseller exclaimed, moving from behind his desk. His expression was torn between outrage and disbelief. "Monsieur, *arrêtez, s'il vous plaît.*"

Henri stopped only when he was certain his tail was nearing the shop. *"Je suis désolé,"* he said, giving the seller a quick nod and heading toward the bookstacks at the back of the store. He knew the bookseller was still watching him, still frowning, but before he could say anything more, a new customer had entered the store and taken his attention. Henri watched their interaction from behind the shelves, peering through the books as he saw the stranger in question refuse offers of assistance, his eyes instead settling on the still-wobbling frame of the staircase, his ears, Henri knew, listening to that slight metallic twang that still filled the air. He turned his attention toward the bookseller, indicating the second floor. The latter nodded, and the man tailing Henri promptly made his way up the staircase, his attention directed above and not below.

Henri took the opportunity to make his exit from the shop.

Down the passageway he went, his footsteps moving at an increased pace, back the way he had come and onto Rue du Faubourg-Montmartre, where he allowed himself to be promptly swallowed by the moving crowd. Henri was reluctant to admit, even to himself, how strangely good the whole episode felt, like he was flexing a muscle that he hadn't used in a very long time. Not that being in the gendarmerie had required so much cloak-and-dagger, but still—he felt as though he had a purpose, something he had not felt since stepping onto that boat.

Henri found that he could not quite contain the smile that was spreading across his face.

He decided on a plan, in the hours after, sitting in a small shop, drinking *café* after *café*.

It wasn't without its faults, wouldn't save him entirely, but it would, he hoped, buy him time if and when it ever came to that—though he promised himself that he would not let things get that far, that he was only being melancholy, mourning his home, and that this temporary madness, this little cloud, would soon pass. And when it did, Henri would take back the money the woman had stolen and return to Spain, ready to resume his duties, whatever they might now be. Yes, he reassured himself, everything would return back to normal, and the wrongs that he had committed against those who had trusted him would be righted, eventually.

Henri paid his bill, asked for the nearest *bureau de change*, and left, head down, just in case anyone was still watching.

The next day, Henri resumed his trail, and on the way back to the hotel that night, he boarded the same bus as her. It was foolish, but the weather was cold, and he was anxious to be back in his room—in a different hotel, just around the corner, so as not to arouse too much suspicion—with a drink and hot bath. He stood in the back, bowler hat drawn down on his face, careful not to be seen. Gradually, however, the bus grew more crowded with those finishing up their long day at work and beginning the commute home, others with bags stuffed with last-minute purchases at the market. It happened slowly—the shifting, the jostling—until he was pushed from his secure spot in the back toward the middle of the bus, until she was pushed in the very same direction. Until there was no distance, no space between them at all. The bus turned, and with it, the passengers were forced to lean, one against another, stranger pressed against the next. She was nearly as tall as he was, so that when they touched, their shoulders were almost matched. He felt the back of his hand brush against her own. The bus righted itself and so did everyone else. Not once did she turn to look over and up, in his direction. There would have been nowhere to hide if she had.

Only after stepping down from the bus did Henri, watching as she disappeared into the warm glow of the hotel before him, release the breath he had been holding.

FOUR

LOUISE

Her gaze is still fixed on a spot behind Henri, where the man in question is seated.

"Yes," she says again, bringing the napkin to her mouth, trying to muffle her voice. "He is most certainly watching us."

Henri exhales. "Oh?"

She attempts a smile. "Either that or he's very bored."

"Perhaps he has a tiresome companion."

She glances back. "There doesn't appear to be any companion to speak of and—" She stops.

"And what?"

"I'm almost certain I saw him at the train station as well." It's true. She had seen him lurking, just outside, had felt her skin prickle at the sight of him, something warning her that he wasn't right, or the situation wasn't right, so that she had clutched her satchel closer to her body. She had told herself she was only being paranoid, that her instincts were off, after everything that had happened in Belgrade. Now, her instincts tell her that she was right all along.

Christine Mangan

Her dining companion only shrugs at this added bit of information. "That seems reasonable to assume, considering he's on the same train."

"What I mean is," she begins again, trying to make him understand. "I'm almost certain I saw him there—watching."

"Ah." Henri leans forward then, makes a small movement with his elbow, and sends the silverware beside him clattering to the ground. A waiter rushes over and at the same time he bends over, turns, casting his eyes around the room.

She is certain that he can tell which man she is referring to—for one thing, he's the only person dining alone, for another, he's staring straight at them. Of course, so are a number of other people now, watching as the waiter apologizes and bows, rushing to retrieve a clean set of silverware. Henri smiles, assures him there is no rush.

He turns back to Louise. "Yes. I see him."

She wonders then whether he already knows about this man. Something tells her that he does—of course he does. This was his line of work, after all, all cloak-and-dagger, mobsters and dolls—wasn't that what they called them in America? Louise purses her lips, moves to say something, then stops herself. What can she say, after all, given the impossible situation that they have found themselves in, a creation of their own making, but still. Instead, she lets out a small laugh, tries to lighten her tone. "You always hear such horror stories. Naïve tourists falling prey to villains intent on taking their money. Perhaps he's selected us as his next mark."

She can feel the disappointment emanating off him. It's clearly evident that he wishes she would have said what it was that she first intended, instead of reverting back to this, whatever it is they are playing at. She can't decide, feels as though she doesn't quite understand the rules. She wishes, for a moment, that they could speak openly, freely. To speak about the past fortnight, to discuss what happened in Belgrade, which is, of course, the reason her hands still shake, why she can't bring herself to eat a morsel of food. She puts out the cigarette she has only just lit, noticing the waiter moving in their direction, pushing a cart full of coffee and tea.

"*Naïve* isn't a word I would use to describe you," he says then, with a look that stops her.

"No?" she asks, trying to look surprised, though she can't quite manage to conceal the flit of amusement that crosses her face, even if only for a second.

"No." He pauses. "And I wouldn't use it to describe myself, either."

She wonders whether this is supposed to be a reprimand, the equivalent of a rap across her knuckles. She balks at the idea. Grinding her cigarette into the glass receptacle, she remains still for a moment. "Well," she eventually says, working her face back into an implacable mask. "One can never be too careful, I suppose."

He looks away.

BEFORE

In Paris, outside the Gare de Lyon, Louise stopped at a *bureau de change*. There she exchanged some of her pounds for francs, telling herself that she wouldn't spend too much, that she couldn't, reminding herself of the way the money had disappeared so quickly before, in Spain. She held her breath when the clerk frowned at the fifty-pound banknote, wondering if it was all over before it had begun, but then he looked up and asked what denominations she would prefer. She let out a slow exhale, bought a few traveler's checks as well, deciding it would be better not to carry large amounts of bills on her person.

After, Louise found a hotel just off the Rue des Martyrs—the name of which she recalled from her mother's letter—on Rue Victor Massé. She rented a room for one night, and although she requested one with a bath, the concierge informed her that both showers and baths were on the landing only. She wondered whether she should find another hotel, but then figured it would take too long and in the end, it didn't really matter, she only planned to be there the one night.

She paused when the concierge placed the registration card in front of her, pretended to fumble in her bag and frown. "I must have packed my passport in my suitcase by mistake. Could I bring it down to you later, once I've unpacked?"

The hotel clerk hesitated—but she knew he would relent, knew this was the type of place where these things happened. It was why she had selected the hotel. It was decent, not the sort of seedy place one often found in the heart of Pigalle. This was nearer the Abbesses station, which meant it could claim a three-star rating, while still retaining an air of scruffiness that the other world entailed. "*Oui, mademoiselle.* That will be fine. If you could just fill this out to the best of your ability."

She nodded, wrote down a fake name, then filled in the passport number. "I think that's right, but a number or two might be off. I'll check with my passport and come down to correct it later."

He nodded, handed her a key. "Will there be anything else?"

She thought for a moment. "A cognac, please. If you could send one up."

"*Oui, bien sûr.*"

She turned to follow the bellhop to the elevator. Her hands were shaking.

She had only intended to spend one night in Paris before taking the train onward to Istanbul—one night to marvel at the city, to see if she could glimpse what it was that had enthralled her mother— but then there had been a strike, as there always was in this city, according to those who seemed to know of such things. The result of which was that, because the train could not go that day, and it was not scheduled to run again until the following week, Louise found herself with more time in the city than she had planned. After a moment's hesitation, she decided not to dwell too much on the missed connection.

First, she returned to the hotel she had only just left and asked for the weekly rate, then she went to the Louvre, where she ignored the *Mona Lisa* and instead marveled at *Diana the Huntress*. From there, she wandered to the Tuileries, which she had seen an advertisement for in the station, and because it was autumn, she ordered *vin chaud* at one of the cafés, sitting in one of the dozens of green chairs that lined the pebbled pathway, watching as the leaves scattered beneath her feet, the taste of spices—of nutmeg and cinnamon—in her mouth. Later, she wandered the Marais, sipping cider and eating crepes, the buckwheat flour rough against her tongue. She went back to the ninth arrondissement, to the Rue des Martyrs, and spent hours walking the length of it, from bottom to top, glancing into bakeries and *fromageries*, her breath becoming more labored as she reached the steps leading to Sacré Coeur. The next day, she treated herself to cream puffs in the Latin Quarter, visited the Natural History Museum, and after spent hours wandering the Jardin des Plantes.

She went to the bookshop that her mother had written to her about and whose address she still recalled, at 12 Rue de l'Odéon, fixed in her mind. Stepping through the door, she tried to imagine her mother doing the same. She looked at the other patrons, searching for any trace of something she might recognize. As she moved, her eyes fell on a particular novel, the author of which had inspired her current alias. On a whim, she decided to purchase it. It was as she was peering at a shelf of translated French literature that she noticed a man—more of a boy, really, certainly no older than university age—watching her from one of the shelves. She held his gaze and he approached, offering her a cigarette.

"*Non, merci,*" she said, shaking her head.

He laughed. "What, English girls don't smoke?"

"I'm not a girl," she responded, though her voice was soft. Reaching out for the cigarette, she waited for him to light it, then inhaled gently. It had been years since she had tasted French cigarettes. She had saved up once, from the money she made at the local laundry, had purchased a pack and smoked them, sparingly, one a week, willing them to last. She never bought them again, knowing that everything afterward would only be a disappointment. If she couldn't afford them all the time, then she didn't want them some of the time. It was best not to fool oneself, after all.

"*Je m'appelle* Guillaume," he said then, smiling down at her. He was tall—so much taller than the boys she had known back home, and lanky, too, his hip span slightly smaller than her own. He was, she thought, the type of boy that girls loved at first sight, and she felt a stab of regret that she had not had the opportunity to meet someone like him when she was still young. The sun was setting by then, but it seemed to her that it was strangely light in that little corner of the bookshop.

"Perhaps I can be of assistance?" he asked.

She let herself laugh at the idea, at the barest hint of insinuation. "No, I don't think so."

He seemed undeterred by her response. "Have you read much French literature?" he asked. To her surprise, she told him about her mother's Françoise Sagan novels, and he shook his head, reached for a book, and said, "Try this instead."

She looked down at the book and saw the author's name, Marguerite Duras.

They made plans to meet the following night. In the hours between, she read, on a bench in the park, curled up in her hotel room, the darkness outside gradually growing light. The next day, she didn't expect him to show, but when he did, they found seats in the dark corner of a crowded bar, and she told him she had finished the book in one day.

"And what did you think?"

"I liked it," she said, suddenly shy, worried that she wouldn't be able to explain why, if he asked. And he did, just as she had known he would. She had wanted to shrug, to reach for the glass of pastis that he had ordered for her—she still couldn't drink it without a slight grimace, though she was working on it—and pretend that her answer didn't mean anything, that his question didn't either. Instead, she frowned and said: "They're not good."

He laughed. "Who?"

"The women. I don't mean that they're bad, but they aren't good. Not like heroines usually are."

"Heroines should never be good," he agreed. "Only in fairy tales."

Louise nodded, told him that was what she liked most—the realness of these women, the sturdiness, so that if she brought them to the light and examined them, she was certain they would not be hollow, but something real, something she could hold. That it reminded her of Jean Rhys, who wasn't French, but had written about Paris, based on her experiences there. She blushed then, certain it was only the drink that made her talk like that, but Guillaume did not laugh, only smiled and nodded, encouraging her to say more.

Louise felt, for the first time in quite a while, something close to content.

The next day, Louise turned in bed, only to find the other side empty. At least her belongings were still there—she wasn't entirely certain they would be as she had fallen asleep. Thankful now to have a few moments to herself, she took in her barren surroundings.

The night before had been fun—certainly more fun than she had had in a while. The boy, despite his age, had not been a novice. She slipped on her dress, looked around at the mattress on the floor, the stack of books beside it. She allowed herself a small smile.

Stepping onto the street, Louise found her way to a café and ordered a *café noisette*. When she was finished, she stopped into a boulangerie for a baguette. From there, she wandered. Up one street and down another, tearing off the bread, piece by piece, until all that was left were crumbs. In all these wanderings, never once did Louise take the metro or a bus, preferring instead to pass the days on foot, the soles of her shoes against the cobblestones underfoot a familiar hurt that both ached and soothed.

On a whim, she walked into an atelier and bought a pair of sunglasses. They were light pink, plastic, and sat quite large on her face. Louise looked in the mirror, ignoring the shopgirl's insistence that they suited her. She had been drawn to them because they reminded her of a pair that Elizabeth Taylor had worn, in a movie she had once seen at the cinema. The movie had been in black-and-white, so she didn't really know what color the sunglasses were. Still, these had a similar design engraved on the temples. She wasn't entirely certain whether they looked right on her, if she looked hip or like a child playing dress-up, but she handed over the francs anyway.

Afterward, Louise walked toward the Seine. She was in a giddy mood, with her recent purchase and rosy-colored memories of the night before, and she thought she might stop for a glass of wine somewhere along the way, or even a bottle, perhaps taking it with her to the Right Bank, to sit alongside the others. She could see it then—her new life stretching out before her, days spent in leisure rather than labor, nights spent with strangers—and a smile began to pull at her mouth.

But when she arrived, bottle in hand, a bit of cheese from a *fromagerie* and a baguette from a neighboring boulangerie, there were only couples dotting the bank. Perhaps it was the fading light, the crispness of the air, but there was a romantic mood that cast itself over the scene. Louise stopped, dismayed. She pulled her coat toward her. It was getting cold, and the only coat she had brought, a trench she had worn since she was young, was proving far too thin. She looked around and felt suddenly alone. She took off her sunglasses—they seemed silly now, childish even—and threw them into her purse.

Gazing into the water, Louise felt something take hold of her. A despondency, perhaps. A desperateness, almost. A hopelessness, despite her attitude of only moments before, her excitement for the future. She remembered Granada, before she had found the money. She hadn't allowed herself to think then of what would come next. Homeless. Penniless. What would she have done, what would she have been willing to do, if the money, this reprieve, had not fallen in front of her? She took a step forward, daring herself closer to the water. She didn't know what she intended, didn't allow herself to think too much. Perhaps she simply wanted to stand on the edge, to peer down below her and know that she had a choice, that it was her decision now, not anyone else's.

It was then that she noticed him.

A man, standing just to the left of her. She couldn't be certain, but she could have sworn he was watching, had moved a step closer when she had moved a step away. She frowned, took another step. From the corner of her eye, she saw him move forward again. She hesitated, uncertain. To make sure she was not imagining things, that she hadn't lost her mind somewhere between the atelier and the Right Bank, she took one last step, bringing her right to the edge of the embankment.

He took another step as well.

That was when she saw his face, poorly concealed under a bowler hat, and realized she had seen it before. She frowned, thinking. It wasn't someone from back home—she would recognize them easily enough. Having spent her entire life in the same village, she knew each and every one of its inhabitants by a quick glance. No, this wasn't someone from home—which meant that they had to be from Spain. Someone who had stayed in her hotel? No, she didn't think so. And it wasn't anyone she had met in a bar or café. Suddenly, it clicked into place. She let out a small gasp at the realization.

It was the man from the bus, the one who had given her the sandwich.

It was uncanny, her being in Paris at the same time he was— which meant that it was anything but that. Louise was smart enough to know that such coincidences in life did not happen. His presence was no mere accident—he was there for her.

She laughed then, the sound sharp. If anyone heard it, they did not look up, did not react, which was just as well, as they would most likely have presumed that she was mad. She could see herself from their perspective—a woman standing on the edge of the bank, the wind pulling back her hair, her face lifted to the sky, laughing. She took a step backward, just in case anyone decided to look up at that moment.

His presence in Paris didn't surprise her. In truth, she had been expecting him—or if not exactly him, someone. First, when she departed Granada, then later, during her long journey out of Spain. It had never occurred to her that it might be him—he was not what she had conjured, not mean enough, not threatening enough—and then somewhere along the way, perhaps at the border crossing, she had forgotten to look, had stopped glancing over her shoulder.

She wondered, standing there on the Seine, the cold October wind whipping her hair, her trench, so that she felt all at once as if it would sweep her up, up and away, how long he had been following her, whether it had been from the very start. She tried to remember the station in Granada, but it was a blur, lost in the frantic moments that had followed the discovery of the money. Was he there, she wondered, tucked into some corner of her memory, standing just to the right, or perhaps to the left, watching as she purchased her ticket, as she made her way to the bus platform?

She knew that he had been, that it was the only explanation for him at the rest stop in Spain, and standing, just a few paces away, watching her now. What she could not understand was why he had not already approached her. After all, the money was not hers, they both knew that, and yet he continued to watch her hand over banknote after banknote, for restaurants and hotels, for train tickets that would take her farther and farther away. She wondered what it was that he was waiting for. He had the perfect opportunity in Spain—her mind rattled from the heat, her thoughts and actions disorientated. He had noticed. Surely, he had. She wondered at the strangeness of this now, this act of kindness. Withdrawing a packet and lighter, she lit a cigarette and exhaled into the air around her, watching the cloud billow and disperse. She didn't know what she was doing—giving him time, she thought, an opportunity. She smoked slowly, watching as the rest of the sun disappeared before them.

The man remained standing, never approaching.

Eventually, Louise turned from the water's edge and walked away, back into the bustle of the city, back to the living—and him, somewhere, just there, over her shoulder. She found she did not have to look back and check, though once in a while she would see him—in the corner of her eye, reflected in the display of a storefront. Before long, she felt as though she could feel him, so she knew that he was always just there, somewhere at the periphery.

The fact comforted her more than it should have.

That next night, Louise placed a call through the switchboard at her hotel.

After, she set the telephone onto the receiver and waited. She swallowed a luminal tablet. Nearly an hour passed before the telephone rang again. When they had been connected, she said, in reference to their first conversation: "I'm hoping you might be of some assistance." It was a risk, but one that she suspected would pay off. Three hours after that, there was a sharp rap on her door. She took a deep breath, then approached.

"I didn't expect to hear from you again," Guillaume said, walking into the room and looking around him.

Louise wondered what the boy would say if he knew she could afford more, a room better than this one, what he would do if he knew the amount of money that was here, even now, in this room with them. She wondered whether she would be able to trust him with that information—knew instinctively that she would not.

"As I mentioned on the telephone, I'm in need of some assistance."

A look of uncertainty crossed his face.

"I'm in trouble," she pressed.

At this, he frowned. "With what?"

"I need a passport."

Louise had thought it through during her walk home the night before. She wasn't certain if the man following her knew anything about her, about her name, but on the slight chance that he might know something, she reasoned that it would be smart to have false documents that supported the alias she had been using. That way there would be fewer questions all around. With a new name, she could create her past, she could decide what her future would be. It would be an opportunity—a real one—to leave everything else behind. To disappear.

"How much time?"

He didn't ask why she needed a passport, and she didn't expect him to, had been counting on the lack of questions.

"A day, maybe two."

He shook his head. "That isn't enough."

It was, and they both knew it. Just as they both knew that what came next would be a negotiation of price, that he would demand an exorbitant amount, and that she would agree, in the end, because she needed the papers and because they had shared a night together, had been kind to each other in a world that often was not. And he had told her—a confession, or a boast, she wasn't certain—about the things he did to survive, had told her how he had started out as an art student only to find the assigned work dull and tedious, his inspiration for original art less than he had once previously assumed, while his talent for imitation, for forgery, was something else entirely, something that would take him out of the maid's quarters and into a second-floor flat.

"I don't have more than that. It has to be then."

He shook his head. "I don't know anyone who could work so quickly."

"I can pay."

He appeared to consider. "I don't know."

He knew, she thought, he knew that he would accept, knew that money put her at the top of the list. She tried to imagine him, then, in ten years' time. Perhaps he would be taller, broader, the thinness of youth disappearing into the adult version that he might become. She found herself saddened by the notion, found herself hoping that he found his way out of this life and into another, perhaps the one he had imagined before he had grown disillusioned with the institution that was supposed to inspire, but had only smothered.

"Two days," she said, naming a price that was too high for him to argue with. She didn't want to leave any room for negotiation.

"Two days," he agreed. His eyes fell on the bottle of cognac and two glasses she had rung for earlier, after ending her call with him. She didn't say anything, hadn't decided where or how she wanted the evening to end. Instead, she handed him her passport, along with the agreed-upon price. He looked down at the document, opening it to glance at her photograph. "Can I ask what it is you're running from?"

She shrugged. "You can ask."

He smiled, gave a tiny nod.

Afterward, Louise poured them a round, followed by another.

"No plans on coming back to Paris, then?"

"No. I'm almost finished with Paris." Her cheeks were flushed from the drink. She thought again of those couples on the bank and poured another round. As she drank, she looked up at the boy in front of her, wishing she were younger. She tried to imagine what it would have been like, to have been with a boy who smelled like French cigarettes, Gitanes mostly and Gauloises sometimes, instead of the country boy who had been her first, so that afterward she had only been grateful that it was over, that it was something she no longer had to think of, to worry over.

She poured another drink, telling herself to stop thinking of the past. If she allowed herself to become lost in it, she might never find her way out again.

Now, she gave the boy in front of her a small smile and let herself be led to bed. It was different than she remembered from the night before—but then, they were a little bit less of strangers now. She didn't know which she preferred, but found she missed some of the excitement of that first tryst. This was like returning to a place that she already knew—there were no mysteries, nothing new to be learned, but there was a comfort in that as well. He knew what she liked, and she him.

"You're certain you can't stay," he said afterward, buttoning his shirt.

"No." She shook her head, and he did not press her further, although a part of her wanted to ask if he would like her to, if he would be happy for her to remain. She suspected she already knew the answer, suspected that it would be the same as her own.

Later, at the door, he said, "It'll be ready in two days. I'll telephone you."

She shook her head. "You can leave it at the front desk."

He nodded, looking only vaguely disappointed. Perhaps he had expected her answer. He leaned over, kissed her on both cheeks. "*Au revoir*, Lou."

Louise nodded and closed the door, placing the chain back into its place. Only when she heard the clang of the lift, the closing of the doors, did she move away from the door.

FIVE

HENRI

Henri cannot stop thinking about the telephone call he made from the train station in Belgrade. He does not want to dwell, not yet—but the man that she spotted on the train has complicated matters. Even now, back in the relative safety of their compartment, he can see that it still occupies her mind, as it does his own. He wishes he could say something to alleviate her worry, to put them both at ease, but he knows that there is nothing he can say without lying.

Henri turns to the window, watches from the corner of his eye as she takes out a book and begins to read. He wants to say something—anything—that will take them back to where they were before, in the dining car, the conversation light, teasing, even. But all he can hear are the words spoken to him earlier that morning: a threat, whispered softly into the telephone.

The truth was, in Spain, they were done waiting.

They had been done for a while, which Henri knew and had tried to ignore. Instead, he continued to tell himself that he just needed another day, another hour—but soon, he would not have even that.

Standing in the terminal that morning, public telephone in hand, Henri had nodded, had made promises to the voice on the other end of the line, knowing that he would do what they asked when it came down to it—or a version of it—that he was a man of his word, if nothing else. He knew, too, that there was no other conclusion. No other way for the story to end.

"It has to be Istanbul," they had told him that morning. "That's the end of the line."

Henri had agreed. Only this time, it was different—everything was different after Belgrade, he thought. Something had changed between them, had shifted, locked into place, so that there was no longer any way to deny the connection. The only uncertainty was just what he was willing to risk to protect it—to protect her.

BEFORE

Henri looked down into the folds of his wallet and cursed. Berated himself for leaving his flat in Granada with so little money. His sleep had been disturbed, he reminded himself, he had not been thinking that morning. Still, even if he had left with more, it would not have been enough, would not have made any difference to his current predicament. He was out of money, he was running out of time, and a decision had to be made. He looked down at his wallet again. He would need to retrieve the money, use what was necessary to make his way back to Granada, and then pay what he owed from the bills he kept hidden under the floorboards in his miserable flat.

The thought of the latter made him stop and frown. He wasn't ready to go back yet—he didn't think *back home*, because Granada was not that to him—wasn't ready to face what he knew was waiting for him. And while Henri had hoped to avoid making any real decisions, to convince himself that this detour was only temporary, that he would soon right the situation and return, money in hand, he knew he could avoid it no longer. He was cold and hungry. He wanted a warmer coat, something to eat to steady his hands, to calm his racing mind. Money was the only thing that would remedy this. He cursed again. There was one way he could access more money—he was just uncertain whether it would work.

On the sidewalk in front of the bank, Henri paused.

He took a moment to glance around him, but there was no sign of the man from the other day. He wasn't foolish enough to believe that he had shaken him completely, but maybe now the man realized that he had been spotted and had decided to take a step back, to rethink.

He looked up at the bank again.

The truth was, he didn't know what would happen when he tried to use his account—if using his account was even a possibility. Perhaps it had been frozen, perhaps all accounts belonging to those who had been extradited were frozen. There was a danger in what he was about to do, he knew, a risk in handing over his real papers, which he still kept on him, foolishly, a talisman against the ghosts of his past, an insurance that left him only more vulnerable. There was a danger, too, in accessing an account that had lain dormant ever since he had abandoned his post. Henri had taken what he could before he had set sail across the Mediterranean, enough to survive, to begin again, but not enough to arouse suspicion, to alert anyone who might have been watching.

In the bank, the man behind the counter called for the next customer in line.

Henri hesitated, knowing that if he did this, if he took one more step forward, it could not be undone.

"La personne suivante, s'il vous plaît," the teller repeated, looking, Henri thought, somewhat vexed by his hesitation.

He took one deliberate step forward, then another. Henri reached into his coat's breast pocket. "I would like to make a withdrawal from my account," he stated, handing over his passport. To his own ear, his words sounded strange, hesitant, almost childlike. He was speaking the language he had always spoken, the language that had been his own since birth. And yet, somehow, there was something different about it here—the accent, the words, he didn't know—but he could feel it, the way that it changed him and the way he was able to express himself. As if when he spoke, it was someone else, a new Henri, who was speaking, one unable to articulate himself in quite the same easy manner in which he had always done so back home. To the unaccustomed ear, he had no doubt that he and the man before him sounded the same, but Henri could hear the difference—could feel it, he thought—so acutely that he began to sweat, as though what he was doing was criminal, as though his very presence there was wrong.

Henri tried not to stare as the man opened his documents, glancing down at his name, at his picture. But then, he realized that perhaps it would look strange not to do so—after all, he had been taught that averted eye contact was the first sign of deception, and so he returned his gaze to the man and the document he held.

The teller looked up, frowning at Henri's direct stare. "The account, it's held where?"

Henri tried to quiet his breathing. "At this bank."

The teller raised his eyebrows. "*En France?*"

He shook his head, lowered his voice. "No. In Algeria."

"Ah."

"Is there a problem?" Henri asked, already knowing the answer. Of course there was a problem—he had read the news, searching out French newspapers while in Spain, had seen the rhetoric flooding the stories. He knew that people like the man in front of him blamed people like him, though for what he wasn't entirely certain. For losing a bit of the empire, apparently. For starting a war, most certainly. And he was guilty—he knew that too—he was guilty by mere association. But then, he wanted to ask, wasn't this man also complicit? Wasn't this shame he carried also carried by others around him by mere fact of nationality and what they had then all allowed to take place before them? Henri told himself to breathe, heard the sound escape his lungs, short and ragged.

The man before him responded with a pursing of his lips and what looked to Henri like a terse shake of his head. "*Non*, monsieur. Of course not."

Henri released another breath. "*Bien.*"

"One moment, please."

The teller disappeared into the back, out of Henri's line of sight.

In the man's absence, the feeling of unease crept over Henri once again. He blinked against the brightness of the bank's lights. There was something about them—about their glare, about the vast hollowness of the space—that reminded him of another time and place, the memory setting his teeth on edge. He had tried so hard to keep it all at bay—though nights were still a different matter—but now, he felt it threaten to overtake him. Or perhaps it was only having to take out his passport, to connect himself so thoroughly with the person who he had once been and the things about home that he had tried to forget, the things that he had tried to eclipse with other memories. He took a deep breath, told himself to remember those other things instead. He remembered the bougainvillea. He remembered his parents. He remembered the hot summer sun and the smell of the Mediterranean. But the rest—flashes of red, the lingering smell of gunpowder—they were always there, just underneath.

Life among the gendarmes had never held any particular appeal to Henri. He had taken on the position to please his parents, and then, when they were gone, he had continued as a way to honor them. But he had never liked it—had liked it even less as the years went by and the events between the Algerian rebels and the French forces escalated. Henri found himself frequently called upon for his ability to speak Arabic—a number of the other officers could as well, though his was always the most reliable—but in those months before he left, in the days after the protests began, the interviews had shifted, transforming into interrogations, the people he was forced to question often civilians.

He was not unaware of misconduct—there had been more than one arrival during his time who had mysteriously been transferred from France without any real reason except for the obvious need for their presence to be expunged from the city where they had come from. He knew, too, that it extended to both sides—the rebels had their Algerian smiles, and the French their *crevettes Bigeard*. The whole thing made him ill, made him want to run, far away, but instead he kept his head down and did as he was instructed. Still, he always felt as though he was being forced to decide, to pick a side—between the nationality he had been ascribed at birth and the place that he had been born. He could feel it as he decided what to translate and how, what words to leave out, what emphasis to ignore, and what others to include. He hated the responsibility, felt it weigh on him, a heavy burden he did not want to bear.

He knew that eventually it would happen, that the day would come when the face sitting across from his would not be that of a stranger. Still, he was taken aback when it finally arrived, so that it had taken him a moment at first, maybe longer, to recognize the face before him.

The passage of time, of experience, had made the man before him a stranger. But it was him—the boy he had once known, who he had once played alongside. Aadir. It was him, his childhood friend.

He was certain. He was older now, as was Henri himself, and sat before him, bleeding and broken. *Suspected FLN*, they had told him before entering the room, referring to the rebels held responsible for inciting civilians to protest. Henri had nodded, had understood what would be expected. But at the sight of the man who had once been his friend, at the sight of his blood, blackened and crusted at the corners of his eyes, which were now staring back at him, wide and unflinching, Henri had hesitated.

Now, Henri placed his hand on the counter to steady himself, to remind himself of where he was—hundreds of miles away, in a bank that was all dark wood and copper polish.

And yet, when he looked up again, the face he saw was still Aadir, in that room, across the Mediterranean. He saw his eyes, watching, felt the sweat bead on his forehead. "We know each other," he had said to him that day, in Arabic, knowing he was not at risk of being understood by the others in the room. "I remember you."

The man had not responded, had only continued to stare, so that Henri wondered then whether he was mistaken. The protests had stretched on for days, and he was tired by that point—they were all tired. Perhaps his mind was only playing tricks there, in that room with the bright lights and the sounds that echoed across its emptiness. The scratching of the other officers' pens as they recorded Henri's translation, his words saving or condemning, a weight that he could feel more than anything, crushing him with its responsibility. So yes, perhaps he was only mistaken. Perhaps his tired brain was sparking and forming connections where there were none.

"Monsieur," the man began.

Henri frowned. He didn't remember Aadir speaking French—no, it had only been in Arabic, that was why he had been requested. Something wasn't right. He wasn't remembering correctly—

"Monsieur," the voice intoned again.

Henri blinked, saw that his hands were still clutching the wooden counter before him, his knuckles now white. He saw, too, that the teller had returned and was watching him, a frown stealing over his countenance. Henri released his grip. *"Je suis désolé,"* he said, wiping his palms against his trousers, then reaching to retrieve his documents, along with the bills he had requested, which the teller had now placed onto the counter.

"Will there be anything else?" the teller asked, his eyes still narrowed.

"Non, merci," he assured the man, taking a hurried step back.

Outside the bank, Henri loosened a breath, tried to ignore the burning sensation in his right-hand pocket, where he had placed his papers. He thought instead of *her* and wondered what it was that she was doing at this early hour. It had soon become apparent that she was not an early riser—part of the reason he had been at the bank's doors exactly at opening. He glanced at his wristwatch. It was half past ten. Surely by now she would be awake, would be descending from the lift into the lobby. He turned in the direction of the hotel, found himself wondering where she would lead them today—and was thankful for the distraction it promised.

She came to a stop in front of an ornate gate, beyond which was a cemetery.

Henri had been following her for several hours, during which time it had been near impossible to stay hidden, given the amount of public transportation she had used. And yet, she hadn't seemed to notice him, hadn't seemed to notice much of anything beyond the slip of paper she removed from her pocket every once in a while, staring down at it for so long that Henri found himself half-tempted to lean over and see what it contained. He didn't, of course. Instead, he wondered where she was going, wondered if it had anything at all to do with the money. Where her movements during the days before had seemed random, unplanned, as though one place had only led her to another as if by happenstance, this seemed more deliberate. He recalled her, earlier that morning, studying the city map in the metro.

Perhaps she was meeting someone—a partner with whom she would split the money. Henri had thought her to be a loner, like him, but perhaps this was not something they had in common. He thought of the man who had approached her in the bookshop. Perhaps he had miscalculated, had only imagined such similarities, desperate to see his own loneliness, his own unhappiness, reflected in another, just as he had seen his own sadness, his own rage, reflected in her that day in the garden.

He found the possibility depressed him more than he supposed it should.

It was a smart choice for a meeting, he thought, stopping on the other side of the road, out of her line of sight. The cemetery was empty, save for a stray mourner or two, but even then, they would be likely too consumed with their own grief to notice what was taking place.

He looked to his left, to his right, saw no one else approaching.

Perhaps they were late.

She remained still, standing outside the gates, looking up at the sign.

Henri thought he saw something then—a shake, or a tremor—as it ran through her body. A chill, most likely, he reasoned, pulling his own coat closer to his body. He had bought the coat that morning in one of the passages, after he had left the bank, had balked at the price, then paid it anyway, knowing there was no other recourse.

But no, he thought, taking a step closer, it wasn't the cold. He squinted, thought he heard something lost on the wind to the noises of the city. He couldn't be certain, but he thought perhaps she was laughing.

And then, with an abruptness that startled him, she turned and began walking back the way she had come. For a moment, Henri remained still, dumbfounded. He crossed the street, his eyes taking in every detail, looking for something that was strange or out of place, looking for evidence of the money or a note left by her or an as-of-yet-unseen accomplice. But there was nothing. Just the cemetery itself, stretching endlessly beyond. He didn't understand. It made no sense. But then—she made no sense, this whole situation, including himself, none of it made any sort of sense.

She had the money, he was certain of that, but she had yet to spend anything more than what was absolutely necessary. And he knew she had it, knew that it must be taken back, and yet he did nothing but follow her. No, that wasn't true anymore. He had done more than that. He had risked his own safety by stepping into the bank that morning, by reclaiming a name and identity he had long since cast aside. And he continued to further such risk by ignoring those back in Granada, who waited for word, for their money, with growing impatience. He wondered what she might say, if she knew. Whether she would call him mad, or whether perhaps she might understand this reluctance of his to return, this fascination he had cultivated for someone before ever speaking with them. The whole thing defied order and reason, those things he had always placed so much faith in. But then, look at where that had led him, he thought, to that empty room with the bright lights.

He shook his head, working to dispel such thoughts from his mind. Instead, he looked to the woman in front of him, whom he could just still manage to make out in the distance. He would need to hurry, or he would be in danger of losing her.

Readjusting his bowler hat, he cast his eyes downward, against the cold, against his memories, and pushed on in pursuit of the woman ahead.

SIX

LOUISE

Louise has been reading for the better part of an hour.

At first, she had only taken out the book for something to do with her hands, to steady herself, after their return from the dining car. But then he had turned away from her, looked out the window, and she hadn't known what to say. If she could, she would tell him that it was a waste, when they had such little time left, but he has been distracted since their return, agitated even, no doubt because of the man Louise had pointed out.

She wonders whether Henri had recognized the man, wants to ask, wonders whether there is any point to this pretense.

In the quiet, Louise finds herself thinking of the woman he mentioned before, Marianne. She feels jealous of this woman she does not know. She whispers the name to herself, imagines someone with long, dark tresses and an old-fashioned dress, down past the knee. She imagines Sunday lunches and trips to the ocean. She does this sometimes—imagines other people's lives, the way they might live, the happiness they might have experienced.

Louise herself can't recall ever being happy, or at least, if she was, she can't remember what it felt like. Which isn't to say there have never been moments, interspersed among the rest, just no one like Marianne, no one she looks back on and wonders what might have been. They were all just clumsy fumbles, mostly in the seconds, the minutes, she was able to get away from home.

"What is it that you're reading with such intent?"

Louise nearly drops her book, startled by his voice. She looks up, finds that he has been watching her, and she wonders what he might have seen, what she might have revealed, lost in her reverie.

"Just a novel."

He glances at the cover. "What is it about?"

She wonders whether he is actually interested or only inquiring to be polite. His mood seems to have passed, she thinks, or he has decided to push it aside for the moment. She glances down at the book. She had purchased it back in Paris, though she has not opened it until now. "A governess, pretending to be someone she is not."

"Ah. And how do you think it will end?"

She frowns, wishing he hadn't asked. Perhaps silence would have been better. "I don't know, I haven't decided, but I suppose it must end the way all of these stories end. It makes reading them a bit tiresome after a while." She shakes her head, not wanting to explain. "But the heroine in this one isn't your typical heroine, so the beginning and middle bits are quite good."

"How is she not typical?"

She tries to think of how to explain, remembers another conversation, in another city, not so very long ago, and wonders what this man in front of her might say. "She's bad, I suppose."

"Bad?" He frowns. "How so?"

She considers. "She isn't innocent. That's the main thing she's guilty of, and so she thinks and schemes her way into a better life. Which means she'll most likely be punished, in the end. Women almost always are." She pauses. "Sometimes I wonder how I would be written. In a novel, I mean. I'm certainly not innocent—or particularly kind, if it came to that."

"You seem perfectly kind to me."

"That's only because you don't know me. Not really." She turns toward the window. "Tell me, Henry, why is it that men are allowed to be absolutely wicked, while women are considered monstrous for acting as they do? Condemned to death, or worse."

"Worse?"

"Yes. There are fates worse than death, I think." She wonders, then, what he might say, what he might think, if he knew. "Tell me," she says, setting aside her book, "what is the worst thing you've ever done?"

"A strange question." He frowns. "Are these the type of novels you read back home?"

She turns away. "I don't want to talk about home."

She takes out her cigarettes, lights one. She doesn't usually smoke this much, but she tells herself that the day calls for it. "I'll tell you the worst thing I've ever done." She won't. She'll tell him something else, a lie. She can't possibly tell him the truth.

She remembers, as a child, her father forcing her to go into the confessional box at church, how she fought the entire way there, unnerved by the idea of being stuffed into that closet, a disembodied voice demanding the revelation of her secrets and sins. She wondered, at the time, what others had said. If they actually told the truth. She herself had lied every second she had spent in that damn box, refusing to part with her secrets for anything.

"My father died," she begins, "before I left England."

"I'm sorry."

"I'm not," she responds, her mood turning sour. It's all this talk of endings, she thinks.

She can almost hear her father now, muttering to himself, the words, the accusation, unmistakable: *You're just like her*. And Louise knew what he meant—that there was something wrong, just as there had been with her mother, that there was something rotten inside her as well. Something that meant she would never be happy with what she was given, that she would always want more. *Don't think too hard*, her mother had said—not an admonishment, she had realized over the years, but a warning.

Now, the man across from her raises his eyebrows, and she knows that whatever shape he had molded her into within the confines of his mind, it is wrong—knows that it is the impression of a girl, of a young woman, who does not actually exist. She supposes it is cruel to say these words to him, but she finds she wants to be, feels a familiar lick of rage flare up within her, so that in this moment she wants nothing more than to shatter whatever image he has created. To burn it all to the ground.

"It's the truth. He died and I was happy, relieved, even. He had been ill for years, and I was his caretaker. All those years, I resented him, blamed him, and then—" She stops, snaps her fingers. "Suddenly, it was over. My imprisonment had come to an end." She exhales, tries to calm her shaking voice. "But that isn't the worst of it."

"No?"

She meets his eye. "No."

BEFORE

That morning, Louise took out a slip of paper from between the folds of her passport, looked down at the address written there, and felt a familiar sensation clutch at her heart. She had found it—a seemingly innocuous piece of paper—tucked away among her father's things, hidden, she thought ruefully, after his death. At first she had thought to throw it out, her eyes sweeping over the contents without reading them—but then she had snagged upon something familiar, her mother's maiden name, and she realized what was written underneath was an address, on the outskirts of Paris. She hadn't known, in that moment, didn't yet know, whether to be enraged at her father for hiding this from her, enraged at her mother for never reaching out, or something in between, which was sadder, colder, and sat more heavily on her shoulders.

After a quick *café*, Louise walked to Gare Saint-Lazare, a twenty-minute journey from her hotel, and took the train to Saint-Germain-en-Laye. At the station, she became disorientated and was forced to stop and ask the departing passengers for help, explaining that she was looking for her mother, pointing to the written address she held in her hand. They seemed to frown when they saw the number she showed them. Perhaps she was only imagining it, or perhaps they were irritated by the foreigner pestering them for directions.

It felt colder outside of Paris, without the buildings and the crowds to keep her insulated. Louise pulled her coat closer to her chest, made a note to buy a winter one before she departed.

After nearly an hour of walking, up one street and down another—noting to herself with a certain amount of derision that her mother must have done well for herself to be able to afford living in such an area—Louise arrived at the address. She stood, looking down at the slip of paper she held in her hand, then back up again.

She let out a sharp laugh. It had to be a mistake, she thought, staring at the cemetery gates in front of her. She wondered whether her father had known, decided that he must have—known that she would find the piece of paper, known that it would lead her here.

Louise experienced the strangest sensation then. Until that moment she had toiled under the assumption that there was still someone out there. At the knowledge that neither her mother nor father nor anyone else who was tethered to her through the permanence of blood still remained, she felt suddenly adrift. It was, she thought, like the first time she understood death as a child.

The concept had frightened her, terrified her, in fact—not the actual dying, not the idea of pain or anything that most people associated with it. No, what had unsettled her, enough to spend several nights awake, afraid to close her eyes, was the thought that that was it—her body would simply return to the ground and whatever existed would be no more. She had never been religious. Her father's early attempts had quickly faltered, then ceased altogether when he fell ill, his bitterness taking root, causing him to declare to anyone who would listen that God had turned his back on him. And her mother, when she was still there, had gone only occasionally to church, with the inconsistency of someone who believed only because they were afraid to do otherwise.

Louise, however, had never been afraid, had never been a believer in that sense. Instead, she believed that there was one life, the life that was given to her now. Still, it terrified her—the idea of no longer existing, the idea that everything she suffered, everything she had fought for, would one day mean nothing because she would not be there to remember it. Losing both parents felt the same. It felt as though some finality had been reached, that there was no turning back, that whatever had come before no longer mattered because her mother and father were both dead and buried and there was no resurrecting them—even if she had wanted to.

Louise did not bother to search for her mother's grave. What was the point? she thought. All the words, all the accusations that she had been ready to fling at her—the portrait of a woman who had traded her daughter's life for her own, the ultimate villain—none of them meant anything now. There would be no release, no cathartic moment to be realized. The truth was that her mother was gone, just as her father was now gone, and she had not mattered enough to either. Louise had always wondered if it was only because of her father that her mother had left, or if it had been her as well. She supposed now, through her mother's silence, her final act, she had her answer at last.

Stumbling away from the graveyard, Louise headed back to the station. She boarded the same bus, going the opposite direction now. Stepping aboard, she recognized the driver, saw a question form on his lips, but she turned away. The ride back went by faster—too fast. Within minutes, it seemed, she was already back at one station, boarding a train and then transferring to another. She moved slowly, her steps leaden. She was in no rush now. Her mother was dead, her father was dead, and she was entirely alone.

Afterward, Louise felt like she could not get warm. She arrived back in the city, hands shaking. She took a luminal tablet, then a second, and because she could think of nowhere else to go, could not think of anything less appealing than her hotel room at that moment, she exchanged a few more francs for a paper ticket, stepped onto the metro, and rode it over to the eleventh arrondissement. She walked to a tiny bar located on the Rue Richard-Lenoir, the one her mother had once written her about.

Louise pushed through the doors and grimaced at the smell that greeted her—something old and musty, something stale and comprised mainly of cat piss. She peered through the darkened space. Every surface of the tiny bar seemed to be covered. Old Franprix papers, photographs, sepia-toned and aging, covered the bar counter, while bottles with sediment that floated at the top lined the shelves. Birdcages, dozens of them, covered both barstools and floor. The little light there was came from the windows—Louise wondered if the owner couldn't afford the electricity—which were covered with enough grime that she was surprised any light filtered in from outside at all.

An elderly woman, her back bent and hunched, appeared from a door behind the bar and stumbled toward her. She twisted her head to the side. *"Puis-je vous aider?"*

Louise felt herself hesitate over her response as she sat down on a stool.

The old woman's face crinkled. "What—you don't speak French?" she demanded, making a disapproving noise, somewhere in the back of her throat. "Come back when you learn."

Embarrassed, Louise slid from the barstool, prepared to slink out of the bar. But then she thought of the day, of all that she had learned, and she felt her courage return, filled with a determined sort of anger as she demanded a glass of wine from the white-haired woman behind the bar.

"Good girl," the old woman said. "Now try this instead." She poured her a glass of pastis, pushed it across the counter.

Louise took a tentative sip, anticipating the taste of licorice that would coat her tongue. She noticed something crusted on the side of the glass—cat food, she suspected. She tried to discreetly wipe the offensive matter away, although she thought it didn't matter, thought that the old woman would be unable to notice such a small gesture.

The door opened behind her, but Louise didn't turn. She was surprised anyone would come to the bar as an intended destination, though she supposed it must happen. Perhaps it was a loyal patron who refused to abandon the old woman in her time of need, or, more likely, she thought, a lost tourist, who would sit for an hour over an untouched drink, confused and vaguely horrified by their surroundings, wondering where the charming brasseries that their guidebook boasted of were. Louise hoped they would not try to engage her in conversation, to commiserate in their poor choice of establishment. She wasn't in the mood for company.

She turned slightly, eyes narrowed, ready to apprise the intruder—when there he was.

The man who had been following her.

He began to order—*un verre de* Pernod, madame—and Louise cut a quick glance to him, shook her head slightly, indicating her filthy glass. She nodded to the row of beer bottles. He frowned, clearly puzzled, but soon amended his order—*pardon, une bière*, he finished. She didn't know whether it was a safer choice, given the dust collecting on them, but figured it was better than risking a glass smeared with cat food. Louise wondered how her mother had written of this place with such affection and surmised that it must have changed greatly since the first time her mother had pushed through its doors.

The old woman reached for a bottle on the shelf. She struggled to open the top. "A busy day. Where are you both from?" she asked, looking between Louise and the man, who sat on opposite ends of the bar. It was a tiny space, only a few stools separating them.

"England," Louise responded first.

The man gave a small nod and replied, "Oran."

The old woman frowned. "Where is that?"

He seemed to hesitate. "The coast."

The old woman looked unconvinced. "And what are you doing in Paris?" she asked, once again not bothering to address either one in particular. Louise wondered how well she was able to see them through the darkness of the bar, her eyes milky and unfocused.

Louise took a tentative sip of her pastis. "*En vacances.*"

"Ah?"

"*Oui.*"

"Better places for it."

Louise laughed at the unexpected response. "Yes, I suppose that's true."

"You should go to the sea. That's where people are supposed to go on holiday. Not to a city." She turned to the man. "Tell her about the place you mentioned, on the coast."

He looked startled by the woman's request.

"Well?" the old woman prompted again. "Don't you know your own city?"

He cleared his throat. "Yes, yes, of course."

Louise waited, found herself enjoying the uncomfortable look that had crossed his face upon entering the bar and that was still there, even now.

"You could walk the corniche," he began, slowly, as though he were considering where to begin. "There are date palms that provide shade, and then there is the port, just beyond."

The old woman scoffed. "She's on holiday, why would she visit a port unless to board a boat?"

He nodded, sipped his beer—looked as though he regretted it. "There is a particular garden with sloped terraces. From there, you have a view of the whole city—the mountains, the water, the, the port," he said, stammering over the last bit. "It's filled with a number of trees. I remember the fig trees used to scare me as a child, because when the fruit cracked open it would look like a monster hanging there, above my head." He paused, smiled. "And there is a fort, Santa Cruz, high in the mountains, so you have to take a motor trip or a cable car to reach it—there's no better view. When I was younger, I would linger in the fort, let the darkness dull my senses, before I would head toward one of the arched windows and it would all suddenly come into view—the mountains, the sea. A deep blue, a blue unlike anything you can imagine."

The old woman was frowning at him again. "Where is this, did you say?"

He hesitated. "Oran."

"I don't recognize the name."

"It's a small city. It doesn't attract many tourists."

She made a noise.

The man turned back to Louise and continued: "There's a place just outside of the city, on the coastal road. A restaurant built into a cliff. My father would take us there—my mother and I—every so often." He paused, frowned. "My parents died on that road, on their way to the restaurant. They had wanted me to join them that weekend, but I was too busy, and my father, his eyesight—" He stopped abruptly, the silence lingering, hovering in the air around them. There was a look of surprise, she thought, on his face. As if even he was taken aback by this confession. "If you ever go, you should order *creponne.*"

"*Creponne?*" Louise repeated.

"Yes, it's—well, *sorbet au citron*, really. But it's made differently there, not like the sweet, sticky stuff they serve in a *gelateria*, but—it's hard to explain. It's different. Unique to Oran, I guess. Perhaps that's why I always think of it with fondness."

"It sounds beautiful," Louise said, after a few minutes had passed, meaning it. She didn't know how she would respond if pressed to tell someone about the place she had been born, doubted she would be able to come up with a single recommendation, a single good word to say. She envied the man in front of her for his memories, however tainted with sadness they seemed.

"I visited my mother today," she said then, switching to English, surprising even herself, in that moment, at her words. She wasn't certain whether the man understood, was less certain whether or not she wanted him to. She didn't mean to tell him, but he had mentioned his parents, had mentioned death, and now she could not keep out the day's events any longer, felt them well up inside her, in front of this stranger who wasn't really a stranger but something she could not put into words.

"The address took me to a cemetery. I didn't go in. I don't even know when she died." She took a quick sip of pastis, flinching only slightly. "She's the reason I came to Paris, the reason that I've gone to the places I have. The museums, the bookshops, even here, to this bar. She described them once, in a letter she wrote. The only letter she ever sent. And so I came here, to these places, searching for any trace, and all that time she was already gone. And really, I'm glad, because the real reason I was looking for her was to tell her what a horrible mother she was to me." She looked up at him, trying to gauge his understanding. "I'm a horrible person. A wretched person, really." She took another sip of pastis. "But then I think you might know that already."

"*Qu'est-ce que tu dis?*" the old woman asked, leaning over the counter. She turned to the man. "Can you understand her?"

Louise didn't wait to learn. Instead she stood, pushing the nearly empty glass back across the bar counter. "*Merci,* madame," she said, opening her purse.

"What, finished already?" The old woman raised her eyebrows. "You don't want another one?"

Louise shook her head. "No, not today."

The woman stared. "You look familiar. Have we met?"

"No, I don't think so." Louise didn't know the last time her mother had visited the bar—ten years or ten days—but she didn't think it could be her that the old woman was mistaking her for. No, she didn't seem cognizant enough for such a recognition.

"It's been years, but I never forget a face. You looked sad then too." The woman tilted her head to the side. "Nothing has changed, *hein?*"

Louise dug out several coins, placed them on the counter. The amount was more than her bill. "*Merci,* madame," she said again, putting on her coat. "*Jusqu'à la prochaine fois.*"

The woman looked down at the money and shrugged. "You should save your money, use it to buy yourself some warmer clothes." She looked back up and smiled. "At least your accent has improved."

Louise smiled, then turned and headed for the door. She did not look back.

The cold air felt good as she pushed through the door. Outside, the day was nearly finished, but Louise decided to walk rather than take the train, despite the distance, despite the encroaching darkness. Her head felt muddled and strange. From her purse, she took out two luminal tablets, swallowed them dry. She supposed she should be worried about the man inside the bar, but she wasn't—not in any immediate way. They had met twice now, and each time when he could have confronted her about the money, he had not. Somehow, though she wasn't able to explain why to herself, she did not think he would do so tonight.

Louise passed a small park, pausing to watch a group of pensioners playing *pétanque* in the dying light. They were laughing, arguing, drinking from a bottle of wine that had been left open on a picnic table. Louise felt the sudden urge to join them, to step out of the strange and suddenly complicated life that she was currently living and into theirs. The sunlight began to wane, and she could feel the chill—colder now—pressing against her. She took another tablet, left the old men behind, and began to walk.

The streets of Paris had a calming effect, she had found, one that seemed to soothe her when she could not get her mind to rest. Now, Louise pushed on, down one street and then the next, not recognizing names anymore, but not worried about becoming lost either. She had worked out the blueprint of the city, knew the arrondissements were laid out clockwise, in a spiral, the city often likened to a snail shell. Knowing that, it seemed hard to be afraid of being lost, of other things, when she knew she was wrapped up safely within a mollusk.

She passed a market then, the lights within casting a glare onto the darkened streets. The sun had set, and commuters were now searching for bakeries that still had loaves of bread, for bottles of wine that would not cost too much, before tucking themselves into the warmth of their homes. She imagined their lives as fuller, richer than her own.

Louise came to a stop outside an atelier. She stood in front of the window, gazing at the coat displayed on a mannequin. Here it was, at last, she thought, what she had been looking for in all of the fabric shops but had yet to find. It would be perfect.

She saw something from the corner of her eye, turned to look, but there was no one.

Louise told herself to stop feeling disappointed and pushed through the shop's doors, blinking at the lights inside. They were brighter than she anticipated, almost garish. She felt dazzled by them, so that she found herself blinking, once, twice, a third time, before it seemed like anything would come into view. She tried to recall how many tablets she had taken, suspecting it was too many. She would need to be careful, she thought, feeling the shopgirl's gaze upon her, sharp and alert. *"Puis-je vous aider?"* she asked, standing.

"I want that piece," Louise said, knowing even as she spoke that her voice was too loud within the small shop, too harsh.

The shopgirl looked startled by her brashness. "Of course. If you want to try it on—"

"No need, thank you," Louise said, trying to soften her tone. "I can tell it will be perfect."

The woman still looked taken aback, but she nodded and went to take the coat down from the mannequin. It was black, with raglan sleeves and a wool collar, circular gold buttons running down its front. The woman held it out for Louise's inspection. "Cashmere," she said, a hint of pride in her voice. "With a satin lining. The collar is lamb's wool."

"It's lovely, thank you," Louise said, her voice a whisper. She raised a hand to touch one of the three buttons that ran down the center, then instinctively pulled back. She didn't want to dirty them. "If you wouldn't mind wrapping it. It's a present. For my mother."

"Oh." The woman smiled. "Of course."

Louise wasn't certain why she lied, regretted it almost instantly when she realized it meant she would have to spend a longer amount of time in the shop, waiting as the woman folded it with maddening precision and then began the process of wrapping and cutting and taping. She nearly gasped when she heard the price but managed to stop herself. Louise reached into her pocket, extracting the bills. She had intended the money she placed there earlier that day to last her the next week, but with the purchase of the coat she would have to dip into her traveler's checks. She reminded herself once again just how quickly the money had gone in Granada, made a promise that this would be the last big expense. After all, a heavier coat would be necessary, and while this one might be more style over substance, it would still be warmer than the trench coat she had been shivering in for the past few days. And the money would do her little good if she were too ill to enjoy it.

Outside, she breathed deeply, wiped a hand across her forehead. She was flushed, she knew, fanning her face with both hands. She blamed the lights inside the shop, the excessive heat. She caught the eye of a man passing by on the street, thought he was looking at her strangely.

There was still no sign of the man from Oran.

Pressing her new package to her chest, Louise hurried into the darkness.

By the time she reached the hotel lobby, she was shivering.

She stopped at the desk for her key, and while the clerk was busy searching for it, she asked, "Is there hot water in the bathroom?"

He looked slightly affronted by the question. "Yes, mademoiselle, of course." He paused. "Would you like a pot of tea sent up as well?"

She considered. "Cognac," she replied instead. "A double, please."

Upstairs, she grabbed her dressing gown and a towel and then headed down the hallway to where the bathrooms were located. Once inside, she undressed in the small space. She was shaking now, her teeth rattling against one another. The water was mercifully warm—she had started it before she began undressing—the steam billowing in the cold air. She placed a hand underneath the faucet, and it scorched her, her fingers turning white from the heat. Ignoring the pain, she tossed the water around the enamel tub, knowing it would be ice once she got in and not wanting to let it touch her body until it was warm. As she did so, she told herself it was only the shock that was making her feel so strange. The shock of finding her mother, of meeting, once again, the man who had been following her.

As she lay in the bathtub, minutes stretching into longer, she found herself almost expecting him, waiting for an interruption. One came, fifteen minutes later, but it was only another guest wanting to use the bath. She told them to scram.

After some time, her skin pink and wrinkled from the water, she walked back to her room, dressing gown tied tightly around her waist. The glass of cognac she ordered had been left on the bedside table. She drank half, waited for another knock on the door. When it did not come, she told herself she was relieved. Lighting a cigarette, her hand shaking as she brought it to her lips, she finished the second half of the cognac.

As she swallowed the remainder, the liquid burning first her throat and then her belly, she moved toward the bed in her dressing gown. She felt the moment the liquid hit her, warming her, turning her thoughts soft and rounded, all the hard, jagged edges finally covered over, at least for a little while. Her head on the pillow, she began to drift to sleep, whispering, as she did, the same lie she had been telling herself all night long—that it was not over yet, that there was still a chance.

Just as she whispered to herself that she was happy there had been no knock on the door that night.

SEVEN

HENRI

The train comes to a stop.

It was scheduled, one of those quick pauses in another small town he has never heard of and that seems to allow hardly enough time for any departing or embarking passengers. It happens just as Louise has finished speaking, the sudden motion causing her to start, as if the movement had startled her from a trance.

He watches now as she leans forward, peering out the window, hair falling across her face, obscuring her expression. He can tell that something has shifted—he doesn't know if it is because of what she has just said, the confession she has just made, the promise of another, or whether there is something more behind her sudden silence. He racks his mind for the correct response, tries to think of what to say, how to bring her back.

She stands, the quickness of the motion seeming to unsettle them both. "I think I'll go freshen up while we're stopped."

He watches her leave, giving a slight nod of the head, listening as the carriage doors shut behind her. For a brief moment, he wonders whether she has really gone to the toilet, wonders whether she is instead making a hasty departure from the train. It would not be the first time. He stands, presses his face against the glass. He looks from right to left, but cannot see any departing passengers. He likes to believe that they have arrived at a truce—at least until they reach Istanbul, where he will no longer be able to ignore his job, particularly not when they are being watched—and that any such tricks or attempts have been put aside until then.

He sits back down in his seat, tells himself that she is still on the train.

And then his eyes fall onto her satchel.

In her haste, she has forgotten to take it with her. It is an oversight, surely, for he cannot believe that she would have left him here alone with her single piece of luggage, the only place that the money can be hidden. Or perhaps this is intentional. A test. He doesn't know. He glances toward the compartment door, trying to estimate how much time he has already lost. Surely there is enough for a hasty examination. Still, he waits, certain that she will come back any second—wanting her to, so that he does not have to do what he is about to.

He stands, takes a step forward.

The satchel is a recent acquisition, he can tell—its leather stiff and still smelling of the tannery. He wonders whether she picked it up in Granada, in one of the souks, wonders, too, what became of the suitcase she had been holding in the gardens. His hand brushes the zipper on top, but still he does not unfasten it. Cutting his eyes back to the hallway, he is surprised to find that there is still no sign of Louise—or anyone else, for that matter.

He opens the satchel.

BEFORE

Henri reached for his cognac, drank, ordered another.

Their final day in Paris had rattled him. No, it had done more than that. The graveyard visit, the bar afterward. He cursed. It was careless of him. He would never have gone in had he known how small the establishment was. He drank, berated himself for lying. Regardless, it didn't matter, he told himself—he had seen the look on her face when he walked in, had seen the recognition. She knew who he was. He thought again about what she had said in that bar, those words she had spoken to him in English. He hadn't known whether she had wanted him to understand or not, had sat frozen in the moments after, uncertain how to respond. And then she had left before he could.

Henri put his head in his hands and wondered, not for the first time, just what the hell he was doing. Part of him wanted to retreat to the room he had rented, to pull the curtains and sit in the darkness, to not emerge again until he had sorted it all out in his mind, once and for all. This business with her, in Paris, the business with his family, back in Granada. Instead, he drank. Tried not to think how he had let this go too far, how it had only been a bit of a lark, at first, a break from the tedium of his life. But no—that wasn't entirely true, wasn't anything, really, except a lie. He remembered the look on her face that day, in the moments before the money had fallen, before everything that had happened after. He recalled, too, the words the men back home had spoken to him. He looked up, signaled to the bartender. *Another.*

Henri had become a fixture at her hotel bar over the last few days, so that his presence seemed almost expected now. At the start, he had tossed the bellhop a couple of coins to keep him informed: of any telephone calls, of any visitors. There had been only one thus far—one telephone call and one visitor, the latter of whom had visited the hotel twice, though the second time he had not gone up to her room, had only left a small manila envelope for her at the desk. Unlike the first time, when he had spent several hours in her bedroom. Henri recognized him as the same man she had met in the bookstore, the one she had then met at a bar, later disappearing into his flat. Henri didn't like to dwell. That was her business, after all. Nothing to do with him. Another lie. He finished his cognac.

Henri paid his bill and left the hotel, pushing into the cold night air. He should go to sleep, he knew. In the morning she would be headed to the train station—another tip from the bellhop, who had eagerly informed him that a taxi had already been arranged. Henri still didn't know what train she had booked, and neither did the bellhop, his information ending at the Gare de Lyon. He suspected the concierge would know, might even know the contents of the manila envelope, but he was older, more stern looking, and Henri suspected he wouldn't be willing to part with information for just a few coins. No matter. He would sort out the train business the next day, and as for the envelope—well, it could wait. The smart thing to do now, he knew, would be to go upstairs and get some rest to be prepared for the morning.

But Henri was tired—tired of looking over his shoulder. Tired of worrying—about himself, about her, about what he had done, even though he still did not know exactly what that was or where it would lead. He was tired of thinking about decisions, the ones he had not yet made, the ones he would have to—and soon.

So while he knew that the smart decision was to get some sleep, to think over and plan what his next steps would be, he also knew that he would do the opposite that night. That he would do anything to avoid another fitful sleep, interrupted as it always was by those eyes that peered at him from the darkness, watching him. Aadir waiting for him to decide his fate.

No, Henri wouldn't be going back up to his room tonight.

Instead, he continued into the darkness, up the Rue des Martyrs, looking for distraction.

It felt strange to be out on his own in Paris.

He had been alone before, but it had been different. He had always been tethered to her, so it had never really felt like he was alone. Now, he felt exposed in a way that shook him. The year before, after the events back home, he had read about what had happened in Paris. He knew about the curfew that had been imposed for young Algerian men, knew, as well, there had been a protest, that it had turned deadly, particularly at Pont Saint-Michel, the question of whether those involved had jumped or been pushed still unanswered.

He knew that it didn't extend to him, this scrutiny, at least not unless someone knew the specifics of who he was, where he had come from. He knew that he could walk the streets and blend in with the rest, and yet he had never felt more acutely aware of the fact that he did not belong, that he was a stranger in this country that should have been his own, by rights of birth alone, but that he felt was not, could never be.

He walked, found himself in the heart of Pigalle. Streams of people crowded the streets, obscured by the darkness, by the flashing of neon lights. Normally, he would have despised it—the noise, the clatter—but he found himself grateful for the beat of the music, for the shrill of laughter that drowned out the thoughts and worries that refused to be still within his mind. He wanted to be overwhelmed by it, swept up, so that it obliterated everything else.

"*Entrez, entrez,*" someone shouted to him, grabbing at his arm.

Henri started at the stranger's grasp. The clubs didn't interest him, he didn't really want to go in. But then he paused, remembering the bars of his youth, listening to the *chebs* and *chebas* sing their provocative lyrics, remembering the nightclubs, how they had stayed out all hours of the night, searching the streets for the vendors at the first sign of light, their cry of "*Carantica, carantica,*" followed by that first bite of the cumin-flavored flan-like dish, the added harissa hot on his tongue.

Henri relented, let himself be led inside, and took a seat at the bar. He ordered a pastis, reminding himself of the drinks he had already consumed, of the early morning he would have. He looked up to where a group of five—three men and two striking women, a blonde and brunette, both older than himself but a good deal younger than the men they were with—had edged their way closer to the bar, to where Henri was seated in the corner, doing his best to avoid having to engage with others. The group, it soon became clear, had been at it for a while. They were heavily intoxicated, speaking loudly, gesturing broadly. American, he thought, though their voices were largely lost in the roar of music around them.

The one in charge ordered a drink, turned to Henri, and said, "Give this man a drink as well. He looks as though he needs it."

Henri, realizing what was happening, started to protest, but the man waved him off, smiling, laughing, too drunk to accept any protestation. After that, they left him alone for a while. The group stayed close, neither including him in their conversation nor excluding him either, so that Henri was left on the periphery, nodding along when it seemed to be necessary, content to let their words wash over him for the most part. He ordered another drink, let the man pay for it again. It felt odd, allowing a stranger to buy him drinks, but the day had already been strange, and the night stranger still, so he found he didn't mind much. His concern continued to lessen as he finished one drink and then another.

Henri couldn't remember the last time he had drank so much—the night he decided to leave Oran, maybe, though he pushed that memory from his thoughts. Instead, he tried to recall the name of the man who had bought him the drink, certain the man had told him at one point, but the crowds, the music, had washed it away. The same for the rest of the group, of which he found the men indistinguishable from one another, all older, balding, covered in a sheen of sweat, leaving the women, the blonde and the brunette, frowning with distaste. He thought they must be their wives, as they didn't seem to be showing the men any more attention than what was necessary. At one point the brunette leaned over, asked whether all men were this beastly when they were on holiday. She laughed then and he smiled. He didn't think an actual response was required.

At some point he became aware that a decent amount of time had passed. That it was late, early morning, most likely, and he began to think again about the following day—*this* day, he realized—about the tasks ahead. Henri tapped the lead man on the shoulder, meaning to ask him if he had the time.

At his question, the man's face erupted in laughter. "Ah!" the man cried, obviously delighted. "You speak English!" He turned to the rest of his friends and cried, his face turning a strange shade of red at the exertion, "He speaks English!" He turned back to Henri. "You can be our tour guide now."

Henri shook his head. "I'm not from here."

"You're not French?" The man frowned.

"No—I mean, yes—but—"

"Well, which is it?" The man looked confused, even slightly irritated at this. "Are you French or not?"

"Yes," Henri said, not bothering to explain then, certain the man in front of him would not understand the peculiarities of nationality and kinship, suspecting that, in general, such things were not as complicated for most.

"Well then, tell us where we should go and we shall go!" The man turned around, summoning the rest of his friends, urging them to finish their drinks as fast as possible.

Henri didn't really want to go with them, could have easily extracted himself from the situation. They were drunk, they didn't have any real sense of time or place or people. He could have walked away from the bar and that would have been it, his presence would have been forgotten in only a matter of minutes. But then he thought of the hotel, of his empty room, of the look on her face when she had spoken to him in English. He signaled the bartender, slipped him a few francs, and asked what the best bar in the area was and how exactly to get there.

A few minutes later, they were all squeezed into a taxi.

The ride, though brief, was extremely uncomfortable, trapped as he was inside the suffocating back of a taxi along with five other passengers, his limbs folded in on themselves. Both the women, it was decided before setting out, would have to be seated on someone's lap, the brunette making for his own. "You don't mind, do you?" she asked, in her flattened accent. She smiled and he felt himself returning the gesture. Somewhere along the way, Henri began to realize just how drunk he was. It was as though in the absence of a drink, all the rest had time to settle, to take hold. The lights he had been drawn to before now seemed harsh and intrusive. He felt blinded by them, found himself blinking, trying to dispel those flashes of red. "Got something in your eye?" the woman above him teased. Henri laughed, though he didn't know at what. It was all moving so fast—the car, the woman's voice, the laughter ringing in his ears. Henri felt as though he couldn't keep up. The car felt hot and stuffy, but despite this, Henri told himself that perhaps the night wouldn't turn out too poorly.

Getting out of the taxi, he tripped, heard the others laugh, one of the men calling, "You better watch out, Gretchen, you've got a live one there." At least that's what he thought they said. Their words were tumbling fast now, too fast, and he struggled to translate in time to respond. He wanted to ask what the man meant, what a "live one" was, but before he could, they were being ushered into the address that he had given the driver. Inside, as they pushed through the doors of the nightclub, stopping at the coat check just to the right, Henri wondered if the bartender who had given him the address had done so only as a laugh. Glancing around, he saw that the place was all red velvet and heavy gold. It looked like a bad impression of something from a bygone era. He turned to his company, embarrassed by the mistake, only to find them grinning as they took in their new surroundings, gasping with excitement, exclaiming in admiration.

He thought of his parents then. It was a strange and sudden thought, but standing there, he wondered at the disappointment they would no doubt have felt at seeing him in such a place, with company such as this.

He turned to the bar, just to the left, and ordered another drink.

"Dance floor is downstairs, apparently," the lead man called to Henri, once they had been relieved of their coats.

Henri held up his drink. "I'm fine here at the moment."

"Come on," the man urged, but Henri found himself tired, wanting only a quiet drink or two before heading back to the hotel.

"I'll sit with him," a voice said.

Henri looked over to find the brunette slipping into the seat beside him. He started to protest, to say something, anything, but before he could, the rest of the company had disappeared, the man giving him a small wink before following the rest downstairs to the discotheque.

"You shouldn't let me keep you from your friends," he said, certain his words were slurred.

The brunette smiled. "I don't mind."

"I'm not the greatest company tonight."

"Neither are they." She sipped her drink—something fizzy. Champagne, he thought, but the color was all wrong, a garish pink. He couldn't remember her ordering it. "You're not from here, are you?"

"Where?" he asked, confused.

"Here. Paris, I mean." She paused, then explained, "I saw you ask the bartender for directions."

He wondered who else had noticed as well. "No, I'm not," he admitted. He indicated their surroundings. "You really like all this?"

"Sure, why not? It beats the view at home." She inched closer. "I'm Gretchen, by the way."

He paused, then said, "Nice to meet you."

She let out a laugh. "You're certainly different than the other men I typically meet."

"Oh," he responded, wondering what others she meant.

"Yes, a lot less eager."

He wondered then what it was, exactly, that was happening, how he had found himself so easily invited on this night out with strangers. He meant to ask, but she placed a hand on his arm and said, "Don't look so serious. Have another drink."

"I think I've had my fill."

"Mind if I finish yours, then?" She drank the rest of her champagne, reached over, finished his drink as well. "Ready?"

He frowned, but stood, following her out of the club, trailing her to a taxi. "This is me," she said, handing the driver a card with the name of her hotel. She sat back, smiled at Henri, who noted that she hadn't asked him to translate, had done it by herself. He found himself marveling at her ingenuity—which he knew, however distantly, was an indication of just how inebriated he actually was in that moment.

In her hotel room, she poured them each a drink.

He knew why she had brought him to her room, that they would go to bed together, but he still found himself surprised when it happened. There had been women in Granada, but only after a long night's flirtation, sometimes more. This seemed too quick, the encounter too brief, and in the end, he felt lonelier after it was over than he had before.

"I'm going to take a bath, but don't feel rushed," she said, reaching for her dressing gown. At the door to the bathroom, she stopped, turned to look at him. "And I left you something, just there, beside the bed."

At first, he didn't know what she meant, but then he glanced over at the table and saw the stack of notes. He wondered when she had time to put them there, whether they had been there all along, and felt himself flush. "*Merci*," he murmured, anxious to be done with the conversation, to be out of the hotel room.

She flashed him one last smile. "Thanks again for a wonderful evening. I haven't had this much fun in ages." She gave a laugh, which Henri thought seemed suddenly too brash, too loud in the confined space around them. He wondered how he hadn't noted it before. "Night, darling."

In the lobby, he glanced at the clock. It was too late to go back to his hotel and try to sleep. It would only make getting up again that much more difficult. He would sleep on the train—once he figured out what train he was supposed to be on.

In the meantime, he wandered, followed his nose, the smell of yeast already beginning to flood the neighborhood. He found a bakery that was open and ordered two baguettes. He ate the first quickly, suddenly ravenous, the alcohol sour in his stomach. The second he ate at a slower pace, savoring the crackle it made each time he pressed his fingers against it, pulling it apart. It was different than the bread he had grown up with. Perhaps, though, he reasoned, it was a bit like *kesra rakhis* with the crisp sound it made when broken.

He went in search of a *tabac* then and ordered two *cafés*, drinking them in quick succession. His right eye twitched, and he wondered whether it was the tiredness beginning to pull at him or whether the caffeine had begun to work.

At the hotel, he grabbed his things, checked out, and walked to the Gare de Lyon, waiting at the taxi stand, determined not to miss her when she arrived. It was cold outside. The initial warmth that the bread and coffee had lent him began to leach out, so he moved farther into the station, but still close enough to the road that he would see the taxis as they drew up.

Fifteen minutes passed, then five more. He glanced at the board overhead. According to the information he had been given, she should have already arrived. He wondered if the bellhop had been wrong, or if she had changed her mind. He began to worry that if she didn't arrive soon, he might not have time to purchase a ticket. He began to pace, both from the cold and from his nerves.

Another ten minutes passed before she finally emerged from a taxi. She stood, clutching her wool coat to her neck with her left hand, while her right held her leather satchel. He had grown used to the way she had of walking—a strange bob up and down, arms at her side, her height ensuring that he could always find her in the crowd if he ever lost sight of her. She was, he could see, wearing those idiotic-looking sunglasses she had purchased the other day. He thought they made her look like an easy target with the child-ishness they seemed to suggest. He wished she would take them off. Besides, it wasn't even summer, and the sun only came out for brief intervals. If she was trying to blend in, to not draw attention to herself, this was certainly not the way to do so.

Henri trailed behind her, careful to keep just out of view, wishing she would speed up, that she would get to her platform sooner. He didn't know whether he would be able to make it back to the ticket counter in time.

Finally, she came to a stop.

He glanced up at the platform board. *Istanbul.* Turning, he rushed back the way he had come, to the ticket counter. He called out his order, pushed his money toward the affronted-looking worker, not caring what he looked like, only conscious that the small amount of time he had left before the train departed was dwindling.

He rushed back to the platform. She was still there. He could see her, leather bag clutched in her hand, face turned expectantly to the train, which had already begun to board.

"*Billet*, monsieur," the man at the entrance to the platform asked.

Henri showed him his ticket, walked through the barricade and toward the train.

And then he stopped.

Standing on the platform, ticket in hand, he wondered what would happen if he just let her go. He realized how easy it would be. A crowded train station. A missed connection. They would be furious in Spain, of course. The money she had taken was substantial, but he suspected that it was more out of principle that they had wanted him to retrieve it, to retrieve her. Things like this didn't happen to them, after all. They wanted to know who the girl was, who she was working for. He didn't think that they would ever be satisfied with the truth: that she was no one, that she worked for no one. That the whole thing had been one big mistake.

There was another possibility, he told himself: he could stay in Paris. He had liked it well enough these past few days. He could stay and disappear into the crowds, just as he had done before. Or he could return to Spain, go to Alicante instead, and start again there. He had heard of others like him in that area, those who left Algeria after the events and couldn't bear the thought of Marseille, of France in general. The name the French had burdened them with, ensuring that they would always be outsiders, something separate from the rest. But then, this all assumed that they would just let him go, or that the shadowy figure tailing him was one who he could shake, and not just for a moment or two, that others would not follow. Henri knew this would never happen.

A train announcement reverberated overhead. The train would depart soon. He waited, let the crowd around him swell and then disappear, along with his sight of her. He remained standing. A minute passed and then another. The train would be leaving soon. He would have to make up his mind. He would have to decide.

He wanted to laugh then, feeling the tiredness of the night before weighing on him. Of course he would board the train. He had made up his mind long ago. He couldn't just let the money go—no, the truth was, he couldn't let *her* go. He was only lying, once again, and only to himself. Henri placed one foot on the step leading to the train, hesitated only a second longer, then stepped inside, the doors closing firmly behind him.

EIGHT

LOUISE

In the toilets, Louise berates herself. She should never have mentioned her father, never mentioned her secrets—even if she only hinted at them. Looking at her reflection, she raises a hand, smears her palm across the surface of the mirror. She cannot bear to look at herself another moment.

When she returns to the compartment, Louise is certain he is stealing quick glances at her leather satchel, a look of guilt shrouding his features. She knows then that he has opened it, has looked, at last, for what it is that he is searching for, what has brought him across Europe, even though she still does not understand why he has not yet taken it back. She doesn't imagine it is his—no, he strikes her as someone who follows orders rather than gives them. Not because she doesn't believe that others would obey him, but because he doesn't seem hard enough—ruthless enough. Otherwise, this would have ended long ago. Perhaps this is what decides her, in the end.

She sits, takes out a cigarette, and tells him the rest. "After my father died, I didn't tell anyone," she begins without preamble. If he is taken aback by the continuation of her narrative, despite her temporary absence, he does not betray it. Louise pauses, pulls a tiny fleck of paper from her lips. "Instead, I crept up to his room and opened his safe. And then I took what money I could find. I took what paltry amount he had kept hidden away over the years—from me, from the creditors. I took every shilling, every single last pence. Forty pounds is what it all amounted to in the end."

She can still remember that night—every detail of it. The way she had done her best not to look in his direction. He was dead, she knew this, and yet she could not stop the rising feeling of panic—of horror, even—as she turned her back toward him, his figure slumped in his wheelchair, frightened that he might open his eyes at any moment, might lunge toward her, might grasp her by the wrist, the shoulder, the neck, and never let go. She had told herself to focus, to stop being so macabre, as she moved the lock on the safe first right, then left, then right again. She knew the combination—had known it for years, watching him when he opened it each week to give her money for the groceries, for the mounting bills—but even so, her fingers trembled as her hands touched the metal. At one point she had thought she heard a creak, whirled around to find him still there, unmoving, his wheelchair stationary.

In the beginning, when he had first been confined to the chair, he had made her mother throw away all the rugs. It had turned out to be both a blessing and a curse—she knew exactly where he was at all times, but she found herself simultaneously haunted, followed by the creak of his wheels upon the wooden floorboards, so that she often found herself starting at the slightest noise—a cupboard closing, the house settling—certain that it was him, that he was there, lurking somewhere just behind her. The safe clicked open, and she had let out a breath she hadn't known she was holding.

Now, she watches Henri—for a grimace, a frown, anything that will tell her that he is disgusted, that she is changed, altered forever, in his perception of her.

He doesn't respond right away, reaches instead for her pack of cigarettes, lights one for himself. "If he was dead, then the money was yours, *n'est-ce pas*? An inheritance."

She laughs at the word, wants to remind him just how little was hidden away in that safe so that he will understand how ill fitting the word *inheritance* is, so that he will, perhaps, understand why they are here today, together, on this train. She remains silent.

"It wasn't stealing," he insists.

She blinks, startled by his response. "Yes, but that isn't the point, is it? I took the money and I left." She pauses. "I left him there, left his body, for someone else to find. It might be days, weeks, even. I don't know if they'll ever find him—or what they'll find when they finally do. There won't be money for a funeral, not a proper one. He'll most likely be buried a pauper, in an unmarked grave, unless someone decides to be charitable. And they won't, not for him."

He nods and for a moment does not respond. She wonders if she has shocked him into silence at last, finds herself both elated and simultaneously weighted down by something else—a feeling she refuses to give name to.

"You say you spent your life taking care of him," he begins. "Maybe now it is someone else's turn."

It's a simple response—reasonable—without any hint of re-proach. Louise watches him, tries to decipher what is behind the carefully arranged features, the equally measured tone. She thinks she would hate to play him in a game of poker. "You're not hor-rified, then?" she asks, a certain desperation in her words, despite the forced lightness of her tone. She hears it, knows he most likely does as well.

He shakes his head. "No. I think you were in an impossible sit-uation."

She lets out a sharp laugh. "I'm not sure anyone else would

agree with you. In fact, I think most would be of the opinion that I deserve the very worst, an end like the women in these ridiculous novels eventually meet," she says, raising her book and letting it fall to the cushion next to her. "I certainly don't deserve to be here, on a train, with nothing but the pursuit of happiness on my mind."

"And you will find this, in Istanbul?"

The question startles her. "Yes, I think so." She thinks for a moment about herself and the idea of happiness, of what such a thing might actually mean for her. "I'll visit the Hagia Sophia and eat fish sandwiches on the Bosphorus. I'll walk the Galata Bridge and watch the sunrise." She will be anywhere that isn't there. She will no longer be trapped.

Louise wants to ask whether he can understand this, whether he can understand what made her take the money that she knows he is after, whether he might consider letting her walk away. She knows it's impossible, the money doesn't belong to her after all, and besides which, she wonders whether he can really understand the feeling of being trapped. If she were a man, she would only need to step into the world, to decide what suited her, what type of life, instead of being told, instead of being limited, relegated. She would never have been prisoner to her father's illness. The word *no* would have been at her disposal any time she wanted. It's an indescribable feeling— being excluded from the world based on gender alone. She wonders what he knows of it, if anything, decides in the end that it's not worth mentioning, not worth taking the risk. "Who wouldn't find happiness in such a place?" she asks instead, willing him to defy her.

He only nods, though she thinks he looks unconvinced. She wonders then, and not for the first time, what he is really doing, what the last fortnight has been about, what this now—the two of them here together—is for. She wonders whether he is trying to get the measure of her—if he is trying to decide whether she is a good person who has only done a bad thing. If he is playing judge and jury. If so, she wishes he would just ask. That he would come out with it and they could end this charade, once and for all.

Louise feels suddenly tired. She isn't good, she would tell him. Yes, she did a bad thing, but it is only one of several bad things she had done in her life. She doesn't want to talk anymore, wants to tell him that the past bores her and the future terrifies her. The present she can manage well enough, if she takes it one day at a time.

Instead, she lights another cigarette and turns away.

BEFORE

She had a dull, throbbing headache.

They had only left the station an hour before, but already, she wished she was back in Paris. Perhaps it had been a mistake—the ticket to Istanbul, the determination to get as far away from everything she knew. She wondered whether she should have stayed.

She turned to the window, lit a cigarette, watching as the scenery drifted past.

No, she would not have been happy there. Not in a city where her mother's shadow would have followed. It made her think, then, of her other shadow—made her smile, despite her foul mood. Louise had seen him, the man from Oran, that morning, standing on the platform—had seen the look of indecision that had crossed his face. She knew that he was debating whether or not to follow, had been startled enough by the idea that he might not that she herself had paused as she boarded the train, had caused a minor collision, the person behind crashing into her and the person behind them doing likewise. It had taken a few moments of sorting out, of apologizing profusely to the others around her, which only seemed to anger everyone more, before they were able to start again, making their way to their respective compartments.

A part of her had been furious. She wondered what had made him hesitate, whether he had finally lost interest, whether meeting her in that dim little bar in Paris had shattered whatever fantasy he may have conjured. She told herself she didn't care, didn't wait to see whether he decided to board, or whether he had turned around and gone back to Spain. She told herself that she hoped he had—then the money was truly hers and she had no more reason to worry.

She ground out her cigarette and stood.

If she had to sit alone in this suffocating compartment one more minute, she thought she might go mad.

In the dining car, the waiter was struggling to find a table for one.

Louise stood, trying to look more irritated than embarrassed. In truth, she didn't know how much more rejection she could stomach. On her way to the dining car, she had done her best to look for him, taking her time, walking slowly, pausing to admire the scenery out the windows in the corridor, though she didn't give a damn for the empty fields and trees they passed by. It reminded her too much of home. She longed instead for the city, to be back in Paris or to be arriving in the next city listed on the way to Istanbul. She tried to recall them all. Milan. Venice. Zagreb. Belgrade. Sofia. Anything was better than the empty, wide-open space that made her stomach turn.

She hadn't seen the man from Oran as she passed the other compartments, though a few passengers had been hidden from view, curtains pulled for privacy. He could still be there, but she wasn't as certain, not like she had been in Paris when there had been the feeling of him just behind her. Now, she felt only the emptiness. The place where he had once been.

"I'm sorry, mademoiselle," the waiter said to her now, a sheen of sweat on his forehead. The dining compartment was packed with voices, the clink of silverware, plates, and glasses filling the room. It felt better than the quiet of her compartment. "I can't seem to find a place for you. If you don't mind sharing with other passengers, perhaps I could see—" he began hesitantly.

She was about to tell him it was fine, that she wasn't that hungry anyway, when a voice called out: "She can sit here, with us. We've got a spare seat."

Louise and the waiter turned. A party of six—consisting of three young men and three young women—sat just to the left. One of the young women—she looked barely older than twenty, Louise thought—was waving her hand with a good deal of enthusiasm. "You can sit here, next to me."

Louise glanced at the other faces at the table, which ranged from amused to indifferent to a small frown of distaste at their friend's offer. It was the last one that decided for her. She nodded to the waiter and moved to take the empty seat. "Thank you," she said, turning to the girl. "I didn't know how hard it was to be a party of one until just now."

"That's our Iris," one of the young men broke in, though Louise had directed her comment to the young woman alone. "Always taking in strays."

Louise narrowed her eyes. "I don't think I've ever been likened to a feral cat before."

Laughter broke out across the table, although the boy—Louise decided he wasn't anything like a man, not even a young one, just a spoiled, coddled little child—only pressed his lips together firmly.

Louise thought it wasn't a good look for him; his lips were thin enough. He had, she thought, that pasty countenance that often plagued certain classes and seemed to speak of complicated family lines, inbreeding, and wet nurses.

"I'm so glad you decided to join us," the young woman broke in. "I'm Iris."

"Vivien," Louise replied without hesitation. "But you can call me Vee."

After that, introductions were made all around. The two other girls—both better looking but decidedly more dull than Iris—were called Mary and Susan, and the boys—potentially all absolute bores, Louise decided—were Michael, David, and John. It was Michael who had made the rather pointed comment when she first sat down.

"Tell us about yourself," Iris prompted.

Six expectant faces turned toward Louise. "There's not much to tell, I'm afraid." And then, when she could see that wouldn't work, that she would have to give them something, she said, "My parents recently died, and I decided it was a good time to go away for a while." It was near enough to the truth, she thought.

Her words were met with a round of nods. Louise felt herself relax a bit.

"So, you're not in want of a fortune, then?"

Louise looked up. It was Michael again. His tone was teasing, and the rest of them were smiling—but she detected a hint of uneasiness there as well. His eyes, she thought, looked particularly sharp. "No," she responded, making her words short, punctuated. "I am not."

Iris leaned closer to her. "You'll have to excuse Michael, he's always had the most appalling sense of humor," she said, leveling her gaze toward the end of the table. She turned back to Louise. "Where exactly are you headed, Vee?"

"Istanbul," Louise replied.

Iris's eyes widened. "Such a long way!" she exclaimed. "And all by yourself. I can't even imagine—all the connections, the different languages. I don't think I could ever do it all on my own."

"I'm sure you could," Louise said, wanting to add, *If you had to.*

Iris shook her head. "My parents would be absolutely livid." She stopped then, raising a hand to her mouth. "Oh, I'm sorry, Vee, I didn't mean to—"

It took Louise a moment to realize what it was that she was apologizing for. "Don't be silly," she said. "You'll have to do a lot more than that to offend me."

Iris smiled. "Do you know, you remind me of someone, I'm certain. You don't suppose we might have met before?"

Louise bit back a laugh at the absurdity of it. "No, I don't think so."

"You don't know the Actons, do you? Or the Bells?" Iris pressed. Louise shook her head.

"What about the Hutchinsons or the Russells?" a voice broke in.

Louise turned to Michael, who was obviously determined to listen in on their conversation. "I'm afraid you can list all the surnames you want, but I doubt very much I know any of them."

"Were your parents very solitary, then?"

Louise thought of her father. "They hardly ever left the house."

"I had a cousin who was a recluse," one of the girls broke in. "Refused to leave the house for anything at all."

A murmur of agreement went around the table, in remembrance of said cousin. Iris turned back to Louise. "Why Istanbul?"

"Oh, I don't know," Louise replied, wondering if she herself even knew the answer to that question. "It seemed far enough away."

"It certainly is," the girl called Susan observed. "We're only going to Belgrade, and even that trip takes ages. Why not fly?"

Before she could answer, Iris interjected, "Because the train ride is part of the experience, isn't it?"

Louise agreed, deciding that there was something about the girl seated next to her that she liked, which didn't often happen and never nearly so fast. Perhaps it was the act of travel itself that lent a more immediate intimacy. Whatever the reason, Louise found herself glad that she had accepted Iris's invitation.

"I've heard an awful lot of artists make that journey," one of the other boys at the table observed.

Michael looked at her. "Are you one of those?"

"Am I what?" Louise asked, simply because she thought he was the type of person who did not like having to repeat himself. The thought of needling him, even just a small amount, gave her unexpected joy. "Oh, do you mean an artist?" she asked, when he made only a vague sound of irritation in response. Louise thought and then decided—oh, why not. After all, she was in a far better mood now than she had been earlier, and there were still hours of time stretching out between now and her destination. Why not have a bit of fun with the others at the table? There was nothing—or no one else—currently present to occupy her time. "I happen to be a writer, actually," she said, which was met by a chorus of exclamations, none more enthusiastic than Iris herself.

"How wonderful," she declared.

"And would we be familiar with any of your work?" Michael asked.

"No, I don't think so." Louise could see that the sparsity of her response had irritated him. To the others, she swore that it wasn't as glamorous as it sounded, that long hours were spent with only her typewriter for company.

"You must write down your surname for us so that we can remember to look, when we're back in England," Iris said.

She promised, though warned them she only wrote under a pseudonym. That way, Louise figured, she could have her pick, explaining why any photograph or biography didn't happen to match. And anyway, by the time they checked, she would be long gone, a brief reminder, a funny anecdote that they told one day. Louise sipped her champagne, bit back a smile. With the exception of Michael, she found herself warming to them all, despite her intentions.

And so too did Louise find that she was drawn to the idea of herself as a writer. Perhaps that was something she could actually do, under a pseudonym like she had mentioned. Perhaps no one ever needed to know about her past—she could write herself a new one. The idea delighted her, and she found herself accepting the offer to refill her champagne glass, ordering the *oeufs frits Catalan* for lunch, though she was disappointed when it arrived, finding it had none of the flavors she remembered from Spain. This tasted mainly of grease, so she only poked at it along with the side of wilted leaves.

At one point, the one called David asked, "And are you planning to stop off anywhere first, on your way to Istanbul?"

"No, I'm staying straight on," she replied.

"Oh, that's a pity," Iris breathed beside her.

"What is?"

"That you're not stopping in Belgrade. We're there for just a few days, before heading on to the mountains to a spa. I wish you could join us."

"I wouldn't want to intrude," Louise said, trying to be polite.

"Oh, but you wouldn't," Iris said, jumping at her words.

Louise looked around, found that most of the group had gone back to talking among themselves, though Michael appeared to be watching her and Iris out of the corner of his eye. "But you don't even know me," Louise pressed.

"I know you're a writer." Iris grinned. "And the rest I'll learn. It's an even better reason to join, so we could get to know each other."

"Perhaps," Louise said, though she didn't really mean it.

The door to the dining compartment opened just then and a man walked up to the waiter. Louise couldn't see his face, but she was certain it was him, the man from Oran. He had the same strict posture, the dark hair swept away from his face, the suit and tie arranged just so. She leaned over, trying to get a better look.

"And maybe it'll inspire you."

Louise realized that Iris was still speaking. "What?"

"The city," she said. "For one of your stories."

"Oh, yes. Maybe." She was on the edge of her chair now, but still the man before her remained a mystery.

"Have you seen someone?"

Louise turned back to the young woman beside her. "What?"

"You look as though you've seen someone you know."

"No," she said, feeling herself blush. She pushed back firmly in her chair. "I thought, for a moment—but no, it wasn't who I thought it was." And it wasn't—she could see the man in question plainly now, realized that he was only a stranger.

"I'm sorry."

Louise took a sip of her champagne, smiled. "Why would you be sorry?"

"I'm not sure," Iris said, frowning. "You just looked—when you thought it was that person—I don't know how to describe it. You're the writer, you tell me."

"I don't think I looked any particular way." Louise worried that the others were listening now, wished that the girl would leave it alone.

"You did," Iris insisted.

"No, I didn't." Louise didn't mean to speak harshly, but the words came out sounding like a reprimand. The rest of the table turned and frowned. Michael, she thought, looked particularly delighted. "I'm sorry," she said quickly, then turning to Iris, she said again, "I'm so sorry. A splitting headache has just come on all of a sudden, and I can't seem to manage my way around it."

"Oh, that's terrible. I have some tablets," Iris said, reaching for her purse.

"You're kind, but I have some as well." Louise took out a luminal tablet from her purse, figured it wouldn't hurt, and swallowed it with the last of her champagne. "I think I'll head back to my compartment for a bit, perhaps try to get some rest."

"You'll be all right on your own?"

Louise gave her a smile. "I always am." She rose, but was prevented from leaving by Iris's hand on her arm.

"Shall we meet later for a drink or two, in the smoking saloon?"

Louise frowned. She found she really did have a headache now, from the champagne, from the stuffiness of the dining car, from the strain of having to smile and pretend. She found herself eager to get away. Iris must have read the hesitation on her face, or perhaps she saw the quick glance she sent in the direction of Michael, for she lowered her voice and said, "Just the two of us. I'll sneak away from the others."

"Will they let you?" Louise asked, trying to lighten her tone.

"They'll have to." Iris smiled. "I'm the one who's paying."

On her way back to the compartment, Louise spotted him.

The man from Oran was sitting in a compartment with several other passengers, looking distinctly uncomfortable. She wondered whether all the overnight berths had been purchased by the time he had made it to the ticket counter. A part of her had wanted to give him more time—she had even risen earlier than needed that morning, planning to depart for the train station so he would have at least a half an hour to figure out where she was headed, to make the necessary arrangements. Her hand had been on the hotel door-knob, gloved and ready to go, when she stopped, looked around her, and wondered just what in the hell she was doing.

This man was after her, she reminded herself, and the money. It was a dangerous game she was playing, and she needed to put an end to it. She had removed her coat then, along with her gloves, sat on the bed, and made herself wait until the absolute last minute, until she was certain that she would have just enough time to make it to the platform and onto the train. If he managed as well, there was nothing she could do about it—but she wouldn't give him any hints, wouldn't make it easy for him.

He glanced up then, saw her watching from outside his compartment.

She looked away, moving quickly down the corridor, back to her own berth.

Iris was alone in the smoking saloon that evening, as promised.

"Oh good," she exclaimed when Louise entered. "I worried you might not come."

Louise sat, took out a packet of cigarettes. "I always keep my promises."

The smoking saloon was smaller than she had expected— nothing more than an assortment of blush velvet chairs and low tables, a single waiter hovering over it all. Still, Louise found she preferred it to the clutter of the dining car, with all its complicated silver and glassware. Here, there was simply a bar, a few glasses to accommodate different drink orders, and paper napkins replacing the formality of the starched linen. She settled into the velvet backing of her chair, felt herself relax for the first time in days.

"I ordered us champagne," Iris said. "I hope you don't mind."

"Not at all." Louise hesitated, remembering her earlier words. "I'm curious, Iris, whether you were serious before?"

"About?" she asked.

"When you said you were paying for all this." Louise paused and added somewhat disdainfully, remembering the look of suspicion on Michael's face, "For them."

"Oh," Iris began, pausing when the waiter appeared with a bottle and two coupes. She waited until he left. "I should never have said that. I'm not sure why I even did. I was only trying to be funny. And it isn't like I pay them to be my friends or anything like that. We've known one another all our lives, all our families are old friends. It's just that theirs have happened to fall on hard times, and well, mine hasn't. So you see, I have a little more than the rest at the moment, though I'm sure it won't stay like that forever."

Louise thought her explanation sounded rather too rehearsed— and long. "And you're happy to spend your money on them?" She frowned. "They're happy to let you?"

"I know they seem a bit ghastly sometimes, particularly Michael, but they're protective of me, that's all."

Louise considered. Most of the animosity she had experienced was from Michael, and it had seemed tinged with suspicion more than anything else. And Iris apparently had a tendency to be over-familiar with strangers, judging by the fact that she had so readily invited Louise to join them in Belgrade after knowing her for only a few minutes.

"All right," Louise said slowly. "I suppose I can imagine that."

Iris smiled, reached for her drink.

The doorway to the vestibule outside their car opened just then, and a man, tall, his face momentarily obscured, stepped in. Louise sat up straighter, just in case.

"Are you certain you're not expecting anyone?" Iris questioned.

Louise turned back toward Iris. "Of course not."

"All right, I suppose I can imagine that," Iris said, mimicking her earlier words.

Louise smiled but turned to the window, willing the chill air she could feel through the glass to cool her flushed face. "When do you think we might cross the border into Yugoslavia?" she asked to change the subject.

"Sometime in the middle of the night, I think."

She turned back to Iris, wondering if she might be able to answer something she had been worrying over, ever since boarding the train. She hadn't thought of it, not at first, but as they crossed border after border, custom officials stepping on board to check passports and throw cursory looks at the luggage, she began to worry what might happen at night, when she was not awake to monitor their search. "How exactly do they deal with customs, in that case?"

Iris shook her head. "It's always such a bother, isn't it?"

"Yes," Louise replied, hoping it sounded like she knew what the girl's comment meant.

"On the night train, it's never that bad. The conductor lets them on, and they go through everything while we're asleep."

"Everything?"

"Luggage, I mean."

"Oh."

Iris frowned. "Didn't the night attendant ask you to hand over the key when you checked your trunk?"

Louise decided there was no point in lying. "I don't have a trunk. I don't have a suitcase. Just a small leather satchel that I carried on myself."

"No trunk when you're going all the way to Istanbul?" Iris smiled. "The boys did say you were a bit unusual."

"Apologies for that." Louise emptied the rest of her glass.

"Don't apologize. They say the same about me." Iris waved away the waiter, pouring Louise's glass herself. "I imagine they'll probably search your bag when they do checks, then."

"Checks?" Louise frowned. "I thought the sleeping attendant took care of all that. He took my passport at the start of the trip."

"Yes, and their word is sufficient if you're in Western Europe, but from what I've heard, the same isn't true once we cross into the East. They want to see the person in question, I guess, in case someone is aboard the train who shouldn't be, trying to cross borders. It hasn't happened yet, but I'm waiting for the day when they take someone away in handcuffs. Wouldn't that be a story to tell?"

"Yes," Louise said, trying to match the look of delight that had crossed the girl's face. "It certainly would."

"Anyhow, I imagine they'll search your bag then." Iris looked at her. "Anything you need to hide in the meantime, Vee?"

For a moment, Louise wasn't certain if she had spoken in jest. "Just a bloody knife I suppose I should dispose of," she teased, making them both laugh.

"So—Istanbul," Iris whispered. "I can scarcely imagine."

Louise smiled. "Have you never been?"

"No, though I would love to. One of my absolute favorite authors spent a good deal of time there."

Louise tried to riddle out who she might be referring to, but soon gave up. "Who do you mean?"

"Agatha Christie." When she saw Louise's face, she asked, eyes wide, "Aren't you a fan?"

"I'm not, I have to confess."

"Why not?" Iris demanded, and with such an affronted expression that Louise was tempted to laugh.

"All her novels seem the same, in the end."

"That's not true—they're nothing alike."

"Perhaps not the novel itself, but the outcome I mean." Iris frowned and Louise continued. "The bad ones always get it in the end, don't they? I can see that the how and the why might be interesting, but ultimately, the killer is revealed and taken away, punished for their crimes. Justice is achieved. *Finis.*"

Iris smiled. "I think that's a bit reductive, but I can see what you mean, I suppose. Still, I think you should read her—and I also think you should start with *The Murder of Roger Ackroyd.*"

"Must I?" Louise asked with a laugh.

"Yes, you must. I suspect you'll like it quite a bit actually, and I also think you'll be rather surprised," Iris promised. "Now, where are you staying in Istanbul?"

"I haven't the slightest. I'm not very good at planning, so I thought I would ask a porter when we disembarked."

Iris was shaking her head. "No need, I have the perfect place for you. When you arrive, you must stay at Pera Palace, in room 411."

"And why specifically room 411?" Louise asked in amusement.

"That's where Christie wrote one of her more famous novels. Staying there might just bring you good luck."

Louise blushed. She had forgotten the lie already. "Yes, perhaps it might."

"At the very least it promises to be absolutely beautiful, with sweeping views of the city. Or so I've read."

"You seem to know a lot about Istanbul."

"I told you, I'm awfully envious." Iris reached for her champagne. "For the most part, my adventures are confined to the pages of the books I read."

Louise smiled. "That's something I can relate to."

"And another reason why you'll love Christie. She'll take you everywhere without ever having to leave."

"Yes, but don't you want to see those places for yourself?" Louise pressed. After all, it wasn't as though Iris didn't have the funds to do so. She wondered what it was that might hold back an heiress from doing exactly as she pleased. It seemed a waste of a fortune, if it still meant being confined to one's own home.

"Perhaps one day. In the meantime I'm not too bothered to be confined to London and the occasional jaunt to the countryside. Even Christie loved Devon." Iris finished her drink. "And a trip to Belgrade—I suspect by the time we get there and back, any itch for travel will be well and truly scratched."

Louise smiled. "To Belgrade, then," she said, lifting her coupe.

Before long, the bottle of champagne sat empty, and while Iris offered to order another, Louise demurred. "I haven't had much sleep these last few nights. I think I need a few hours to close my eyes."

"And some time to pack."

Louise raised her eyebrows.

"So that you're ready to depart the train tomorrow with us," Iris insisted.

"You're relentless."

"So I'm told."

They kissed each other good night, promised to meet in the morning, no matter Louise's decision, and parted. On her way out, Louise passed the only other occupants of the smoking saloon. Up close, she could see that neither looked anything like the man she had hoped they might be.

It was curious. After her father had died, Louise had wondered whether she would be haunted by him—not his actual ghost, but people who looked like him, who reminded her of him in some fashion, however small. She had thought, at first, that she would never forget the sound of his wheelchair against the wooden floors, that it might follow her to the grave. To her surprise, it had all vanished from her mind rather quickly, as though it had never existed. Memories of that time seemed strange now, as if they belonged to someone else. Even her father's face was difficult to recall unless she concentrated.

Now, she wondered whether it wasn't something else that would haunt her. Or someone, rather. She didn't know what would be worse, to continue to have the man from Oran following her every day—or to know that it wasn't him at all, only a figment of her imagination.

The next morning, Louise stood looking at her leather satchel, trying to decide what she ought to do. The train would arrive in Belgrade within the hour, according to the timetable. If she was going to depart and join the others, she would need to decide. It was ludicrous, of course. The mere idea. Altering her plans at the last minute. Joining a group of strangers who were, in fact, just that—strangers, persons unknown to her except for a few stories traded over glasses of champagne. Louise would never have entertained the idea, would never have even given it a second thought, under normal circumstances.

Though she very much doubted whether anything would be normal again.

She was tired. That was the problem. What little sleep she had managed to get had been interrupted, as Iris had promised, by the customs officers. The whole affair had been quick and perfunctory, but she had trouble falling asleep afterward. It didn't help that in the hours before their arrival, she had barely slept at all. Returning to her compartment after meeting Iris, she had taken out the needle and thread she purchased in Paris, had begun work on what she had meant to start much earlier, letting her mind drift, entertaining different possibilities as she thought about the two options ahead of her. Alone in Istanbul or surrounded by a bunch of strangers, save for Iris, in Belgrade. Neither of them seemed particularly appealing. She felt the sourness of the champagne in her stomach. By the time she turned off the light and closed her eyes, she had slept for only an hour or so before a banging on her door had heralded the arrival of the customs officer.

Now, in the cold Belgradian morning air, her nerves felt frayed, raw. She thought ahead to Istanbul, and she felt tired, more tired still. Belgrade didn't seem a much more comforting offer, though she would have a few more hours to spend with Iris, who continued to be surprising and whom Louise had already decided she liked quite a bit. But then, she reminded herself that Iris didn't know her, not really, and if she did, she certainly wouldn't be inviting her to come along with her friends on holiday.

Back home, Louise had never experienced that type of close, intense friendship that she read about in books. But then, she often thought, those types of relationships were reserved for the good characters—the kind and sweet and blushing heroines—while the others, the ones more like her, were solitary creatures. It didn't help that the others in her school had avoided her, cupping their hands to one another's ears, whispering about the girl who was so terrible her own mother had abandoned her.

There had been the start of something, once. A new girl to their village, one who didn't know all the secrets, all the whispers and rumors, the taunts and accusations, that came with growing up with the same group of people, who knew everything from birth until the present day. Before she could ask, Louise told her that her mother had died, that she lived alone with her father. She didn't know why she had said it, exactly, but she knew enough to realize that such things mattered, that this—an absent mother, a disabled father—made her into something that was different from the rest. This fiction lasted only a few short days. The girl must have spoken to someone, must have listened to the voices that said she, Louise, was not a person worth knowing, that she was not a person worth anything.

"Why did you lie?" the girl demanded, in the days after their friendship soured.

Louise had only frowned. "What does it matter?" She shrugged, meaning it. For what did it matter whether she had told the girl or someone else? The end was always destined to be the same— Louise, alone, on her own.

She thought of her classmates then, of the smugness upon their faces at the collective judgment that she was worth less than they were. She suspected that some members of Iris's party already felt similarly toward her, and she found herself bristling at the insult.

And then she thought of the man from Oran, thought of the hesitation—a judgment of both her and her worth, she felt—that she had seen cross his face at the Gare de Lyon only the day before, and she felt something cold and steely start to build within her. It was something akin to what she had felt back in the village after her mother had left, walking the same pathways she had always walked, feeling those same eyes upon her. Louise peered into the watery morning light. It was decided, then. She glanced at her wristwatch. There were about ten minutes left before they were due to arrive at the station.

Louise began to pack.

NINE

HENRI

She is still staring out the window, cigarette in hand.

He tries to imagine it: her, in Istanbul, among sultans and mosques. Her in Ephesus, walking among ancient ruins. He can see it, these different versions of her, these imagined and potential futures. And yet none of them seem to fit the contradiction of the woman in front of him. He wonders what she is looking at now, wonders whether she is looking only in order to avoid him, for the sky has since fallen dark and little more than one's own reflection can be seen.

He wonders, too, at her story, decides it is unlikely she is telling him the truth—perhaps a sliver of it, but not everything—not yet. Still, he is surprised that she has chosen to confide even this to him, suspects that such a confession was prompted by what happened in Belgrade. He wants to tell her that he understands—the desire to run, to flee, to find a place that is not reminiscent of the past. He knows what it is like to be displaced, and while hers is of a different kind, a chosen exile, it is still that all the same. He opens his mouth, determined to inquire—about her past, about *their* past, perhaps about both. Instead, he finds himself asking, "Are you hungry?"

She turns to him, looks taken aback by the question. "No." And then with a frown, "No, I don't think I could eat."

He doesn't imagine he would be able to either, feels embarrassed for having mentioned it, now that he can see disappointment stretching across her face. It is perhaps not the response she wanted, but he finds himself uncertain how to proceed. He has always been a man of few words, one who has been content to exist within the silence of others—but now, here, with her, he no longer wishes to remain there. He wants, instead, for her to speak, to tell him another story, whether filled with half-truths or outright lies, he doesn't care. He will take them, will sift through their contents, searching for whatever truth she decides to give him.

He knows this means that his own silence must be broken. And so he clears his throat, sits up a bit straighter, and says, "I suppose it's my turn."

She turns to him in surprise. "For what?"

"To confess the worst thing I've ever done."

She seems to consider before giving him a nod, leaning back into her seat, crossing her arms across her body. "All right, then. Let's hear it."

BEFORE

The train from Paris was turning out to be an absolute nightmare.

All the overnight berths had been sold out by the morning of departure. The only ticket available was for a small, overcrowded compartment that reeked of body odor. Looking around in dismay, Henri had sunk back into his seat. He was exhausted, his mind and body spent. He told himself it was only from the night before. He couldn't remember the last time he had stayed out all night— surely not since before he had joined the gendarmerie.

He grimaced at the memory, pushed it away. He was too tired, too ill to entertain such thoughts. In fact, he really thought he might be ill, sitting among the smell of everyone else's *toilette*—heavy perfume, perhaps a touch of gardenias, his eyes turning to accuse an elderly woman in the corner. There was the scent of a body in need of washing, though perhaps that was his own. He felt himself go pale. He needed air, thought he might be sick if he didn't get it. Standing, Henri made his way over to the compartment's sole window, began to crack it open, only to be immediately reprimanded by one of the other passengers, a stern-looking matron with her purse on her lap, fingers clenched white, and rambling incoherently about *mauvais air*. He sat back in defeat.

An hour into the journey, Henri abandoned his seat, anxious for the fresh air he had been denied and somewhat desperate to discover where *she* had secreted herself away, if only to reassure himself that the endurance of the journey ahead would be worth the misery. He reasoned she had probably purchased a berth, her own ticket selected days before the departure, but suspected that peeking into private rooms would only get him into trouble that he wanted to avoid. He decided to check the public areas before taking any unwarranted risks. He went to the smoking saloon first, found it empty, save for a few stern-looking gentlemen, then the dining car, which was already teeming, despite the early hour.

As he stood at the vestibule, he noticed her seated next to a young woman who was talking with great enthusiasm. He found himself surprised by this development and then somewhat irritated and embarrassed for being so unnerved by it. She was smiling, was looking amused, even. It felt strange to watch her now. He had never really seen her speak to anyone before—waiters and concierges, yes, but nothing beyond a perfunctory greeting or inquiry. This was different. Standing there, he was reminded of Paris, of that tiny bar off Rue Richard-Lenoir, and he felt strangely affected. As though he had been excluded from something he had never been part of in the first place.

"How many for lunch, monsieur?"

The host was looking at him, tapping his pen with what looked like irritation. Henri wondered how many times he had repeated himself. "*Je suis désolé.* I'm no longer hungry, thank you." He turned away then, anxious not to be seen.

Back in his compartment, packed in with the other travelers, he began to feel ill again. He reminded himself that it was likely only a consequence of the night before—too many drinks and not enough sleep. Still, this felt different from previous hangovers, though admittedly he couldn't remember the last time he had had one. But surely, he would remember an experience similar to this—the sheen of sweat that had broken out over his forehead, the clamminess that seemed to be coating his skin like a film. He remembered dull headaches and maybe a queasy stomach—but he had been younger, his body less susceptible. He thought then of the way she had looked in the dining car—exuberant, perhaps that was the right word—and he felt his heart begin to speed up. It was not the thought of *her* exactly, but the thought of what she had looked like, what she represented in that moment—the happiness of youth, now long dissipated for him, written clearly across her entire person. Those carefree days, filled with love and laughter and friendship—for him, they had ended long ago.

He crossed his arms, told himself to stop being so idiotic, and tried to breathe through his nose and then out of his mouth, working to calm himself.

A woman across from him leaned forward and tapped him on the knee.

He looked up, startled by the gesture.

"*Ça va?*" she asked, frowning.

He gave a curt nod. He didn't trust himself to speak, thought his voice might come out sounding weak and strangled, found himself embarrassed to be on the end of someone else's concern.

The woman—she had to be his own age, perhaps even a little older—was watching him with a skeptical face. Finally, she looked down to her purse and dug around for a few moments. "*Ici,*" she said, looking up at him. She reached across the aisle and offered him a plastic-wrapped sweet. "*Le mal des transports,*" she said, giving him a weak smile. "I get motion sickness on trains as well. Especially when traveling backward."

Henri noticed then, for the first time, that his seat was faced in the opposite direction of travel. He placed the sweet on his tongue—honey, with a touch of heat from the ginger—and murmured, "*Merci*," to the woman. He leaned back and closed his eyes. Perhaps the stranger was right and it was only motion sickness. He remembered, suddenly, those motor trips to the beach when he was a child, how his father had always been forced to pull over at least once so that Henri could empty his stomach. He didn't know how he could have so easily forgotten.

Henri slept little that night, restless. Once more, he found his thoughts filled with the past, with Algeria and those days before. He closed his eyes, and he was there again—in that room, with *those* eyes, staring out of the darkness. A reminder of what he had done.

Henri opened his eyes, let out a breath he had not known he was holding. He felt horribly alone in that moment, was certain he could smell the tang of lemons, despite knowing that it was only his imagination.

Sleep unattainable, he stood, thought to stretch his legs with a walk around the train, and eventually found himself in the smoking saloon, though he didn't really feel like smoking, or drinking, for that matter. That last night in Paris had soured his stomach toward even the mere suggestion of alcohol, and he thought it would probably be a while before he could convince himself to drink anything stronger than a beer. Still, he found the smoking saloon to be a balm on his mind, empty as it was this late at night, and relatively quiet, save for two others—the same young men, he realized, as the ones she had been seated with at lunch. He took up a seat nearest the window, willing the cool air to assuage his lingering nausea.

"I don't trust her for a second," the one was saying.

At this, Henri stilled. They were speaking of her—he was certain of it.

The other—blond, with a sharp, pointed-looking face—gave a quick laugh. "Come on, she's not that awful. And certainly not to look at it."

"Isn't she?" He shook his head. "All that nonsense about being a writer, about going to Istanbul on her own. I don't believe it for a second. In fact, once we reach the hotel, I'm going to telephone home, have someone check her out."

"Michael—"

"No, Iris needs to learn. She needs to be more careful with whom she places her trust in. We won't always be around to look after her, and what then? Some charlatan comes in and manages to take it all away. You know as well as I do that Iris needs to grow up."

"Maybe, but look, we get off the train tomorrow, without Vee, and we're back on our own again, just the six of us. So let's leave it until we get home, shall we?"

The young men departed the compartment after that. So, Henri thought, leaning back into the plush chair that was decidedly more comfortable than those in second class, she had managed to take up with an heiress—and upset her guard dogs along the way. He wanted to laugh, wondered what those two would say if they found out the real reason their friend's new companion was aboard the train. That she was most certainly not in need of any monetary help.

And yet—Henri frowned, wondered if there was something to their worry. He dismissed the thought just as quickly. She could not have known about the young woman's fortune—she wasn't even supposed to be on this train, he reminded himself, recalling the strike in Paris. Besides, something told him she wouldn't be capable of it—he thought of that day in the garden, the look of anguish on her face. No, stealing money from a stranger was one thing, but from someone you had spoken with, laughed with—he didn't think she would be capable. But then, he reminded himself, he didn't really know her. Not at all.

Henri drifted then, his eyes closing every so often, only to be jolted awake by the jerking motion of the train or a noise from somewhere in the distance. He noticed that the bartender had left, the lights in the smoking room dimmed. He wondered what time it was, turned his face toward the window to ascertain.

That was when he saw him.

The sky outside was pitch-black—either late or incredibly early, he was no longer certain of the hour—which meant that the light inside the train was cast against the window, creating a reflection. This was how Henri became aware of the man from Paris standing just outside the compartment, watching him. He didn't think the man could see his own reflection, didn't think that he was aware that he had been observed. Even so, he kept his eyelids heavy.

Henri had been waiting for him to reappear, had wondered why the man had yet to make his approach, why he didn't seize upon this particular moment now. After all, there was no one else in the smoking room. The lights had been lowered. It was the perfect stage for a clandestine meeting. It was this reluctance that made Henri wonder now—that made him worry.

He let his eyes flutter nearly closed, let his head slump back, keeping his attention on the figure reflected in the window. Just as Henri was certain the man was about to push through the vestibule and into the room, he stopped, turned abruptly, and disappeared from view.

Henri remained still, wondering if it was a trap. A part of him worried that if he were to move, to open his eyes and stand, the man might come rushing into the room and then—what? That was the problem. In the end, he didn't know what the man was after, not when he had been following him so long without any approach. The only reason behind such hesitancy that Henri could think of was his familial ties.

He wondered, not for the first time, just how far that would take him.

At some point during the night, Henri must have fallen asleep. He woke the next morning with a sore neck and momentary confusion as to where he was. It quickly came back to him—the stuffiness of the compartment, the trip to the smoking room. The man who had been watching him. He looked around, but there was no one; not even the waiters had arrived yet.

Henri stood, swayed slightly, then realized the train had come to a stop. They must have reached Belgrade. He looked out the window and was startled to find *her*, standing on the platform, calmly looking around. At first, he thought she might only be stretching her legs, but no, she had her leather satchel, and was standing with that group of six—all of whom were now beginning to make their way farther from the train itself, raising their hands for porters, trunks ready to be lifted and transported elsewhere. He wondered for a moment whether he was still asleep. Just then, she turned and saw him, watching from the window. She gave him a rueful smile—and winked.

He laughed, despite himself.

He shouldn't have been surprised to find that she meant to shake him. After all, she had stolen the money that he had been tasked with retrieving. Of course she would do anything to lose him, to get away from him. He moved quickly, back to his compartment, grabbing his coat, his scarf and hat, his single suitcase. The latter he had bought while in Paris, along with a few spare clothes, not knowing how long he planned to be on the road, not knowing, at the time, how far he was willing to allow this to continue.

Stepping into the cold, Henri came to a decision. He would not let her leave the city with the money. He would not let this go as far as Istanbul. Not now that his own shadow had reemerged.

No, it was time, he knew. In Belgrade, he would get to her satchel and the money that was in it, just as he had agreed to back in Spain.

The only question was what he would do with her once he had it.

TEN

LOUISE

Louise doesn't really believe that the man sitting across from her will actually have anything to confess. It seems unlikely that he might have anything to hide at all—but then she remembers that everything about him is a lie, his whole reason for being there, in this compartment with her, obscured behind the veneer of a friendly fellow traveler. Perhaps she is wrong. Perhaps this kindness is only a guise. Perhaps he is a man built of secrets. "What is it, then?" she prompts, anxious to hear what he will divulge.

He reaches into his pocket, pulls out his passport.

She takes it from him and frowns. "I don't understand."

"It's a fake," he informs her.

She raises her eyebrows. Whatever she had expected, it was not this. A part of her had thought he might have been reaching for his official papers, that perhaps this was what the great surprise was all along—that he was with the police, not the people who wanted their money back. Her heart began to beat faster at the thought. He has that look, she thinks. Observant, stern. And then there's the way he sits—his back straight, his posture too exact to be explained as anything else. "Why do you need a fake?" she asks.

"The same reason I suppose anyone does." He pauses, seems to be waiting for something—a response, perhaps. When she remains silent, he says, "So that I won't be found."

"By who? Someone from your past?" she asks, though she doesn't think so, doesn't believe that it fits the man in front of her. He seems somehow too good for the sordid tales of her own life. She can't imagine they might comprise his own as well.

"In a way, yes."

"Really?"

"You don't believe me?"

She thinks. "No, I don't."

This admission elicits laughter. "What do I need to do to convince you?" He leans forward, starts to point to the passport. "Shall I show you how you can tell?"

"No," she says, holding the passport away from his grasp. "Tell me why. That has to be part of the answer. A fake passport isn't enough to explain why it's the worst thing you've ever done."

He seems to consider. "I have a fake passport because I needed to leave Algeria, and I didn't want to be found once I did."

"Why?"

"Because of the way I left."

"And how did you leave?"

He pauses, looks out of the window. For a moment, she's not sure he will respond. His tone, up until now, has been light, teasing almost, but there is a seriousness, just there, underneath. A rawness that suggests he isn't ready to delve into whatever prompted his exodus.

"I abandoned my post." He seems to consider. "I deserted."

She thinks, decides her earlier assumption must be right. "French Army?"

"Gendarmerie."

"And *why* did you leave?"

He hesitates. "I don't know how much you know about what was happening—"

She had read about it in the papers—the Algerians fighting for their independence from the French. It all seemed so distant, unreal—but then, the man before her had been there, in the midst of it, and on the wrong side of it as well. She finds she has trouble reckoning these different sides of him—good, kind, but employed by criminals; earnest, smart, but fighting on the wrong side, the side that history would frown upon and condemn. She wants to ask him to explain, to make her understand, but she says only, "I know enough."

He exhales, looks down at his hands. "I just found that I couldn't do it, the things I was ordered to do."

She considers, decides she doesn't believe that people can change, not really. "All of a sudden?"

"My parents died. That happened first. And then I—"

He looks at a loss for words, and so she offers, "Didn't want to live for them anymore?" She thinks this is something she can understand.

He looks at her. "Yes, I suppose that makes sense. And then there were the protests with the civilians, all the casualties and—" He stops. "I know it sounds foolish, but I really didn't see it for what it was. What others were already calling it."

"War."

"Yes."

"So why didn't you just resign?"

He hesitates. "There was an interrogation. Of a boy I knew. Aadir. Not a boy by that time, of course. We just hadn't seen one another since our childhood."

"And what happened to him?"

He shakes his head. "I don't know."

"What do you mean?"

It takes him a moment to begin, and she thinks she can see the change in him, the retreat, that takes place. When he does speak, it sounds as though he is speaking of something happening now, in present time, not recounting something that has already happened.

"After the protests, I was called in to ask questions, to interpret," he begins. "I didn't even recognize him right away, but when I did, I tried to ask if he remembered me as well—but he didn't respond." He shakes his head. "Sometimes I wonder whether I only imagined it, whether he really was this boy from my memory, Aadir, or whether he was someone else entirely, my mind playing tricks on me. We were only in there for a matter of minutes, and yet, even now, I can't get it out of my mind. I close my eyes, and it's his eyes that I see."

He leans back in his seat. "When he finally started speaking, I couldn't decide what to do, not at first. And then, I was translating, every word. His association with the rebels. His part in the planning. I could have held something back, could have arranged the words different, placed emphasis on one thing. But I didn't. I couldn't decide, and by the time I did, it was too late." He shakes his head. "In the days after, I tried to find out what had happened. Everyone I asked shook their heads, claimed they didn't know who he was or anything about him. It was as if he had just disappeared, as if he had never existed in the first place. And I—I stopped asking." He stops. "And then I left."

"You ran."

"Yes." He gives a weak smile. "It seems we have that in common."

Yes, but it wasn't the same. He had run from an idyllic childhood that had been shattered by war, while she had run from the opposite, a house of anger and hatred and resentment. They weren't the same things at all, she wanted to tell him. He had done a dishonorable thing for an honorable reason. None of her choices had been made for reasons that were good, that were noble.

She had meant to shock him, before, with her admission. But now he is the one who has rattled her, for it is suddenly clear to her just how staggeringly different they are. She turns away from him, wishes that she were anywhere other than in this compartment, with him, with this man who was, who would always be, better than her because he was good, he was worth saving. Leaning over, she hands him his passport and asks, "Is that your real name?"

He shakes his head, then says, "It's actually Jean-Henri."

Even his passport is not entirely a lie. "It suits you." She turns away, unable to meet his stare. Instead, she glances toward the corridor, desperate to avoid him and this conversation. She notices a figure standing just beyond their compartment. "Don't look now," she begins, "but there's that man again. The one from the dining car."

Henri doesn't turn, keeps his gaze directed on her face. "What is he doing?"

"The same thing he was before." She turns back to look at him. "Watching us."

BEFORE

At the front desk of the Hotel Metropol, Louise worried that there weren't any rooms available. Either that or the concierge was taking his time. She would be out of a train ticket if that was the case, as well as a comfortable night's stay in a hotel. Then her hasty decision would have all been for nothing. She turned to Iris, where she stood waiting with the rest of her friends, and gave them a thin smile.

"Ah, yes, mademoiselle, we have a room, at the rate of—"

Louise felt the breath escape her. "I'll take that one, thank you very much."

Afterward, once they had all checked in, they decided to go sightseeing. Louise hadn't really felt like it, had wanted nothing more than a hot bath and good, long sleep—where she could avoid thinking and rethinking her decision, wondering whether *he* had followed—but Iris had begged, pleaded, had practically turned a bright pink in her exertions to convince Louise. In the end, she felt there was very little she could do but nod and smile weakly, telling her new friend that she would be delighted to come with them.

It was decided that they would go to Kalemegdan Park, to see the fortress.

Set among a sprawling green space, the trees were an array of reds and yellows and oranges. A perfect autumn day, Louise thought, pulling her coat closer to her. They had started in the city, on the main pedestrian street, Kneza Mihaila, and walked from there, the buildings slowly disappearing around them. At the entrance to the park, where a few vendors sold gifts and souvenirs, they paused. The young men purchased beer tankards, a set of large knives—something closer to daggers, really—while Mary and Susan bought a few postcards to send back home.

Afterward, walking through the gates of the fortress, they explored what was left of the castle and strolled along the Sava Promenade. They stood and looked out at the city, the view resplendent from atop the cliff. They turned and looked toward the water, where the Sava and Danube Rivers met. After, they stopped by a food vendor and purchased *burek*, which they cut up and passed around their group of seven. The warmth and grease worked to improve Louise's mood.

The group seemed kinder toward her, too, since they had departed the station. Even Michael had ceased in his assault—although Louise still felt an occasional glance thrown her way. She stopped herself from bristling too much, remembering what Iris had told her. Instead, she began to consider that maybe Iris was right about her friends.

They saved the Roman well for last. One of the girls in the group, Mary, shivered upon entering the darkened space and decided almost immediately that she wanted to leave. The rest of them filed out rather quickly after that, though Louise chose to stay behind.

There was a tour group being led around by a rather enthusiastic guide, despite the bleak subject matter, and Louise found herself curious. "Some say that this well possesses a dark history," the guide intoned. A few people in the group stifled yawns, others rolled their eyes. It seemed that the imposed gravitas was boring his audience. Louise leaned in closer. "They say that the well was never used as a well or a cistern," the man was explaining, "but that an alternative use was made of this sixty-meter hole." Louise thought she knew exactly where this particular tale was headed. If history was anything, it was reliable in its repetitiveness, in the dependability of man's cruelty. "According to some, skeletons were discovered below. Prisoners."

Louise looked down.

"An *oubliette* is what they called it. A dungeon that could only be reached by an opening in the ceiling and, in this case, impossible to escape. The prisoner was trapped at the bottom, unable to get out, held at the mercy of his captors."

Louise felt a shiver run through her. *Oubliette.* Presumably, she reasoned, from the French *oublier*, meaning *to forget*. A forgotten place, then. She recognized it from the Gothic novels she had read as a child, the heroines locked away by tyrannical husbands. Louise had never been trapped in a dungeon herself, but she had been locked away all the same, and the escape had seemed just as insurmountable. She felt something turn cold inside her, felt for a moment as though she could not breathe.

She searched for the entrance.

Outside, in the light, Iris was waiting for her. "Where did you disappear to?"

Louise struggled to compose herself. "I was listening to the guide back there, at the well."

"You're braver than I am." Iris gave a shudder. "The boys were saying that one of the locals claimed it was used just recently, that some man tried to get rid of his wife by throwing her body down the well. They didn't find her for ages."

Louise didn't doubt it, but she said, "I'm sure they're only exaggerating."

Iris shrugged. "Maybe. Still, I don't like it. I suppose if anywhere were likely to be haunted, it would be a place like that." She looked at Louise. "Are you all right?"

"I'm fine, why do you ask?"

"No reason, you just look a bit peaked, that's all."

"Nothing a glass of something strong won't cure," Louise teased.

Iris laughed, linked arms with her friend. "Do you know, I don't think a well is that ingenious of a place to hide a body. I would have chosen the Danube, I think. Less chance of getting caught. What about you?"

Louise broke her friend's hold, reached into her purse, and withdrew a packet of cigarettes. "I don't suppose I would. Try to hide it, I mean."

"What? You would just leave the body out for someone to find?"

Louise inhaled, felt the cigarette burn its way down her cold lungs. "Why not? If you're bound to get caught, what's the point of trying to hide what you did?" She blew out a puff of smoke. "And they all do—get caught, I mean. In the end. Your Christie tells us that."

"You're being awfully macabre. Look, Vee. I've still got gooseflesh."

Louise wanted to tell her that was from the chill weather rather than anything to do with lingering ghosts or whatever else she had gotten into her head, into both of their heads now. She told herself to stop being ridiculous, that there were no such things as ghosts. But then she remembered the way she had felt standing there, looking into the abyss. She shivered and looped her arm back through Iris's own. "Come on," she said, forcing a lightness into her voice that she did not feel in that moment. "Let's go find the others."

Once reunited with their party, Louise watched them as they spoke, as they laughed, tiny asides leading to longer anecdotes, the shared history, the familiarity, running between them. She wondered what it would be like to be a part of something like this, a group of people, of friends, who knew one another's faults, their worst bits, presumably, and still laughed and cared for one another. She thought of the way Iris had defended Michael, had not denied his selfish, narcissistic nature, but had declared her love, her loyalty for him, nonetheless. She felt it then—an ache, a longing, sharp and insistent. Felt the possibility of it, something she had never before experienced, so tantalizingly close, a possibility where before there had been none.

It was only a mirage, she knew.

Louise drew her coat closer to her, steeling her nerves against the cold—against everything.

After returning to the hotel, they went to prepare for supper. Louise promised she would meet them all in the lobby at seven, despite already knowing she would not.

Instead, she walked back out into the cold and stepped into the taxi she had asked the concierge to order for her. She knew that Iris would be baffled by her absence, offended, maybe, but it couldn't be helped. Louise needed to be alone. She wasn't certain what it was— that damn well, maybe, reminding her of before, or perhaps it was Iris and her friends, a vision of what could have been. Louise knew only that she could feel it, a type of darkness, threatening to sweep her up, overtake her, wrapping itself around her like a cocoon.

And so Louise left the hotel on her own, needing to dispel the
shadows lurking around her, to cast them off, before she was dragged
down into the oubliette along with them. It would do her no good,
she knew, to sit in her room alone, but nor could she bear the idea
of being the odd one out at dinner, prying eyes and questions constantly thrown her way. She had asked the concierge to make a
reservation for her somewhere in the city, somewhere away from
the hotel, away from the crowds of tourists.

The driver stopped in front of a row of buildings that looked
more residential, in a part of the city Louise didn't recognize.
"Here?" She frowned, stepping from the taxi. Louise wondered if
this was some sort of scam, whether the driver wouldn't now demand money from her to take her back to her hotel, or whether he
didn't have someone else lying in wait. But the driver only pointed
at one of the doors, and when she still did not see—for she was
certain it was a residence, nothing more—he alighted from the taxi,
pressed one of the buzzers on the door himself, and waited with
her until she heard the corresponding click a few moments afterward. Embarrassed, she thanked him, placing an outrageous tip in
his hand.

Inside, the building was almost completely dark, and as Louise
stood in the foyer, she found herself wishing that she had asked
the taxi driver to wait. Glancing up at the wrought iron railing of
the steps before her, she found herself further convinced the wrong
address had been given. She turned to go, but something—a noise,
a fraction of a light—caught her attention. Stepping farther into
the foyer, she glanced toward what she supposed was the garden flat and saw a thin sliver of light emerging from somewhere
just beyond. Louise considered only for a moment, remembering
her words to the concierge, her desire for something local, some-

thing away from the regular tourist haunts, and started down the steps.

Stepping inside, she found herself immediately overwhelmed—by the amount of people, the noise, the smell of the food flooding the cramped space. She felt too warm in her coat, felt the sweat begin to gather on the small of her back.

Louise was shown to her table in a room that looked more like a conservatory than anything else, green plants placed in every corner and hung from above, so that they looked as though they were spilling from the ceiling. The effect was jarring, for while there was no sun in this subterranean flat, it felt as though she were seated outside on a sunny day.

"Hungry?" the waiter asked.

She wasn't, but she was surprised by his crisp English and found herself saying yes. A menu was handed to her, one that was written in Cyrillic, but she found she didn't much care what she ate, so she pointed to a few things, which the waiter graciously translated, and then accepted his suggestion of a honey-flavored rakija.

The drink came first, followed by another round, and then another, so that by the time the food arrived, Louise found that she was starving. She devoured the *cevapi* first—tiny little sausages that came with a flatbread and sour cream. She ate the *burek* next, a coil of pastry so thin it cracked upon touch and was filled with egg and cheese and spinach. The one they had shared in the park earlier paled in comparison—this was warm and left her fingers coated in a layer of golden oil.

She had hardly eaten in Paris, turning away the sweets that usually delighted her, ordering the plainest, simplest of foods instead. Now, she ate greedily, licking the grease from her fingers. Perhaps, she thought, her appetite had returned because she was somewhere that was unknown to her. Here, she could decide who she was and what future she wanted, unlike in Paris, where the past still tied her, tethered her to the person she was before. It was the reason that she had decided on Istanbul. The chance to disappear and start again. To be someone else. She hadn't believed it possible, had thought she would feel the same everywhere, that she would not be altered by the place and people around her.

For the first time, she found herself hopeful that she might be wrong.

Afterward, she walked.

The host at the restaurant had wanted to call her a taxi, had insisted, but she had waved him away, eager for the fresh air against her skin. She turned on Bulevar despota Stefana, toward Skadarska. Back at the hotel, the concierge had recommended a short stroll to the Skadarlija following her dinner, likening the neighborhood to Montmartre. Louise had raised her eyebrows in skepticism at the claim.

"The gypsies lived there, then many artists," he promised her. "Bohemia."

As she walked, she looked for *him*, the man from Oran, wondering again if he had managed to follow her off the train, or if he was, even now, barreling toward Istanbul.

The winding street of Skadarska was livelier than the street she had just come from, despite the darkness, filled with cafés and galleries and restaurants. Louise looked around her, thought of the promise the concierge had made, and decided that he was right. Gone was the severity that had defined other parts of the city. Between the soft glow of the lamps casting their light on the iron benches, the trees stretching over the cobblestoned streets, the tables and chairs pulled outside each restaurant, filled with people eating and drinking, smoking and laughing, Louise could have been in Paris, could have been sitting down at one of her favorite spots in Montmartre.

She came to a stop under one of the streetlamps, where a number of vendors had set out tables, selling a variety of arts, crafts, vintage castoffs no doubt left over from the war. The thought made her feel sad—or perhaps *maudlin* was a better word—but she put it down to the weather, which was colder than Paris, the chill of autumn turning into something more wintery.

At one of the stalls, she lingered, her eyes roaming the articles on display—someone else's ring, someone else's comb, someone else's purse—all glittering under the lamplight. She didn't want any of it, didn't want the responsibility, the weight, of being tasked as the keeper of someone else's memories. Her own were more than enough. Still, she felt the eyes of the sellers on her, felt pity that they were forced to part with items that had once brought someone joy, perhaps even themselves. Louise dug in her purse for some of the dinars she had exchanged for her francs back at the hotel. She bought a clutch threaded with shining silver beads, the inside lining yellowed and torn. In the taxi back to the hotel, she looked down at her new purchase, ran her hand across the beaded design, did her best not to think about who might have done the same before.

In the end, she left it in the back seat, for someone else to find.

At the hotel, Louise lay on the floor in the bathroom. Her stomach churned, but every time she felt as though she might be sick, the feeling retreated and she was left with something even worse. At some point she fell asleep against the cold tiles, woke up shivering, certain she had heard something. She sat up, her eyes searching the hotel room, but there was no one—nothing. She was only imagining it, she knew. There were no ghosts lurking around her, trying to drag her down into their wells. There were no monsters, either, hiding beneath her bed. She bit her lip, frowned. She was the only one in the room—the only thing to be frightened of.

Still, Louise did not close her eyes again that night.

ELEVEN

HENRI

Louise is still watching the man outside their compartment. She had pulled the curtain earlier, largely obscuring them from his view, but every now and then she pulls it back again, just enough so that she can peer into the corridor. "What do you think he's doing here?" she asks, dropping her voice to a whisper, though he thinks she already knows.

"I don't know," he lies.

"What do you think he wants?"

"I don't know." Again, another lie.

"Well," she says, her tone firm. "Perhaps we should ask him, then."

"No, I don't suppose we should."

"Why not? I'm tired of being watched." She turns to him, her gaze hard. Steely, he thinks. "It grows tedious after a while."

There is an edge to her tone that Henri doesn't think was there before. Something is amiss, has been ever since he had shown her his passport, hoping she might do the same. He had found her own— forged, as well—when he had opened her satchel, the piece of identification lying on top, as if waiting to be discovered. The passport itself is good—certainly good enough to get her across the Bulgarian and Turkish borders, and more than good enough to get her wherever she wants to go from there. Still, he can see it—the signs that it has been tampered with, that it is a forgery, however well-done it may be.

He thinks of the young man who had visited her in Paris, spending time in her hotel room. That must be it, he decides, recalling the small manila envelope that had been left for her at the front desk. He wants to ask, to see if he is right—but he can tell that she is not in the mood, that something has upset her, agitated her. Perhaps it is only the man watching them, but then Henri does not think that is all, senses that it came after he told her about his own past. It seems to have divided them, though he cannot understand the reason for this.

"Shall we go to the smoking saloon?" he suggests.

"Why, so that he can follow us there as well?" she challenges.

He sees her point but knows also that their location will not change the man's whereabouts, that he will continue to follow them, to shadow them until he makes the decision to approach. It is only a matter of when, Henri knows. Something stirs in him then. A realization that they are running out of time, that it is all barreling toward an end and they have yet to really start.

"Louise," he says, the name still unfamiliar on his lips. "Louise, what happened in Belgrade, I—"

The look she sets on him stops him cold. They remain like that for several minutes, maybe more—it certainly feels like it, Henri thinks.

"I've had enough," Louise says, starting to stand, and he wonders for a moment what exactly it is that she means. "I think we should ask the gentleman if he's lost, don't you?"

Henri is about to tell her that they won't do that, that it's the most idiotic idea he can think of, when he realizes that she's already standing, already opening the door, an incessant buzzing in his ears the only thing he can hear in that moment.

Louise steps forward, but before she can utter so much as a word to the stranger in the corridor, the night attendant is standing before her. Both Louise and the attendant jump back, startled by the other's appearance. "My apologies, mademoiselle," he begins, covered up by her saying, "No, don't be silly, that was my fault entirely."

They stand for a moment like that, unsure how to proceed. Then the attendant seems to recall himself, looks to Louise again, and says, "We have a compartment in our sleeping car that is empty until we reach Istanbul. I thought that, perhaps, mademoiselle might be more comfortable there overnight?"

He can see the surprise on her face, can feel her turn to him, just slightly. There is only one answer that makes sense, but still, he finds himself hoping she will give another. "Yes," she says. "Yes, of course."

The attendant smiles. "If you will please follow me."

"Now?" she asks.

The attendant looks confused. "Yes, it is ready for you now."

"I'll just collect my things." She turns, steps back into the compartment, avoiding his eyes. She reaches for her satchel—she is still wearing her coat—and hesitates. "Well, I suppose this is good night," she says, looking back toward him.

Henri nods. "*Bonsoir.*"

The attendant clears his throat again. "Shall we?" he asks, indicating the direction in which they should begin.

"Yes," Louise says again. "Yes, of course."

Before he can gather himself to say anything, they are gone, through the vestibule and into the next carriage, leaving Henri alone. For the next few minutes, the compartment is silent, and he can feel the emptiness that her absence has left. He brushes this aside, knowing that he has other business to take care of now, that it cannot be ignored any longer.

He stands, opens the door to his compartment. "Well?" he says to the man standing in the corridor.

The man smiles, heads toward the open door. "*On se rencontre enfin.*" He gestures for Henri to take a seat first. "That was convenient," the man says, indicating the direction in which Louise has disappeared. "Gives us a chance to speak." He's not someone Henri recognizes from Spain, and he wonders if he's been hired for this job, as he seems to speak a little French, though his words are hesitant, unsure, his accent difficult to understand. Henri's own Spanish is decidedly better.

"Yes," Henri replies, wondering if the man had any hand in the compartment that suddenly became available. He wonders whether there is anything to worry about, on Louise's end, whether someone might be waiting for her there—but no, he hasn't noticed anyone else, thinks the man is alone. An assault on this train would likely bring too much attention, he reasons. "Presumably you already know my name. Perhaps you should tell me yours, since this is an introduction of sorts."

The man smiles. "For now, let's say *Fulano.*"

Henri does the translation, smiles back. If he didn't have to dislike the man in front of him, he suspects he might feel quite the opposite. "All right, *Fulano.* Well?"

"Well," the man repeats. "You have the girl, you have the bag. *Quel est le problème?*"

Henri exhales. He has been waiting for this, preparing, and he tells himself to begin slowly, to be careful with his words. He switches to Spanish, to make certain the man understands. "The problem is that the money isn't in her bag."

The man frowns, sits up. He has lost some of his bravado, Henri can tell. Good. He had been expecting that—or hoping for it, at any rate.

"What do you mean it isn't in the bag?"

The question tells him exactly the type of man he is dealing with. This is good also, Henri decides. "I checked the bag. I found this instead."

The man looks down at the carbon receipt that Henri has handed him. "What is it?"

"A wire transfer."

The man looks up, confused. "For what?"

"She transferred the money while she was in Paris."

"To where?"

He points to the receipt. "Istanbul."

The man curses. "Why would she do that?"

Henri tries his best not to frown, to show signs of irritation. "To avoid a situation like this, I would suppose. One where the money is forcefully taken from her."

The man nods. "Let's drag her off the train, then, take her somewhere to get the money."

"It doesn't work like that." Again, Henri measures his tone. He speaks slowly, with authority, but does his best not to condescend. He's met men like this before, has dealt with them throughout his career. He knows their lack of patience, their unwillingness to commit to the smart plan when a quicker alternative is available. He must make him understand that there is no choice here, that there is only one option. "The money has been transferred to a specific bank in Istanbul. It's the only place that it can be retrieved."

"So why don't we jump the train, hurry our way to Istanbul,

and grab the money ourselves? You can tell them that the money belongs to your wife."

"Unless you have the exact identification for the woman's name listed just there," he says, pointing at the carbon copy, "they won't be handing over any money."

The man curses, looks out of his depth. He asks Henri, "So what do we do?"

"Exactly what I have been doing." Henri indicates their surroundings, leans back in his seat, and closes his eyes. "We wait." He means to leave it at that, but between the clanking of the train and the feel of the man's gaze upon him, he struggles to remain silent. "How long?" he finds himself asking. He opens his eyes. "Since Granada." It isn't a question.

The man fixes him with a disappointed stare, crossing his legs, then his arms, settling back into his seat. He says, his voice heavy with disappointment, as if Henri's actions have wounded him, "This was a test, my friend." He shakes his head. "And you are failing."

Henri closes his eyes again. The man is lying.

They aren't friends—and Henri has already failed.

BEFORE

He found himself adrift in the city.

Belgrade. Beograd. The name alone shook him. It felt cold, austere even. It matched the way the city looked. The buildings were heavy, imposing. He could feel himself shrinking from them as he walked down the streets. It was ridiculous, he knew. They were only concrete and mortar, they could not hurt him, and yet he could not explain it, but he felt himself flinch under their shadows. Even the hotel she had chosen—though she hadn't selected it, had only followed the others—the Hotel Metropol, was so severe in its construction that he found himself recoiling from it as he stepped into the lobby.

Now, standing at the window in his room, he searched the view for something familiar—the endless blue of Oran, the pink skies of Paris, even. There was nothing, only clouds and cold and the promise of snow. Three nights, he reminded himself. That was what the bellhop had told him she had booked in for. Three nights and then she was scheduled for a drive to the train station, resuming the journey to Istanbul. Turning away from the window, heading into his private bath, he wondered if that was really the final destination, or just one stop on an endless adventure that would take her across the world. He wondered whether he would follow.

Henri turned the water on, let it run until the steam filled the room.

The city was too damn cold.

At least he knew the day of her departure, which had made the decision to stop following her a little easier. He needed time to think, to formulate a plan, and he couldn't do it while constantly en route. Besides, she was with *them* now. That group of young people she had encountered on the train. It changed things somehow, made the watching seem more illicit than it had when it was just the two of them. The addition of six other people made him uneasy. It also, he realized, made it easier to be spotted. She had noticed him early on; there was no guarantee that they would not as well.

It was best to step back. To take a moment, so that he might think and plan.

And he was exhausted, if he allowed himself to admit it.

After his bath, Henri had lunch sent to his room. He didn't know what exactly he had ordered, had not recognized anything on the menu, but decided it didn't matter, he wasn't hungry. He just needed something to distract him.

Henri had already paid the bellhop to keep him informed of her whereabouts, just as he had in Paris. That had been the first step. And he was grateful to find the boy seemed eager to earn a bit of extra money. But then, he supposed that bribes in Belgrade might be few and far between, for the Metropol certainly didn't inspire the image of scorned lovers skulking about hallways. The boy had already informed him that she was out for the afternoon—with her new companions, sightseeing, of all things—and that they had made reservations in the hotel restaurant for half past seven that night.

There was a knock on the door.

Henri nodded at the waiter, gave him a tip, and then, just as he was leaving, caught sight of a key ring on his belt. In Paris, he had decided against breaking into her hotel room, not yet ready to head back to Spain. And while the idea of returning still sat uneasy with him, he knew that it could not be avoided forever. If there were a way to retrieve the money without having to forcibly take it from her, he far preferred that route.

Henri left the food. He had given it a cursory push of his fork, both sausage and sauce heavy and gray in appearance, the meal rounded out with a lump of unappealing cabbage just to the side. He didn't imagine he could convince himself to take more than one bite, let alone finish the entire plate.

No matter. He had come to a decision—a step forward. Now, finally, he would be the one to lead.

Downstairs, he found the bellhop.

"I need her room number," he began without preamble.

The boy immediately looked nervous.

"Don't worry, it's nothing like that," he assured the boy. "I only need to leave something for her. A note."

"I could take it," the boy offered.

"It isn't finished yet," he said, knowing it sounded like the lie it was. Henri slipped a few more dinars into the boy's hand, in part to cover his own embarrassment.

"504," the boy said nervously, followed by, "But I can't get you the key. They would know it was me. I would lose my job."

Henri smiled, clapped the boy on the back, and assured him that he would slip the finished note under the door, a key would not be necessary. The bellhop looked like he didn't believe him.

Henri took the lift to the second floor, though his own room was on the third, and began to search the hallways. It would be better to do it here, he reasoned, away from anything that might connect him to what he was about to do. But there was no one, not a single guest or housemaid, the latter of which he had been hoping to find. He went back to the lift, took it to the fourth floor. He felt uneasy, worried that he might inadvertently draw attention to himself by moving between floors, but no one seemed to notice. Most likely, he told himself, because there was no one around to notice. It was almost as though the hotel were empty, himself and Louise and company the only guests. He supposed he should be grateful for that at least.

Henri rounded the corner then and found what he was looking for—the housekeepers, with their carts of towels and sheets, still finishing with the morning turndowns. A younger woman was standing in front of the cart, organizing the items. She looked up as he approached.

"Could I please have a few extra towels?" Henri asked, in English. He tried to avoid looking at the outline of keys that could clearly be seen in her front apron pocket.

The woman frowned. No English, then. He tried French, but still nothing, only the deepening of her frown, the start of a worried look, which he had wanted to avoid. As a last resort, he tried Arabic.

Her face lit up with understanding. She smiled and handed him a stack of clean white towels. "Shukran," he said, stepping closer to the cart, leaning to accept them. "Bi s-Salaama."

"Ma'a s-Salaama," she responded.

Henri turned, hurried back to the lift, keys in hand.

He didn't know when she would return, but he knew for certain that she would be at dinner starting at half past seven and figured it would be an hour's affair, at the very least. More than enough time to enter into her room with the master key, search her bag, and take back the money. Henri took a sip of the cognac he had ordered from downstairs to steel his resolve.

He knew it was the right decision—retrieving the money, setting things in motion for his return to Spain—and yet something weighed on him. It was taking the keys from the young woman, he finally settled upon, that was the crux of it. He hoped she wouldn't be in trouble—or worse still, lose her job—when she discovered they were missing.

And then there was *her*. A part of him regretted having to take the money, he admitted to himself, plagued as he was with questions of what she would do, how she would survive when she realized that it was all gone. He didn't think she had another plan, didn't suppose she had any additional money stored away somewhere else. Perhaps he would leave some for her, he thought. Not from the money she had stolen, but from his own funds. He could put it in an envelope and leave it with the concierge. It wouldn't be much, just enough to get her started again, to ensure that she wasn't left stranded. He suspected she wouldn't want to accept it, that her pride wouldn't allow it, but in the end—well, he knew what people did in the end, when they were desperate.

Henri finished his cognac.

He thought he might take another bath, try to warm himself in the hour or so he had left before their dinner reservation. In the bathroom, he turned on the water, waited. Several minutes passed and still there was nothing but cold water. He rang down to the lobby, inquired with the concierge, who was apologetic but offered no solutions, only a vague promise that the hot water would return at some point. Henri placed the telephone on the receiver and cursed.

He would go out and get a drink, he decided. See something of this country besides this damned hotel room. There was still time enough before dinner. Henri called the lobby again, asked for a taxi and a recommendation for somewhere to eat and drink—a place that was less imposing than the hotel, he requested, trying his best not to make it sound like an insult.

Stepping out from the taxi, Henri noticed the change at once. Stari Grad. That was what the concierge had called the area the taxi had been directed toward. It was, he could already tell, markedly different from the place he had just come from. Softer, even. Gone were the concrete slabs, the impersonal buildings set against a gray, drab sky. Instead, warm yellow lights lit the tree-lined cobblestoned streets, the structures here reminiscent of something altogether more European, their façades bathed in warm colors. He found, much to his surprise, that he was actually hungry now, the aromas filling the air different from those of the hotel's kitchen, and he chose a restaurant from among the many lining the street. He ordered, pointing to a few things on the menu, hoping they were neither gray nor covered in sauce like this afternoon's dishes. A small tumbler of clear liquid—rakija, he was told—and a plate of mushrooms, covered, to his dismay, in a gray sauce, were eventually set in front of him.

"Mushrooms with old cheese," he was told by the waiter.

"Old cheese?" Henri asked, looking down at his plate in alarm.

"Yes, old," he confirmed, turning away.

It took Henri a moment before he realized the man must have meant *aged.* It was strange, he thought, taking a bite—thankful to find that it was, in fact, delicious, that it tasted of cheese and garlic and good, strong olive oil, nothing that could be defined as *old*— the way a word could mean one thing but also something entirely different, depending on translation, on context. He thought of

Granada then, of the words she had spoken to him that day on the bus, found himself smiling at the memory.

A scattering of applause broke out in front of him then, causing him to look up. Henri had chosen to sit outside, despite the cold. The rakija, he found, was all the warmth he needed. He turned toward the street, trying to find the source of the noise, where he could now just about make out a troupe of street performers.

What followed seemed to be a reenactment of sorts, with lots of singing and dancing from both actors and audience. Henri hadn't a clue as to what it was about, what the words meant, but he could feel it—it was that same feeling that would overcome him on a night out back home, when the *raï* singers had performed and he had danced with Marianne, pressed close together. The feeling that he was not alone, that there was someone out there in the world who was tethered to him and he to them. That it meant something, moments like this, all of it. He didn't know what it was, exactly, that feeling, didn't know how to describe it, but he thought it might be something like happiness.

Henri had spent the last hours despairing at the futility of his situation, but now, he found himself wondering if perhaps it was for this—for these small moments that made him wonder if he could, in fact, find happiness outside of and away from Oran. Whether home could be a decision rather than a declarative. Whether all this could be a beginning. The past year, he had existed in a haze, feeling neither happiness nor sadness, numb to everything and everyone around him. Now, he felt pinpricks gathering on his skin—hurt, anger, and, yes, moments such as these, moments of contentment and hope for the possibility that his life had not ended the day he boarded that ferry to Marseille. He thought of Marianne and how he had once felt betrayed, how he had accused her of turning her back on the past, on her country, on him. He realized now that she had only found something else, something new—that it did not mean what came before was lost.

Or perhaps, he was only drunk, he thought with a laugh.

He finished another rakija, signaled for the check.

Afterward, he walked for a while, in no rush to get back to the quietness of his room. He came to the end of the street, where Skadarlija turned into Dečanska, and decided it made more sense to return to where he had started, hail a taxi from there.

He turned and there she was, just a few steps away, looking down at a stall of trinkets.

So much for the bellhop being a reliable source of information, he thought. He made a note not to trust his word so easily the next time. He looked around him, searching for signs of the others. From what he could tell, they weren't there—she was alone. Strange, he thought, when the bellhop had said the group had a reservation for that night, the window between then and now growing rapidly smaller still. He didn't know why, but he didn't think it mattered, didn't think she intended on attending whatever gathering they had planned for that evening. He didn't know what it was—something in her face perhaps, the expression on it dulled, somehow—but he was reminded of that day he had first seen her, in the gardens of the Alhambra.

For the first time, Henri found himself tempted to say something—to reach out and touch her. Before, he had enjoyed the distance. There had been a seduction in it, a comfort as well. Now, everything felt different. In Belgrade, standing under the streetlamps, it all fell away—the wall, the barrier, whatever it was that was supposed to separate them—so that he was left with the urge to hasten his steps, to walk beside her across the cobblestones. He told himself that he would, damn the rest. He would cross the distance between them and they would figure it out from there. He waited, one beat, then another.

She turned and began to walk away, in the opposite direction.

Henri stood still, watching her go.

TWELVE

LOUISE

She slips out of her clothes and shivers, despite the heat of the train.

Louise hasn't really allowed herself to think about Belgrade, about what happened, until now. She is furious with him for bringing it up, furious, too, for what he did in Belgrade, for saving her when she had not wanted to be saved—was not meant to be. Perhaps, she thinks, this is her punishment. To sit on this train, knowing what he had done, what he would likely still do, and knowing that she is unworthy of it all.

Louise curses. She shouldn't have left him alone with that strange man. She knows this, and yet that familiar anger boiling inside of her tells her not to care, tells her he deserves it, that there is no other way, not for her or for him or even for the two of them together. He was supposed to stay in the shadows, that was the game—one that was supposed to end with her disappearing into Istanbul. He would be someone she would think of every few years, whom she would smile over, remembering how she had bested him at his own game, and perhaps he would do the same, wherever he was in the world.

Except now there is *this*—and *this*, she doesn't know what it is, only that there is some indefinable feeling that has moved through her and made her question everything she has done and everything she plans to do still. She feels full with this emotion that she cannot name—though there is sadness, anger, regret—so that she feels as though she were ill, as if she were feverish, the electricity of it coursing through her, a sensation just beneath her skin that makes her squirm, makes her feel as though she is on fire, burning. She wants nothing more than to be free of it—free of her body, of her very self, of everything that she is and that has brought her to this moment. She had never thought to waver, never thought to examine or question. And yet now, now she is doing both. She can feel herself, thin as paper, and she hates him, blames him, for making her aware of feeling something that she was already aware of but had managed to ignore.

Louise opens the window, tells herself to breathe.

She finishes undressing, places her traveling clothes onto the chair beneath the desk. She wants to keep them in reach in case something happens that calls for an escape. The hour is late, well past midnight, but she wonders if it even makes sense to change, whether she is only making things more dangerous for herself.

In the end, she decides that she is too tired to care.

She yanks the curtain of the window closed, though it is dark and there is nothing to see beyond the suggestion of shapes as the train continues into the darkness. She locks the door, having heard tales of bandits, of overly familiar conductors and customs officers, then places the chair from the desk underneath the doorknob, bracing it, just in case.

Louise is exhausted. Not the feeling that comes with a bad night's sleep or a day filled with travel. No, this is something more, something deeper. She feels it more acutely than she has felt anything, feels it somewhere at the core of her, the very center, so that even the small space between the door and bed is nearly too difficult to complete. She hasn't slept well since Paris, she realizes as she lies down, feeling her limbs stretch and recoil. She presses her face into the pillow. Exhaustion sweeps over her, immediate and pressing, so that she has barely closed her eyes before sleep overtakes her entirely.

BEFORE

Louise was asleep when the pounding on her door began again.

"Go away, Iris," she murmured into her pillow, her words no louder than a whisper.

Louise had been avoiding her new friend for the better part of a day. After returning from the restaurant the night before, she had gone directly to her room, locked the door, and there she had remained. She had taken all her subsequent meals in her room, alone, ordering breakfast that morning—a hard-boiled egg and a pot of strong coffee—followed by lunch, which was a simple affair of fish with tomato relish and a salad. The first meal she had eaten with a surprising amount of enthusiasm, the second she had only pushed around her plate before setting it outside her door, unable to stomach the smell of the fish as it began to warm within the room. She hadn't planned on ordering dinner, didn't think she could summon up enough energy. Instead, in the intervening hours, she had lain in bed, watching the hours slip by, waiting until it was time to board the train to Istanbul.

Louise was under no false illusions. She knew what would happen when she reached the city, knew that the man from Oran, wherever he was now, would once again make an appearance, the thought of which both terrified and thrilled her. A part of her wished that he was here now, that she could speak to him, as she had in that bar in Paris, convinced that he would understand this strange malaise that had swept over her.

The knock at the door had grown more insistent. Iris, it seemed, had begun to lose her patience. The thought almost made her smile.

Louise knew she should answer, knew that she should at least open the door and assuage her friend's fears, but it seemed somehow too difficult. After all, how could she explain when the truth was that she was embarrassed, ashamed. Locking herself up within her room, refusing to come out. How to tell Iris that it was simply who she was, a solitary creature unfit for the company of others, for the friendship of people like Iris. She blamed their visit to the well. That goddamn hole in the floor that she could not stop thinking of, so that England and everything from before—before the money, before this new chance at life—came roaring back to her and she was unable to forget what she had been there, sad and miserable, lonely and penniless.

A part of her, she knew, would always be trapped there. In that miserable village, in that miserable life, never quite believing that she had made it out. How to explain this to the girl on the other side of the door, how to make her understand that champagne and jaunts abroad, that confidences and trusted friends—these things were not really her, were not part of her everyday life. That she was comprised of dark corners and spaces that smelled like illness, like death, that the stench of it would always remain on her, no matter the names she tried on, the miles she ran.

She could hear her father's voice then—*you're just like her.* And Louise knew what he meant, the accusation in his voice, that she was just like that woman who had refused to accept her place in life. She could hear it. The wheels of her father's chair as he made his way through the hallways of their house, looking for her, demanding her. She could hear it. The strange groans that emanated from the house at night, so that there were times she was convinced his need for the chair was a ruse, that he spent his nocturnal hours roaming, laughing at her for thinking it was his imprisonment, when really it was her own.

Louise sat up, gasping, blinking through the darkness in her room. It was dark outside; there was no light coming through the thin curtains. She must have dropped off at some point without realizing it. She looked down at the scattered pillows, the discarded duvet, which lay in a heap on the floor, evidence of her fitful dreams.

Iris was still knocking on the door.

Louise frowned, wondering how long the girl had been there—surely not the entire time she had been asleep. If she had been asleep. Time seemed to be moving strangely, so that she wasn't entirely certain of when things had happened, if they had happened. She remembered that her father had been there, in her room, walking back and forth—or no, she had only been imagining. Louise shivered. As she stood, a wave of dizziness overtook her. The closeness of the room, she thought. And the rakija, glancing at the number of empty glasses that cluttered the floor. Her appetite for food might have disappeared, but her thirst seemed to have increased.

Louise opened the door, found Iris on the other side. "How did you get my room number?"

Iris only crossed her arms. "Is that all you have to say?"

Louise struggled to find words that might be appropriate for the situation, that would ease the look of anger, of disappointment, on the face of the young woman standing before her. But no—it wasn't anger reflected there, she realized, it was worry. "I'm sorry," she said, though her tone suggested she didn't mean it. Instead, she sounded petulant, like a child who had just been told off. Louise had never done well with apologies, even less so when she was the one making them, but she *was* sorry now, at least as far as Iris was concerned. "I wasn't feeling well. That damn migraine from the train came back again," she finished, pointing to her head.

"You should have told me," Iris said, reaching into her pocket-book. Her face softened. "My mother suffers from them, so I always carry some acetaminophen on me, just in case."

Louise looked down at the two tiny pills that Iris placed in her hand. She felt as though she might cry at the ridiculous kindness that this even more ridiculous girl had shown her, right from the very start, despite the fact that she didn't deserve it.

"What's wrong?" Iris asked, her own face crumpling at Louise's expression.

"Nothing. I'm just being silly."

Iris nodded. "The migraines do the same to my mother. Either she's screaming or weeping. Sometimes both. We've all learned to keep our distance until it passes." She paused. "What you need is some fresh air. You've been trapped inside this dungeon for far too long."

At these words, Louise felt as though she really might have a migraine coming on, something bright and tight at the corner of her eye.

Iris frowned. "Unless you think you ought to see a doctor."

"No," Louise said, thinking of the drinks she had consumed, of the tablets she had swallowed. "No, I'm quite all right."

"Probably best, considering our current location," Iris said, to which Louise attempted a smile. "You're leaving this room tonight, Vee. I insist," Iris said, seizing on her hesitation. "Besides, it won't be any fun without you. It certainly wasn't last night. The boys seem to have nothing but romance on their minds at the moment, which can be rather tiresome. Particularly when no one seems to harbor any such thoughts about you." She admitted the last with a blush.

"I thought maybe you and Michael?" Louise began, thinking about his overprotective nature.

"No," Iris said, blushing further still.

No, Louise didn't think so either, recalling the way he had looked at Susan. "I doubt my company will make things that much better," Louise warned.

"Don't be silly. You don't know what a treat it is to have someone to talk with about things other than the latest fashions." Iris rolled her eyes—but not in a way that was cruel, only teasing. Louise could see how much she cared for her friends. "We're meeting in the lobby at eight and then heading down to the Sava."

The name sounded familiar. "The river?"

Iris nodded. "Apparently the boys managed to make some friends last night, and this particular one has invited us all to have a drink on his boat."

"Out on the water?" Louise didn't like the sound of being so isolated.

"It's docked on some island, so more like a floating bar, I suppose." Iris turned to leave. "Do you know," she said, pausing. "I'm so glad to have met you, Vee. It can be terribly lonely, being the only one without someone." She reached for Louise's hand. "But now I'll have you." She leaned in and smiled. "We'll have each other."

It soon became apparent that the others had started drinking long before they piled into the taxi. The evidence, Louise noted, was written across their faces—Michael, John, and David—all three of whom were bright and shining, cheeks flushed with heat. There was a commotion when Louise first emerged from the lift, as though she were a long-lost friend they hadn't seen for ages, and then again when they arrived at their destination and were greeted by their host and his friends. Everything, it seemed, delighted them to no end that night, and all three girls seemed happy to smile and go along with it, while Louise only glowered. There was something about them, about their boisterousness, that set her on edge that night. She found herself wishing that she had stayed back at the hotel—or had kept on the train to Istanbul.

"They're highly excitable tonight," Iris confided, as they boarded the boat.

"Apparently," Louise responded, somewhat tersely, her goodwill extending only so far as Iris and perhaps Susan and Mary were concerned.

On board, their frenzied level of enthusiasm only seemed to increase. Together, they toasted to new friends—though Louise hadn't bothered to learn the name of the host nor the handful of other attendees—and champagne was passed all around. After the first hour, she wondered whether she had ever seen so much champagne in her life. She wasn't even entirely certain she liked it, would have preferred the smoothness of rakija to the acidic bubbles and tang of the drink she found being constantly refilled for her, all protestations otherwise lost. She learned quickly that it was best to offer little resistance unless she wanted all eyes drawn her way— which she very much did not. And so she continued to hold out her coupe, the glass catching in the light, accepting refill after refill. Louise looked to the others, smiled, and drank.

It did not take long for her to feel the effects of such indulgence. She felt too hot, her dress scratched and itched, so that she could feel welts starting to rise around her collarbone. She had been uncertain how to dress for the night, had selected a dark, loose shift that she had brought with her from home and that looked as though it might not be too terribly out of place, particularly when layered with her coat. And it wasn't, not entirely, not to anyone who wasn't looking. But Louise suspected it only took a knowing glance to see the difference between her and the other women present, to see the quality of the cloth, of the cut, that adorned the others. She should have bought a few other pieces, should have allowed herself an indulgence beyond her damn coat while she was in Paris, she thought, pulling it closer around her, suddenly conscious of just how cheap the fabric might appear.

She drank, raised her glass to be filled again. For Louise, after having spent the last day or so on her own, the whole night was beginning to feel like a bit too much. She did her best to engage, nodding here and there when included in the conversation, but for the most part she only stood and stared, drinking her champagne and waiting for intervals that allowed her to break away from the others and wander on her own, under the pretext of exploring.

The boat itself wasn't what she had first imagined. It was, she thought, less of a boat and more like a giant barge—only with a ceiling and the inside done up like it was someone's living room, complete with sofas and chairs, coffee tables and lamps. The effect was strange—stranger still when one stepped outside and realized how close they were to the water, just a step or two away, the boat floating just above its dark surface.

"Thinking of jumping?" asked a familiar voice behind her.

Louise inwardly groaned. "Evening, Michael," she said, trying to brush past him.

He reached out, grabbed her by the arm. "Have you got a light?" he asked, an unlit cigarette dangling from his mouth.

Louise thought she could read the threat, just there, lurking beneath his words; felt it, too, in the way his fingers pressed into her skin. She shook him off, not bothering to respond, and disappeared back into the boat, into the safety of the others.

Iris and the girls were sitting on the couches while the others seemed to be running circles around them. "Don't they ever tire?" Louise asked, coming to sit next to her friend.

"Eventually," Iris assured her.

"Vee," David suddenly called out. "We were just telling our hosts about you, our most mysterious guest, and now they want to know all your secrets as well."

"My secrets?" Louise did her best to laugh, to match the level of gaiety that they all seemed to be experiencing, which she could only seem to observe from afar.

"Yes, come on, Vee," John called. "Tell us your secrets."

"I'm afraid I haven't any secrets to tell," Louise called back.

The girls smiled along, but Louise thought she saw something else on their faces as well. Irritation, perhaps, at no longer being the center of attention.

They shook their heads, one declaring, "I don't believe that for a second," while another asserted, "Nor do I. Look at her." Another voice rose to match them. "She's all secrets," Michael said, having rejoined the group after his cigarette break.

Iris huffed, called back, "Don't be tiresome." She turned to Louise. "The boys have convinced themselves that you're someone terribly important."

"Have they?"

"Yes." Iris reached for her drink. "Michael claims to have spotted a man watching you on the train while we sat in the dining car."

Louise felt her smile tighten. "Oh?"

"Yes, I told them it was nothing, just an anonymous admirer, surely, but they're all convinced you're a spy or something equally clandestine. Their imaginations know no bounds, apparently."

"How silly," Louise said, hoping the darkness hid her face, hid the blush that was even now creeping over it. She laughed and felt it again—the swell of possibility, the life she might have had. Once more, the feeling of melancholia swept over her. She wandered after that, eager to cool her face, to ease her mind, stepping away from the others and toward the boat's edge, only to find that, once more, Michael had followed, steps behind her.

"Finally, I've got you on your own."

"Have you been looking to get me on my own, Michael?" she asked, teasing.

She saw the glint in his eye then, the way he puffed up in expectation.

"I checked up on you, you know."

Louise sipped her drink. "Did you?" She wondered what that meant, knew he couldn't have managed to get very far, given the name he had. She only wondered whether he had managed to find out the origin of it, though she doubted he would have been able to do so. And presumably that was all he had done, telegrammed home, asked someone to make a few inquiries. He was bluffing, she thought.

"I did."

"And what did you find?"

He shrugged. "Not very much, though I suspect you already know that. Though I also didn't find an author either."

"I told you, I write under a pseudonym."

"Oh, did you not mean the obviously fake name you gave us?" he asked in mock surprise.

She laughed, impressed he was clever enough to have realized. "You certainly expect a large amount of honesty from people you've only just met."

"Well, when said person intrudes upon our holiday—"

"Ah, I was invited," she reminded him.

"Fair enough." He smiled, but his tone, she noticed, had hardened. "Though a word of caution. I wouldn't get too terribly comfortable. Iris does tend to get bored quite quickly."

Another bluff, she suspected. "Perhaps I'll get bored first."

"I wouldn't think so. People rarely do when the bill is being taken care of." He sipped his champagne, obviously pleased with what he believed to be a biting remark.

Louise laughed. "Are you referring to yourself?" His face fell at that. "No one is paying my bill other than myself."

He looked flustered. "Look. It's obvious to us all that you don't belong. Besides that silly coat you wear, the rest looks like it could be from the local charity shop."

The man standing before her was outrageous, she thought. "Is it a crime to be poor, Michael?" she demanded.

He looked furious now, his face a dark red. "It is if you're trying to fleece someone else's money."

For a moment, Louise wondered how he knew, how he had managed to find out—then she realized that he was talking about Iris. She found herself wondering again about his intentions toward the girl, whether he didn't mean to save his own fortune with her as his bride, concerned as he was about strangers interested in her money. She began to laugh.

He looked affronted at the sound, saying softly, but without any real conviction, "You're mad."

"And you're an absolute snob."

"She will tire of you. Shall I tell you why? You're a charlatan, Vee, or whatever your real name is. Everything about you is a lie. And we, Iris included, will always tire of you first for exactly that reason, because you're not real, because there's nothing at all beneath that mask."

Louise stopped laughing then. The boy before her was terrible, yes, the absolute worst, but he was also right. She was not real, not in the way Iris was, in the way the others were. She was a ghoul, made up of rage and anger, subsisting on a dream that would never come true. No, she was not substantive—but then she had never been given the chance, had been robbed of it by others like him.

He was no different, she realized, despite his money and posh accent, from the boys who had taunted her at school, who had teased and picked on her because her mother had done the one thing that mothers were never supposed to do. And Louise was, those same boys and girls had decided, the reason. That her mother had not loved her, that she had left. There was no one to blame but Louise and everyone in town knew it. The boy in front of her, Louise thought then, somehow knew it as well. That she was unlovable, that she was not worthy in the way that the rest of them were. Even here—despite the distance of time and place—she was marked as something separate, as someone who did not belong.

"I believe your train leaves tomorrow," he said.

Louise nodded, fighting to bring herself back to the present. "It does, yes."

"I think it would be best for everyone if you were on it."

Louise had every intention of being aboard the morning train; still, she didn't want the child before her to think the decision had anything in the least to do with him and his pitiful threats. She took a step closer. In heels, she towered over him. "Or what, exactly?" She laughed, delighting in the way he flinched when she drew close.

Louise didn't give him time to respond, only smiled and moved away, his angry words lost in the air behind her. In that moment, Louise hated him, hated all of them—even Iris. She knew it was wrong—cruel, even—for the girl had been nothing but kind. But then her kindness was a part of the reason that Louise resented her, because she had been afforded the opportunity to be nice, because she had been raised in a world that taught her only the good in others, and that had blinded her to reality.

Louise wished for that, desperately, sometimes. She thought again of her mother's refrain to her as a child—*stop thinking*. She gave a slight shake of her head, knew she couldn't stop, that she didn't want to. For while she might pine for the oblivion that a world of wealth might have provided her, she suspected that even then she would have seen through it, seen through the pretense that the others around her so carefully curated.

"What is it?" Iris asked, coming toward her now. "You look upset."

"Nothing, just your ghastly friend," Louise declared, not wanting to be nice. She hadn't wanted to come out, was furious now with Iris for making her, furious at herself for agreeing. She knew what she was like in these moments, in these moods, where nothing could reach her. She was sad and she was angry, and then there was always something worse, right there, waiting. She had only ever allowed it out once before, but felt that tonight, similar to then, she might not be able to stop it.

Iris frowned. "He's not so bad as that."

"Oh, but he is, Iris. He's the absolute worst. Dull and conceited, an absolute snob, if you want the truth."

"That's not fair, Vee." Iris looked hurt.

"Really? I think it's completely fair," Louise snapped, deciding she didn't care about the girl's feelings, about any of their feelings. She wondered just what the hell she was doing there, when she could have been well on her way to Istanbul—already there, in fact. The whole idea to join them had been one of absolute madness, she saw now. She didn't know how she had let herself get so carried away, had let herself believe that this could turn out as anything but a complete and utter disaster.

"I did warn you, about Michael, it's just that he's—" Iris began.

"Protective?" Louise spat. "Yes, so you've said. Protecting his future investment, I suspect, while also looking out for side interests." She nodded to where Michael stood, leering over Susan inside the boat.

"That's cruel."

"It's the truth." Louise set her drink down with a clatter. She cursed. She didn't want to be like this, not with Iris, at least. The poor girl looked ready to burst into tears—she didn't deserve Louise's anger, her barbarism. "I think I might head back to the hotel now," Louise said, anxious to be away from her, from all of them.

Iris's face crumpled. "I've said the wrong thing, haven't I? I always do that, I'm told."

Louise felt something crack through the anger at the miserable expression that crossed the girl's face. "No, don't be silly, Iris," she said, the words sounding cross. She took a deep breath. "The truth is I just can't shake this headache. The champagne seems to have only made it worse. I think I might go back and run a hot bath, see if that helps any."

Iris seemed unconvinced. "You promise you're not cross with me?"

Louise shook her head. "You're sweet," she said, meaning it, knowing it was the perfect way to describe the girl in front of her, knowing as well that the same could never be said about herself. She wasn't sweet, no. She was bitter, like arsenic, a poison, all the way through. She felt her anger ebb then, replaced with something dull and heavy and all at once impossible to bear. "And I'm not cross," she promised. "Not with you."

Louise wanted to tell her then that she didn't always have to do what others told her, that life was simply too short to live for anyone other than herself. But she didn't. She saw the expression on the girl's face and knew that she wouldn't listen to her, or that even if she did, she would only dismiss it when faced with the opinions of others. She was smart, infallibly kind, but she wasn't ruthless.

Iris seemed to hesitate then. She took a step closer to Louise and lowered her voice. "I don't mind, you know. If you do have secrets."

Louise frowned, taken aback. Whatever she had expected Iris to say, it had not been this. "Secrets?" she repeated, not knowing what else to say.

"Yes. Whatever it is—" Iris stopped and frowned. "Whoever you are, I won't mind. That's what I mean."

Louise found herself surprised, as she had consistently been by Iris. She would never have thought the girl to be as perceptive as she had proved. "I see," was all she could manage.

Iris left her alone after that, for which Louise was thankful. She reached into her purse. It was a careless thing to do, she knew, considering how much she had already had to drink that night, but she also didn't care. She didn't want to think anymore, and the alcohol was working far too slow. She swallowed one pill, then another. She grabbed a glass of champagne, drank it quickly, and reached for a second.

Louise glanced around the boat—at Iris, at her friends, smiling, laughing, not a care in the world. She knew Iris was genuine in her invitation to join them, but she also knew that she didn't belong here, and she was tired of pretending otherwise. She took a step away, casting one last look over her shoulder—at what might have been hers, in another life, if the circumstances had been different, if *she* had been different—and walked away.

Standing at the water's edge, Louise stared down into the Sava River. In the darkness, it looked black. Like tar, she thought, or oil. Like something one would fall into and never find their way out of again.

There was something attractive about the idea. She swallowed another tablet, couldn't remember what number that made. The pill tasted bitter on her tongue. She reached for another, swallowed it as well. Her fingers scraped the bottom of the vial. There was no more, just the white residue left on the bottom. No matter, she thought, the lights from the city across the water blinking in and out of focus. She had decided.

She could run as hard as she could, and as far as she liked, but there would always be someone there. Someone like Michael, to remind her that she didn't belong. Someone who knew about the money or who had been sent to retrieve it. She would never be free, not in any way that mattered. No, she would always be trapped in that damn well, the circle of light, of freedom, above her, always just out of reach. She would always, she knew, be left behind, in that forgotten place.

She stepped from the shoreline, into the river. The first shock of water felt like ice. By the time it reached her knees, she was shivering, trembling, but she thought the cold no longer felt as bad. No, she could almost convince herself it was something distant, far away. Something that could no longer touch her. The thought gave her comfort as she pushed ahead, farther into the water.

THIRTEEN

HENRI

When she is angry, the tips of her ears turn red and her cheeks seem to glow, two bright-red spots emerging alongside the blood vessels. He had seen it when he mentioned Belgrade. He doesn't know why he brought it up, doesn't know what he might have said if she had allowed him to finish. His only thought at the time was that he couldn't remain silent—didn't want to in light of their diminishing time, the diminishing distance between here and Istanbul.

Henri is thinking of this as he drifts in and out of sleep, uncertain how many hours have passed since her departure, when he hears a knock. He opens his eyes, still more asleep than not, and looks around the compartment. The man sitting across from him, the one who called himself Fulano, is gone. There is no one else other than himself. It takes a moment to realize that the noise is coming not from inside, but outside, where the sleeping attendant, the same one who earlier had escorted Louise away, is standing, frantically knocking.

Henri stands, opens the door. "What is it?" he asks, wondering if there has been an accident, wondering whether it has to do with Louise, with the man who is no longer in the compartment. He pushes the fear down, rearranges his face into something more appropriate.

"Excuse me, sir, but do you know the lady who was in this compartment?"

Henri knows the man in front of him means nothing more than that, that a simple affirmation is all that is required, and yet, he cannot bring himself to answer right away. Does he know her, he wonders, and if he does, what is it specifically that he knows?

"Monsieur," the man says, interrupting his thoughts.

"Yes, yes, I know her."

"Come with me, then, please, sir." He points in the direction Henri watched her disappear before. "The officers are this way."

They move from one car to the next, and at times Henri can feel himself pushing past the attendant, does his best to slow his gait, to remind himself to let the other man lead. Still, he cannot stop himself from imagining what he might find when they finally end up wherever it is they are heading. Louise, battered and bruised. Louise, dead on the floor. The man gone, vanished.

In the next car, Henri finds two officers standing outside a closed door, looking cross.

"They cannot wake her," the attendant explains. "We've been trying now for some time. And nothing."

Henri looks to the closed door, tries not to imagine what they might find behind it. "Nothing?" he echoes.

The attendant shakes his head. "Something is blocking the door."

Henri feels something heavy on his chest then. It's fear, he realizes. He reaches out, begins to bang on the door. "Louise," he calls, hesitant at first, then louder. "Louise, are you there?" It occurs to him that this is not the name listed on her passport, but he pushes aside such concerns for now. He looks to the customs officers, to the attendant, wondering what it is that they expect him to do. He does not have the answers, he wants to shout at them. He does not have any answers at all.

He turns back and raises his fist. All at once, there is a sound from within the compartment, a scraping noise, followed by a click, and the door swings open. Louise stands, in her nightgown, looking around at the group of men, the expression on her face confused—frightened, even. Henri cannot help but notice how young she looks.

"*Je suis désolée*," she whispers, then again, repeating the phrase over and over. He wonders at the choice of language, wonders whether she dreams in one different than her own, but then he reasons that they are in Turkey now, where French seems more appropriate. Perhaps this has occurred to her as well. "I was asleep, I was dreaming, horrible things, I'm sorry," she says, looking between him and the attendant. "*Je suis désolée*," she says again. She is rambling, he realizes, unable to stop. Her teeth begin to chatter. She places her arms around herself, seems to realize just how naked she is, standing in front of these strangers, this group of men. Turning, she snatches her coat from the compartment, and places it on, pulling it taut against her waist.

"Are you all right?" Henri asks, stepping forward.

"Yes," she murmurs.

"They just need your passport, that's all."

She fetches her papers, her hands still trembling. "I've always been a heavy sleeper. My father used to complain about it, said he could raise the dead before he could raise me," she says to him.

He smiles, thinks that perhaps this particular story is true. "Don't worry, I'm certain they're used to it here. You can't be the first person to fail to answer the door." He looks inside the compartment. "Though perhaps the first person to brace the door shut," he guesses, looking at the position of the chair.

She blushes. "I was afraid of highwaymen."

He smiles. "Do they still exist?"

"I don't know, but I would think it likely to be here, if anywhere." She lets out a shuddering breath. "It's certainly a strange practice, isn't it? Shaking us all awake in the middle of the night."

"The allure of the night train, I suppose."

"Or the reason why train travel is out of fashion."

"You may be right."

The guard standing closest to them—the one with the sternest look—examines her passport. He takes his time, longer than necessary, though Henri suspects that it is not the possibility of forgery that causes him to linger, suspects as well that, in the chaos, the guards did not notice the other name Henri had called out. It is, more likely, only a petty retaliation for having to wait. Eventually, he says, "Thank you, Mademoiselle Virginie."

She takes her passport without a word, but Henri notes the blush that has crept from her neck to her cheeks. He doesn't think anyone else has noticed.

The customs officer standing closest to the door points then and asks, "Your luggage?"

She looks confused for a moment—Henri wonders whether she is still half asleep—and then she starts, says, "Oh, yes. It's just there."

He watches her as the officers enter into the tiny berth and open the leather satchel. She looks nervous, he thinks, far more nervous than when the officer examined her passport.

He cannot help it—he leans forward and whispers: "Worried they'll find something?"

She looks at him, then a grin crosses her face and she laughs, deep and sonorous. The attendant appears taken aback; the customs officers irritated. Soon enough, they depart, leaving Henri and Louise alone in the hallway. There is a sudden lurch, and he knows that the engines have been started, that they have officially crossed the border into Turkey. It will not be long now.

"Would you like a *café?*" he asks.

"Yes, I think so." She looks down at herself. "Give me a moment to dress and I'll meet you there."

"I'll just wait here, outside the door."

He doesn't mean it as a threat, wonders what she hears in his words. He only wants to assure himself that she will not disappear again, for however brief a time.

BEFORE

It was his last night in Belgrade. And he had not had another opportunity to retrieve the money unnoticed. Since the night before, she had remained in her hotel room, never once venturing out and into the city. He had stopped inquiring from the bellhop as to her movements. There wasn't any need. Even if he had trusted the boy's information to be reliable, he knew exactly where she was at every moment. Still, it hadn't stopped him from checking, from walking by her room, placing his ear against the door, listening to make sure that she really was there. He was being ridiculous, he knew. And yet—something sat uneasy with him. He tried to brush it aside, tried to tell himself that it was because he had blown his one opportunity to take back the money without a confrontation.

The train to Istanbul left in the morning, and he was running out of time.

There was a tentative knock at his door. Frowning, Henri wondered if it were possible that she knew he was here, wondered whether she had managed to get his room number, perhaps even in the same way that he had retrieved hers. "Yes?" he asked, at the door.

He heard someone clear their throat, murmur, "Sir."

It was the bellhop. Henri opened the door, tried not to look disappointed. "What is it?"

"You said to come and tell you," the bellhop began, "if there was anything unusual."

Henri frowned. "Yes?"

"She's gone out."

"Gone out?" he repeated.

"Yes, she's left her hotel room."

"Where to?"

The boy shrugged. "The front desk called her and the others a taxi."

"You're certain?" he asked.

"Yes."

Henri considered, then thanked the boy and handed him a few additional coins.

Inside the hotel room, Henri pulled the keys from his pocket. Her room was empty, then, unless the boy was lying, though he couldn't settle on a reason for him to do so, or mistaken, but he didn't think so. The boy had seemed certain, which meant that now was the time to do what he had planned: to sneak upstairs, search the satchel, retrieve the money, and head back to Spain.

He thought again of the way she had looked the other night, standing in that street that had looked like Paris, thought again of how he had wanted to breach the distance between them. He looked down at the keys he held in his palm. Henri cursed.

He grabbed his hat and coat, walked to the lift.

Inside, he pressed the button for the lobby.

Downstairs, as Henri waited for the concierge, he reflected just how much he was looking forward to the train, to the journey out and away from the city. It was true that he had liked parts of it, but the bits he did not—the hotel included—made him yearn to stand in a place where the things around him were not built within the last few decades. There was something not to be trusted in places that did not reflect their history, he thought, that seemed to turn away from it in defiance. Henri could see the danger in that, thought he could never live in a place unmoored by time.

When the concierge appeared, Henri explained without preamble, "You called a taxi earlier, for a group of seven. No longer than an hour ago."

The man shifted hesitantly. "Yes."

"I was supposed to meet them in the lobby, but I overslept." Henri placed several coins on the countertop.

The man reached forward, placing the money in his coat pocket. "They have gone ahead to Ada Ciganlija, on the Sava River, to a private boat."

"Where, exactly?" Henri demanded, anticipating that there were most likely a dozen such boats lined up at the shore's edge.

He hesitated. "I could ring for a taxi and have him take you to the same address."

Henri nodded. "I'll wait in the lobby."

He didn't know why, exactly, he felt compelled to follow her that night. Told himself he was making the wrong choice, that he was being ridiculous. She would be in the company of the others, after all. The thought did little to dispel his worry. Something did not feel right. He couldn't articulate it, but his palms had grown sweaty, his heart had begun beating faster, louder, as though he had drunk too many *cafés*. No, something was wrong. He tapped his foot against the marble floor, his knee bouncing in agitation. It took only a few minutes to procure an available taxi, but by the time Henri crawled into the back seat, he could barely contain his nerves.

"Here," he said, pushing a number of dinars toward the taxi driver. "There's more if you can get me there in half the time it usually takes."

He didn't know if the man understood the words, but he glanced at the money and nodded. Henri looked out of the window, hoping that he was not too late.

By the time he found her, she was already in the water.

He had started his search at the boat, had become worried when he found no sign of her there, though the rest of the group remained. The taxi waited, on his instruction. He didn't trust being able to find another at this time of night, in so remote a location, despite their closeness to the city.

When he did find her, she was only just beyond the boat, hidden by the darkness and the reeds that crept up out of the water, which made it difficult to believe they were not in the country, but only a few minutes away from the imposing buildings of Beograd. He would never get used to this city, he thought. It was unpredictable, just like the woman in front of him. The water reached only to her waist; he didn't think she was in any immediate danger of drowning. Despite this, he threw his coat onto the sandy banks and hastened his steps. He told himself that he was not running.

It was a shock when the water hit him. He hadn't expected it to be so cold, didn't know how she could stand as if it weren't freezing, found himself wondering just how long she had, in fact, already been there. He didn't ask, simply clasped his arm around her waist and began to pull her toward the shore. She offered no resistance, stumbling against him for only a moment, then allowing herself to be pulled away from the water.

On the banks, she heaved, then retched, once, twice, enough times that he wondered what she could possibly have left inside her. Her fingers curled into the sand, and he turned away from the sour smell of alcohol that filled the air, turned instead to find her coat and purse, which had been left on the banks. An empty bottle fell out. He could see that the name on the prescription wasn't hers—he wondered briefly if there was a husband before deciding it was most likely her father's. He hurled the bottle into the water.

"What were you doing?" he asked, turning to her. But she wasn't listening to him, wasn't making sense, either, murmuring over and over, "There's no way out," as she shook her head. He didn't know what she was talking about, didn't think she probably knew either, judging by the state of her. "You're out, I promise," he said, trying to reassure her, to vanquish her fears, however unintelligible in that moment. She turned to look at him then, her eyes bright. He wondered whether she was running a fever. After all, who knew what was in that blasted water. He needed to get her back to the hotel. "Come on," he said, pulling her to her feet. "We need to get back to the taxi before the driver changes his mind about waiting."

She didn't respond, but stopped murmuring those words, at least. He shivered. The water had been cold, and the air felt more like winter than it did autumn. She reached for her coat and purse. The walk back felt longer—he hadn't realized how far from the boat they had drifted—but eventually they found the road where the taxi waited.

The driver protested when he saw the state of them, but Henri pushed more money into his hand so that his objections quickly fell away.

In the taxi, he glanced at her. It had been some time since he had seen her from anything but a distance. He took her in now—the slight wrinkling at the corner of her eyes, the solitary freckle on her right cheek, high up, near the cheekbone. And her voice, when she had spoken on the shore. He had heard it before, but it was different than he remembered from their time in that Parisian bar, even from the rest stop in Granada—less polished, somehow. He wondered whether it had been an affect of some sort. Now, her accent seemed to contain a certain lilt, a fullness that had not been there before. A suggestion of something that made him think of the moors, of farmland and small villages. He could almost smell the damp of wet earth. He was taken aback, then, by how real—how tangible—she was in that moment. It frightened him, more than anything, the thought that he could reach out and touch her as he had wanted to only a few nights prior. She was now that close.

At the hotel, he was relieved to see a face he didn't recognize behind the front desk.

"Room 504," he said, waiting for the key.

The concierge—he must be the night shift, Henri thought—glanced at them, no doubt alarmed by their appearance. Next to him, she shivered, violently, having earlier refused to put on her coat while in the taxi, insisting that it was the only nice piece she had ever owned. He thought it a rather absurd argument, but had remained silent, shifting closer to her instead.

"Should I telephone for a doctor?" the man behind the desk asked.

Henri shook his head. "Just the key, thank you." He was tempted to have a drink sent up, but didn't think she needed any more.

In her hotel room, Henri guided her gently toward the bed. Once he was certain that she was in no danger of collapsing, he went into her bathroom, turned on the water, and waited until it began to steam. She was still shaking, her wet clothes clinging to the shape of her. He turned to tell her the bath was ready, that she would need to undress, but she was already standing, already moving to the bathtub, still clothed. She stepped over the rim and sank down, under the hot water, her dress billowing up and around her. He stood, unable to decide what to do next. Her eyes still closed, she said, "Close the door," and when he hesitated, startled by her voice, she made a noise and told him to turn around at least as she began to undo her dress. He left the bathroom and went to the telephone to call for room service. He ordered a large pot of tea and several slices of dry toast.

After it arrived, he placed the tray on the tiled floor beside the bathtub.

She remained in the water, letting the room steam up and then dissipate several times over. He sat on the bed, still in his wet clothes, and waited. Eventually—he didn't know how much time had passed, an hour, maybe longer—she got out. He had left her dressing gown in the bathroom and now she dried off, making her way over to the bed. She didn't speak, didn't even look at him. She simply crawled between the sheets and lay, shivering every once in a while.

"I don't know what I was thinking," she said, in French.

Her voice was raw, aching.

"I don't think you were," he responded. He waited a beat, then said, quieter, "No more pills."

"No." She shifted in the bed. "That was the last of them anyway." Her voice became more muffled. "But no, no more pills."

He sat, waited until he heard her breath grow steady, until the last of the shivering ceased altogether, and he was certain that she had fallen asleep.

Quietly, he let himself out, making his way back to the lift and to his own room. First, he looked for the maid. He found her on the same floor as his own room and he thought, perhaps, she knew what he had done, why he was there now, for she avoided his gaze, stepping into one of the rooms as he came into view. No matter, they didn't need to speak. Retrieving the keys from inside his pocket, he dropped them on top of her cart and continued walking, down the hall and to his room, which felt cold and empty in the absence of the steam that had flooded the one he had just left. He glanced at the clock. There were only a few hours left before it was time to make his way to the train station. He peeled off his wet clothes, lowered himself onto the bed, and closed his eyes. He would sleep, but only for a moment or two.

He did not want to miss the train, the start of their final journey.

At the station in Belgrade, he approached the ticket counter. "The morning train to Istanbul, please." Henri had glanced at her ticket the night before. It had been on the nightstand, and he had committed to memory the compartment number and seat. "Are there any seats available in this particular one?" he said, pointing to the diagram on the counter before him.

The ticket agent consulted his book. "Yes, all but one seat is still available."

Henri paused. "How many other seats are in there?"

"In the entire compartment? Six total, sir."

"And only one has been purchased?"

The ticket agent frowned. "Yes."

Henri reached into his coat pocket, pulled out his wallet. "I'll take the rest of the seats in that compartment."

"All of them, sir?" the ticket agent asked.

"*Oui.*" Henri had already planned it out. It would take more than a day for them to reach Istanbul, and this would give them time—time to introduce themselves, properly—to plan, to decide what to do with the money, with her.

"There is a single berth that has just become available. A last-minute cancellation. You could purchase one of those in order to have some privacy. And at a much cheaper cost."

"No, thank you."

The ticket agent frowned.

Henri paid for the tickets, placing the papers into the pocket of his coat. Thanking the ticket agent, he turned and searched for the platform, for the train—for her.

FOURTEEN

LOUISE

She is dreaming of the woods—autumn in its peak, all violent reds and oranges, with not a single drop of yellow. The ground, heavy with dew, is dotted with mushroom caps. At first, they are large, billowy white puffs that look as though they could be flowers, stretching up from the grass. But then something changes. The farther she steps into the woods, the stranger they become. No longer white, but yellow, sprawling in size, and then they're no longer that either, but black and sunken in on themselves, with spots of whitish-green mold that rise and fill her nostrils. She recoils. Her back presses against something solid and cold—metallic, she realizes. And then she hears it, that sound, wheels creaking against the grain of hardwood floors. And then her name, on his lips, calling out, begging for help—no, demanding it—her name no longer her name, but something that belongs to him, something that he is owed.

She wakes drenched in sweat, and to the sound of another noise, just as insistent, though the tone attached to it is deeper, sterner, more authoritative. *Mademoiselle*, they are shouting. *Mademoiselle, open this door at once.* And then she hears him, her name on his lips, the same exclamation from her dream but entirely different—*Louise.*

Louise moves from the bed, does not even bother to grab her coat. Instead, she removes the chair and unlocks the door, opening it with trembling hands to find a group of men dressed in uniform standing in front of her. For a moment, her heart stops, her breath catches in her throat. This is it, she thinks, they have come for her at last—but then she sees him, sees the worry etched across his face and knows that she is safe. That the end has not yet arrived.

They are close, but this is not it, not yet.

After, when he suggests a coffee, she agrees. In the dining car, they are both silent for a time. In the absence of words, he places a small amount of sugar in his cup, stirring, while she leaves her own black. The thought of drinking or eating anything makes her stomach ache. He raises the small cup, drinks it in one swallow. She does the same. The coffee is strong and filled with grinds—she can feel them in her throat, between her teeth. She reaches for a glass of water, moving the liquid around her mouth.

He smiles, watching her. "Turkish coffee."

"Is that what this is?"

He sets down his cup. "Before, when they couldn't wake you, I thought maybe you were gone."

She looks to either side of her, trying to make light of his words. "Where to, Henry?" She waits a moment and then says, "You must be wondering about the name the officers read on my passport."

He does not meet her gaze. "Louise suits you better."

She suppresses a smile. "What happens when the train reaches Istanbul?"

He looks at her then, and sighs. "There is something that I must take care of, something that I have been putting off but which I can no longer ignore."

She nods, tries to say the next words with an airiness she does not feel. "I suppose that's the way of things. Always having to do what we don't want to."

He frowns and says, "Yes," and she wonders whether he is thinking about now or before, when he left his home, when he had refused to do exactly that—what others had told him, what he did not want to do. This act of defiance gives her some measure of hope.

"And the man?" she asks, wondering then what has become of the other man sent to find her and, quite possibly, she knows, him as well. "Is he still on the train?"

He raises his eyebrows. "What man?"

She knows he is pretending, trying to obscure something from her vision, but she cannot figure it out, cannot understand. "The one from earlier. The one who was watching us."

"Oh." He gives a shrug of his shoulders. "I would imagine he returned to his own compartment."

She searches his face for any clues, knowing that the answer cannot be as simple as the one that he is offering her. "Henry," she begins, her voice nearly a whisper.

He waits, expectant.

She cannot bring herself to finish her sentence, cannot bring herself to imagine what she might be willing to offer, to concede, to save the man in front of her. Instead, she thinks of the sound of wheels turning on wooden floorboards, feels herself grimace at the memory. She shakes her head. No, she cannot go back, cannot bury herself again. "Nothing," she says instead. "It's nothing."

He gives a small nod, orders another coffee.

In Istanbul they part at the train station.

"I suppose this is farewell." She offers her hand.

He accepts. "Yes, I suppose it is."

"Don't look too downcast," she teases. "No one should be that sad after disembarking an overnight train."

He gives a small laugh. "No, the train I won't miss."

"I suppose we were right, in the end."

"What about?" he asks.

"Train travel coming to an end."

"Yes," he says, nodding. "I suppose its day has passed."

She gives a small nod, doesn't allow herself to say more.

She feels the sun on her face then, hears the sound of prayer in another language rising in the air around them. If this were a story, she thinks, he would save her, and she him. As a child, she had waited for a knight, had imagined him to take the shape of her mother. And when she never materialized, never arrived to save her, when Louise was quite certain she had been abandoned, she had stopped waiting, stopped hoping. She feels it then—something dark and cold and miserable, comprised of all the regrets for the things she has done and the things she will never do because of them—well up deep inside her, and she clutches her coat tight against her chest.

She turns, worried that if she does not leave now, she might never summon the courage. Only once does she allow herself to glance over her shoulder, watching as he sits on the steps outside the station, reaching out toward a stray cat. She knows this good-bye is only temporary, knows what will happen next, the inevitable conclusion, the ending of this story. She sees, standing there, all the ways in which she might stop it, rewrite it, but knows that she will not. She is not good or innocent or pure like the heroines in her books, and the things she has done will always haunt her, haunt him, too, if she were to allow it—because she knows he would, if she were to ask him. This she will not do.

She thinks there is perhaps some good in that, at least.

Louise signals for a taxi and tells him to take her to the Pera Palace Hotel.

Inside, she pauses to take in the imposing marble pillars, the wrought iron staircase, the glittering chandeliers, the red velvet couches. She tries to imagine how she would describe it to Iris, if she were to ever see her again. It's overwhelming, she would tell her. It's everything that she dreamed of while trapped in that suffocating house back in England—and yet, standing here now, she feels as though she cannot breathe. She stares at this marvel of art nouveau and feels trapped by its presence, knowing, as she does, what it means. The end. She dispels the thought, tells herself there will be time enough for that later.

Louise asks for a room with a bath, 411, if it's available, then allows the porter to carry her single bag to the lift and up to the fourth floor. She finds a few pounds and pushes them into his hand, apologizes for not having the right currency. He looks surprised, says thank you, bows a few times, and leaves.

Alone, Louise removes her clothes, feeling a bit like she is peeling off her skin. A part of her wants to remain within the safety of the hotel room, in the hushed stillness, but if this is her last day of freedom, if it is all over once the sun sets, she does not want to waste a single second of it.

Downstairs, she stops in the Kubbeli Salon, orders a cognac to steady her nerves. She looks around her, wonders if Christie once sat here as well, thinking up her tales of deception. Louise wonders what she would make of her own predicament, whether she would have started it with the Alhambra or somewhere long before. She wonders what Iris would have thought of it all, had she known the truth, decides it's impossible to know. Her new friend, it seemed, had a penchant for being difficult to predict.

Louise did not consider herself as one who was easily surprised, but even she had been taken aback that final morning in Belgrade, when she had arrived at the station and found Iris waiting patiently at the gate.

"How did you—" Louise had begun, surprised to see her there, and feeling caught out and unprepared at her presence.

"I had a feeling you might try to leave without saying goodbye," Iris had replied. "I told the front desk my friend had a train to catch in the morning and I couldn't remember the time of her departure. I'm always forgetting things like that, you know. I told them I needed to say goodbye." She looked around her. "I got here early, just in case."

Louise had laughed, though the gesture hurt. There was an ache that seemed determined to persist that morning, the physical reminders refusing to let her forget the humiliation of the scene by the Sava River. "Something tells me you would do just fine on your own from London to Istanbul. If you had to," Louise said, recalling their first conversation. "You're far cleverer than you let on."

"I know." Iris took a step closer, reached for Louise's hand. "So are you."

Louise frowned, remembering the words that they had exchanged the last time they spoke. "I'm sorry about last night."

"Don't be silly." Iris paused. "And you were right. I know how they are, who they are. My friends, I mean. Michael, in particular. And I can't explain it, but there's a comfort there, I suppose. In knowing what to expect from those around you."

Louise didn't agree, thought it sounded the opposite, but remained quiet.

From her purse, Iris took out a slip of paper. "If you're ever in London again—"

"You'll be the first person I ring," Louise cut in, accepting the note, which she could see held Iris's address.

"Promise?"

Louise nodded.

"Take care of yourself, Vee." Iris gave a small laugh then.

Louise watched her, confused. "What is it?"

"Nothing, just—" She had paused, looked at Louise. "Virginie Varens. I didn't recognize the name, not at first, but then I remembered where I had read it before." She gave a small smile. "I suppose a part of me always wished she had gotten away in the end."

Now, Louise pays her tab and heads for the lobby. She won't bother with a taxi today.

She roams the neighborhood of Beyoğlu, in no hurry to arrive anywhere specific, making her way to Istiklal Caddesi, with its shops and cafés. She narrowly misses the tram as it comes passing through, and trips a little over the raised rails. She wanders from there to the side streets, watching her feet as they click against the cobblestones. She tries to imagine herself here under different circumstances and fails. Something feels hot and tight in her throat, and she swallows, trying to clear it.

On one of the side streets, far from the crowds, she finds a café and orders coffee and *menemen*. It is still early in the morning, and she finds she is starving, feeling as though days have passed since her last meal. When the dish arrives—steaming eggs, bubbling olive oil, tomato, and pepper swimming in it all—she eats too fast, cannot stop herself. She takes a bite of the cheese, sharp and salty. It is the first real meal that she has eaten on her own over the last several days. She is surprised to find that she misses the company.

Louise looks down at her food. It has congealed in the minutes since she has paused, the oil pooling in and around the vegetables. She feels something rise in her throat, feels the bile, sharp and acidic. At the station in Belgrade, at Iris's parting words, she had felt herself blanch, had felt herself try and reach for a witty response, wanting to tell her that perhaps this time Virginie would get away with it and have a happy ending—but the words had refused to come, had stuck there, in her throat.

It's almost as if she can feel them again now. Louise struggles to swallow, feels as though she cannot get enough air. Stop being ridiculous, she tells herself. It's only a story. It had nothing to do with her.

But it did, she knows. It has everything to do with her. Because she is the same as all the women in those stories—wicked, with no redeemable traits, with no happy ending in store for her.

Louise hails a taxi, instructs him to take her to the Blue Mosque.

In the courtyard, she follows a group of women to the ablution area, where they each sit, one by one, on a marble stool placed in front of a spigot. Louise falters for a moment, wondering if she is allowed. One of the women, her hair hidden underneath a handkerchief, turns and smiles, beckons with a wave of her hand. Louise isn't certain whether the gesture is intended for her, but she moves forward, takes a seat on one of the stools, and removes her shoes.

The water is cold, so much colder than she expects, as it falls onto her bare skin. She glances around, follows the other women's gestures. There is a strange peacefulness to the moment, she thinks. She finds herself hesitant to follow when they stand and begin to make their way toward the mosque. She leaves her shoes outside the entrance and withdraws a scarf from her purse, winding it around her hair until she is covered.

Inside, Louise walks with a tentative step, feeling the soft carpet underneath her bare feet, worn in spots by others who have made a similar pilgrimage. She stares up at the blue tiles, at the stained glass windows and chandeliers. She closes her eyes against the light. She thinks then of that day at the Alhambra. Of the hours before all this had begun. The way she had felt, standing in the room with the stars in the ceiling, the way the light and shadows had danced above her. She tries to remember what it was that had taken hold of her then—that wanting for something more than she had been given, for something more than life had told her to expect. She tries to summon that same feeling, that same energy now, and fails.

Louise stands with the rest of the women behind the main prayer area occupied by the men, and she thinks of whom she might pray to, if she were someone who believed in prayer. Perhaps life would have been easier if she were, perhaps she would not have done the things that she had done—or at least, perhaps she would feel something more like regret instead of the emptiness that has found its way inside her, hollowing her out. What she had done was unforgivable, she knows. And yet, standing here, in this place, she feels unrepentant. She cannot change the past—would not. The freedom that she has experienced, however brief, even if it is to be for no longer than the end of that day, was worth the price, she thinks. She had suffered for so long in that house that to break free of it was worth risking everything.

At some point, Louise realizes that she has begun to cry. She doesn't know why, doesn't know exactly what conclusion she has arrived upon, how she will reconcile what she has done with who she is, but she feels the tears, wet and hot on her cheeks, spilling from her, onto the carpet. She tries to hide them at first, wiping them roughly from her face, but when they do not stop, she lets them go, lets herself empty out. She feels a hand on her shoulder. She leaves it there, does not turn, does not move to speak. The hand eventually releases her, and she remains where she is, standing at the back of the praying crowd, a bystander, always.

She doesn't know what time it is when she departs the mosque but knows the day is almost at an end. She's not ready. She wants to scream, to rage, to beg for more time even though she has had more than her share. But it isn't enough—she isn't ready just yet to face the consequences, even though she knows there is no other choice, no other way. The ending is close now—she can feel it.

Louise wonders whether he is at the hotel already, waiting for her.

Despite the inevitable, she stops in at a bar, orders one final drink. She waits until the sun has dipped behind the Bosphorus, until the Golden Horn is lit up by the golden sky, the mornings and evenings made up of this dazzling light that she has never before seen and that she thinks she will most likely never see again. She thinks of that moment as a child when she had been terrified of death, of not being. In all the many ways that she had imagined it since then, this scenario had never crossed her mind. She wants to laugh, imagining what her younger self would think if she knew it would come to this, in this strange, foreign city, so far away from everything. It seems fitting, somehow. Perhaps her younger self would have found some humor in it. She doesn't know. That girl who had once dreamed of escape was gone now; she thinks she lost her somewhere along the way.

"Finished, mademoiselle?" the waiter asks.

She looks up at him and smiles. "Yes. I am." She reaches for the bill, taking a few Turkish liras from her purse. "I'm finished."

Later, when he knocks at her door, she doesn't bother to answer, only calls out, "It's open," and stands by the window, waiting until the door closes firmly shut.

When his hand touches her waist, this time she does not flinch, only turns to him, expectant. Pulled into an embrace, Louise raises her chin in defiance and, instead of swooning, instead of relenting, instead of doing all those things she has been taught as a woman never to do, while simultaneously being taught to do them—she confesses. She moves close and whispers to him, tells him that she lied, before, when she told him the worst thing she has ever done. And knowing that this is it, that they have come to the end at last, she tells him the truth that has followed her, has haunted her, so at times it feels like she cannot breathe, cannot move forward, part of her stuck, always, in the past.

She tells him—

It had been a day like any other. She had gone to the shops, had hung the laundry out to dry. She had cooked breakfast, had lifted him from bed to chair to toilet and back again. She had stood by the window and gazed out, not bothering to hope, not bothering to dream. She had already, long ago, given up on things such as that. It was as she was preparing to lift him once again, from chair to bed, that she noticed it. Washington Irving's *Tales of the Alhambra*. The same worn copy her own hands had once held, the pages yellowed from the sun, from dust and dirt and time, lying on his bed, half-hidden by the sheets. The copy her mother had left behind, the one that Louise had always assumed was burned with the rest.

At that moment, the day shifted—*she* had shifted, something moving and rearranging inside of her, rage filling the hole, the emptiness that had lived in its place for so long.

She would like to say that it happened quickly, quietly, that it was all over before she knew what was happening, before she could change her mind. But that wasn't true. It had been slow—arduously slow. In the end, he had more fight in him than she expected, so that by the time it was done—minutes, hours, she didn't know, couldn't tell—her fingers were raw, aching. When she pulled the pillow away, her hands shook with the effort, and with something else. No, he had not gone quickly. He had not accepted his fate. He had fought—as much as his small, feeble body had allowed him. And for this she had hated him even more. As she pushed against him—and he pushed right back—she had been consumed with nothing so much as this hatred, manifesting and transforming itself into the rage that she had kept lodged inside for all those years. She wanted, in that moment, to scream, to demand to know why he was denying her even this, why he refused to go, refused to die so that she could, at last, begin living. For that to happen, the two of them could not exist. Didn't he understand that? she wanted to know.

The end, when it had finally come, had not been quiet. Even now, she can still hear it. That gurgling sound, lodged somewhere deep within his throat, the only sound of protest that he had been able to make. It sounded like someone drowning, she had thought, standing before him, towering over him, the bile rising in her mouth. It was, she realized later, the sound of death.

And then she tells him the worst part. For everything that she has told him up until now is only part of it, only the beginning.

Standing by the window, their silhouettes lit behind the curtain of that hotel room in Istanbul, she whispers to him the rest.

She does not regret it. Not a moment. Not for a single second.

And this, she knows, is what makes her truly irredeemable. The act itself could be written off, explained, rationalized as a crime of passion, a temporary madness. It was none of those things, she knows, and her lack of remorse is proof of that. What she did was calculated, what she did was without feeling, because afterward she felt nothing at all. She only felt that she had taken care of a problem that had long plagued her. If anything, she felt relief. Because for the first time she could see it—a future, the possibility of life outside the house that had imprisoned her, that had sentenced her, long before she even knew it for what it was, a prison of her own making.

She should have left, she knows, years ago. Should have put herself first instead of being weighed down by his wants and needs, drowning in them, so that in the end there was nothing left. Until even she was not left. He had taken that from her—her sense of self, her sense of worth, and for that she could never forgive him. For that, she could not mourn his death, could not feel guilt for what she had done. Standing there, looking at his frozen face, the hours passing by, his body turning cold and blue, she had felt nothing. Nothing at all. Only regret for the life she could have had.

Her gaze had fallen on the book then—one of the few things she had left of her mother, one of the few things that she had loved and cherished and that he had taken away, despite knowing this and, perhaps, she thought, in spite of it—and that was when she had decided that she would go and see the Alhambra at last.

She tells him all this so that he will know, so that he will understand. There is nothing redemptive about her. That is why she took the money in Granada. She had already committed the ultimate sin. How could something as silly and inconsequential as theft make any difference to her, to her fate. And so, she had reached down and taken the money, already knowing what the end would be. She has made a kind of peace with it.

And yet—

Louise cannot stop herself from hoping that the end has not yet been written with such finality. It's the same reason she answered the knock on the door, the reason she leads him now to her bed— she cannot convince herself to accept her fate, but continues to want, to fight, knowing she should submit, but refusing to do so, even for a moment.

FIFTEEN

HENRI

Henri wakes to the call for prayer.

He hears the crackle of the loudspeaker first, followed by the voice of the muezzin. His eyes closed, he remains still, listening, and for a moment, he is back in Oran. He feels the sun on his face, feels the breeze from the port spilling in through the opened French doors. He hears his parents, his father opening the newspaper, the sound of the printed page rustling in the breeze, his mother at the stove. He smells the sharp scent of lemon flooding the room.

Henri opens his eyes and returns to the present, to a hotel room in Istanbul where he lies, alone. Where he has managed to pass an entire night without any nightmares, any disturbances at all. He can tell already, even before rising, that she is gone. Her leather satchel is also missing, which means she does not intend to return. He should have suspected, should have been prepared, but it feels as though she is always one step ahead, that he is only following her lead. He searches for his clothes, finds them on the floor near the room's only window. Morning light filters in and he pauses for a moment, allows himself to linger in the slice of warmth that pours through the curtains.

He had stood in this same spot only the night before, had pushed the coat down and off her shoulders, had known—finally known—for certain, what he had suspected for days. The money was not in the leather satchel, only her passport and a few odds and ends—including a needle and spool of thread. He thought back to that first day on the train, from Belgrade to Istanbul, as they had made their way to the dining car and found themselves momentarily thrown against each other, the way she had flinched when his hands reached for her waist. She had been wearing the coat then, had probably worried that he would feel it, the stacks of money sewn into the lining. No wonder she had never taken it off, had made sure to wear it wherever she happened to be. Except that night by the Sava, when she had left her coat lying on the bank. He wonders whether she knew he would be there, that he would find her, eventually.

He had felt the weight of the coat last night, had seen the look in her eyes—watching, waiting, to see what he would do, how he would react. A challenge. Henri had let the coat fall to the floor, had not looked down at it again.

Later, in bed, he asked her, "Do you remember the first time we spoke?"

"In Paris."

"No, before that."

"The rest stop," she said. "When you gave me your sandwich."

"Yes. And do you remember what you said to me, on the bus?"

She laughed. "Something about being able to take care of my-self, I think."

"You said, or you meant to say, 'Keep your coin.'"

She frowned, looked as though she were trying to recall. "And what did I say instead?"

He thought back to that day, how he had known she wasn't French just from that one expression, though her accent had hinted at it as well. "You said: 'Keep your corner.'"

She shook her head, reaching for her cigarettes. "*Mon français est bon.*"

"*Oui, c'est très bon,*" he allowed. "And yet, *coin,* as you meant it, is actually *pièce* in French. While *coin* is—"

"Corner," she said, exhaling.

"False friends." She frowned then and he tried to think of how best to explain it. "Two words that look the same but have very different meanings." When she raised her eyebrows, he admitted: "I studied linguistics for a bit at *université.*"

She had laughed then, and he watched her, his face turning gradually more serious. "I need to tell you something," he said. "About the man following us."

But she had shaken her head, had refused to hear more. "Not now. Later."

Now, as he dresses, he curses himself for not insisting. He had meant to, the words on his lips, the plans he had begun to form, but then they had all fallen away. It had been easy to pretend that they weren't who they were, that the situation wasn't happening. It had felt good, indulgent, even if only for a few hours. Now, he regrets remaining quiet—though not the moment itself—berates himself for not telling her about what he had learned in the hours before he joined her at the hotel, the ones he had spent with the man who called himself Fulano.

At the train station—only the day before, he has to remind himself, for to Henri it seems somehow much longer, as if days and weeks have already passed—he had lingered, had not followed her, knowing the man would eventually emerge. He had wanted their conversation to take place as far away from Louise as possible. He had positioned himself on a stoop outside, where a gray-and-white cat was sunning itself. Absently, he stroked the cat's fur and waited.

Henri was right. It did not take long.

Fifteen minutes later, as the sun began to near its zenith, the man had rounded the corner, had joined him on the stoop, bending down to stroke the stray's head.

"*Ça va*, Fulano?" he had asked.

"*Ça va*," the man replied. "Too many cats here," he said, after a moment's reflection, cupping the creature's head. His fingers tightened.

"Leave it," Henri warned, in Spanish, to make sure the man understood.

The man paused, the cat hissing between his grip, then let it go, holding up his hands in mock surrender. He leaned back against the wall, lit a cigarette. "Tell me the plan."

"The plan?"

"We're in Istanbul. Isn't this where the money will be?"

Henri nodded.

"So why didn't you follow her?"

"There's a date on the wire transfer. It's for tomorrow. An address as well."

The man paused, then nodded. "All right. We'll keep each other company until then."

Henri had expected as much. "And what do you propose we do with the whole day ahead of us?"

"What the tourists do." The man shrugged. "Let's see the sights."

They had walked after that. Without any real purpose, any real aim. They slipped between French and Spanish, sometimes reverting to hand gestures when the words refused to translate, Henri still reluctant to acknowledge just how proficient his Spanish was. He thought that the man was clever enough not to take anything personally; after all, they weren't the ones giving orders, only obeying and disobeying. The man did not ask if Henri knew where Louise was, and Henri did not offer any information to indicate whether he was in possession of such knowledge.

They walked to the Galata Bridge, watched the fishermen in the early morning light, casting their reels into the Bosphorus below. They followed the shouts of *balik ekmek* to where a number of boats sat in the water, vendors grilling fish and placing them between bread. They ordered two, along with a drink—something violent red that tasted both salty and sour. They stood eating, the man spitting out the tiny bones, one by one, Henri crushing them between his teeth. After, they walked through the old district of Sultanahmet, to the park that lay between the Hagia Sophia and Blue Mosque. They stood in front of the great red mosque and its dome that seemed to fill the sky, the blue of the Bosphorus at its back. They turned around, took in the view of the Blue Mosque and its legendary six minarets. They stayed outside, never venturing in.

"I don't know you well enough," was the response the man had given when Henri had asked about purchasing a ticket. "Too many people, too many distractions. Lots of opportunities." He had cocked his head to the side and said, "Let's see what happens after." They ordered a *café* from one of the stalls, drank standing up with the locals, the man complaining all the while that the coffee was too sweet, that everything in this country was too damn sweet.

Eventually they tired, and the man said, "Enough with the postcards. Let's find a place to drink." They asked around for somewhere local, somewhere cheap, and they were directed to the city's Anatolian side, across the Bosphorus. They bought tickets at the

Eminönü dock for the ferry to Kadiköy, and on the ride over, Henri fell asleep—only for a few minutes—but he jolted awake with such force that the man turned to him and laughed. From there, they selected from one of the many bars that lined Yeldeğirmeni, sat down, and ordered beers. They sat for a while then, drinking, eating *lahmacun* and *pide*, not speaking much. The smell of hookah tobacco wafted around them.

"I'm curious," the man said at one point. "Why didn't you take the money?"

"I told you, the wire transfer."

"No." The man shook his head. "I mean before."

Henri considered lying, telling the man something that would not arouse suspicion, but then he figured that it didn't matter, not really. He thought back to that moment, standing in the gardens of the Alhambra. "I was curious, I suppose," he said.

The man drank. "About?"

"I don't know." He searched for the words to explain. "Her, I guess. What she would do, where she would go. And how far I was willing to let her get, so that I didn't have to return."

The man didn't respond, only continued to sip his beer. The weather was cold, but not as cold as where they had come from, and so they sat outside, on a wooden bench, watching the people as they went about their day. There was a market nearby, and many of them passed carrying bags filled with groceries. It seemed strange, Henri thought, to be faced with such normalcy, given the situation they found themselves in. At last, his curiosity got the better of him and he said to the man, "It's a long journey home."

The man nodded in agreement.

"How can you be so sure you will be able to get her back? There's a lot of opportunity for her to escape, to make a scene."

The man sipped his beer. "I agree."

Henri stopped. "Oh?"

"Yes, that's why everything will be resolved here." He cut Henri with a glance. "As you said, too many opportunities. Too many loose ends," he said, though he tried to say the expression in French, saying *threads* instead. *Too many loose threads.*

Something occurred to Henri then. "And the woman? From Granada, I mean." He hadn't thought of her since, but now, with all this talk of threads, his mind was humming, remembering, as he tried to work out what the past meant for the future.

The man met his gaze. "Taken care of, same as what we'll do here." He leaned back, sighed, and looked around them. "We should start to look for a hotel. Somewhere close to the address on that receipt. You still have it on you?"

Henri nodded, said yes, wondering if the man meant to shock him with the casualness of his words, if that was the point. Or perhaps he really did believe him, about the wire transfer, about waiting for the money. He didn't know, found it impossible to read the man in front of him. He waited for another twenty minutes to pass, for them to finish and settle the bill, before he said, "I need to find a toilet first."

As he rose, the man reached out and grasped his wrist. "Just make sure you don't take too long."

Henri held his gaze, nodded.

In the restaurant, he looked for an exit and found one next to the toilets. He made his way through the crowds, through the market, ignoring the vendors' calls, pushing away hands that reached out—holding up an olive to be sampled, a piece of fish to be marveled at—back to the port, where he bought a ferry ticket that would return him to the European side of Istanbul. Standing on the ferry, he removed a crumpled piece of paper from his pocket. *Pera Palace Hotel.*

He had found it after they had said their goodbyes, in the breast pocket of his coat, no idea when she had placed it there. It had been careless of him to keep it, particularly when the other man could have demanded to search him, but he had not wanted to part with it, liked, even now, looking at the cursive handwriting—strong, unrushed—knowing that she had decided, somewhere along the way, to pass this on to him. That it had not been a last-minute, hastened impulse.

He looked up, out across the Bosphorus, where the sun was already beginning to set. He didn't yet know how he would get her out of the city, how he would get himself out, away from the man who called himself Fulano. An indication, perhaps, that he was only one of many.

Henri pushed such thoughts from his mind. He would only think of the night ahead. That was enough. It had to be.

Now, in the lobby of the Pera Palace Hotel, Henri tells the concierge, "My wife was supposed to leave instructions for me." The man behind the counter obviously does not believe a word of what he said. "I'm supposed to meet her. Room 411," he hastens to add.

Something shifts in the man's face as he says, "The lady from 411 asked for directions to Lale Restaurant this morning."

Henri narrows his eyes. "Could you write down the address for me, please?"

The concierge does so, then hesitates—and Henri knows for certain that something is amiss. "What is it?"

"I feel I should tell you, monsieur. You are not the only one to inquire after mademoiselle this morning."

Henri stops. "What do you mean?"

"There was another man, shortly after mademoiselle left. He spoke to the bellhop, asking where she was headed." The concierge pauses. "He's new to the hotel and young. He didn't know what to do."

"He told him?"

"Yes."

Henri curses. "Call me a taxi." He fixes the concierge with a stare. "A good one. Someone who will take me straight there, no detours."

"Yes, of course." The concierge hesitates. "Should I ring the police, sir?"

"No police." Henri doesn't ask how long ago this conversation between the man and the bellhop took place, but he knows it's been long enough, knows there is a good chance he will arrive to the restaurant only to find both of them already gone.

The restaurant is nondescript, tucked into a larger building that houses a hotel on one side and another restaurant on the other. For a moment, he wonders whether he is in the right place. For while he was not surprised to find her gone from the hotel, he is surprised to find that it is only to this restaurant in front of him. He had imagined she would have used the time to make her escape—that she would have by now boarded a ferry or bus out of the city. That she had stopped for a meal beforehand was a decision that he cannot work out—she is clever, Henri knows, too clever for this. Which leaves him wondering just what it is that he is missing.

On his way in, Henri passes a board of notices and his eyes drift to the handwriting there. He stops to read a few of the messages. Missed connections, mostly, but there are others too—rides offered, journeys overland, to places like Kabul, Nepal, and farther, even. Her choice of venue starts to make sense. He wonders whether she has had time to connect with anyone, whether she has managed to find a ride out of Istanbul, after all, away from all this, from him. He wonders whether he will even find her inside, whether she is already across the border, gone.

He pushes through the restaurant, where there is no sign of her. Eventually, he finds her in the garden, a milk pudding in front of her, uneaten.

Louise smiles when she sees him, though her face is pale, and he thinks there is a slight tremor in the hand that holds her coffee. "What took you so long?" she asks, her voice aiming for lightness, her words cracking slightly.

He takes a seat beside her. "That man," he begins without preamble.

"I know. The one from the train." She takes a sip of her coffee, careful to leave the grinds. "Why do you think I'm still here?"

He curses, calls for the waiter, and orders a coffee. "Where is he?" Henri asks, scanning the area.

"Outside, presumably. I only noticed him when I got out of the taxi. For some reason I didn't think to look before. I rushed inside the restaurant as quick as I could, then headed outside to the garden. He hasn't shown his face since."

"He's waiting."

"For?" She raises her eyebrows in question.

"I fed him a line about the money. Told him you didn't have it on you, that you had wired it to Istanbul from Paris."

It had been a last-minute decision, spurred on by the incident in the bookshop in Paris, where he had confirmed the suspicion that he was being followed. After, he had sat in a *tabac*, the caffeine from his *café* flooding his system, and come up with a plan. He remembered a *bureau de change* he had seen near the train station, and when the waiter returned with his coin, he had asked where the nearest one could be found.

Henri had followed the waiter's instructions, which took him down one street and then left onto another. Once at the exchange, he had asked for a wire transfer receipt, requested it be stamped, flashing his credentials at the young woman behind the counter, hoping she would not inquire further or ask to see the piece of paper up close. She hadn't. Instead, she nodded dully and called for the next person in line, her eyes red and tired. Henri thanked her and moved on. He filled the rest out later, back in his hotel room.

"That was smart," Louise observes. "But what do we do now? Surely at this point he's realized you've lied."

"We need to lose him," he says, considering how it will affect his plan. "How far away is the Grand Bazaar from here?"

She looks confused by his question but does not ask him to explain. "Ten minutes, maybe, on foot. Less in a taxi."

Henri nods, drinks the coffee the waiter has only just placed before him, and thinks some more. During that time, neither of them speaks. They sit and stare at the view, the Blue Mosque and the Hagia Sophia just beyond, fighting for attention. Eventually, coffee finished, grinds coating the bottom of the cup in a thick sludge, he signals to the waiter, speaks to him in hushed Arabic.

When the waiter departs, Louise leans forward and asks, "What did you say?"

"I asked him to call a taxi."

"And then?"

"We head to the Grand Bazaar and do our best to disappear." He leans back, gives a weak smile. "Isn't that what you said you wanted, to disappear into Istanbul?"

She returns the smile. "I said sail away across the Bosphorus."

"Not so dissimilar, then."

She looks at him. "Why don't you just hand me over?"

He holds her gaze. "Why don't you just give me the money?"

She gives a smile in response. He thinks she looks sad—regretful, maybe.

"Come on." He stands. "We'll make a run for it now."

"He'll only follow."

"I know."

"And even if we lose him in the bazaar, he won't give up."

"I know."

"Then—" She stops.

"Then what?"

She shakes her head, refuses to finish.

He knows, though—or at least, he thinks he knows—what it is that she was about to say, to ask. She wants to know what the point is, whether this whole thing is futile, because in the end, if this man does not catch her, then another man will be sent, and another after that. He wants to tell her that he has been thinking the same thing, that he has been trying to figure it out, that he may have even found a way—but there is something else he needs to know first. "Have you found a connection yet, out of Istanbul?"

"What?" The surprise is evident in her voice.

"Louise," he intones, his voice sharp. "Did you?"

She shakes her head, avoids his gaze. "There wasn't time."

He nods, disappointed, and also relieved.

"We run," he says, his voice filled with more conviction than he feels. "We run, into the heart of the city, and then, when it's safe, we leave. I have a plan, or the beginning of one, if you're willing to trust me." He watches her as he speaks, carefully, searching for anything—any sign of deception, any betrayal that she does not feel the same at this proposal that explicitly means, without actually saying the words, that they are in this thing together, for however long they might have left.

"Partners, then?"

He thinks he can hear the hesitation in her voice. "For now," he says, with a small smile.

She returns his gaze, then gives a quick, sharp nod.

It's enough, he decides. He stands, offering his hand. "Then we need to be quick. I don't suppose he'll wait much longer."

She stands, motioning to the exit. "Gentlemen first."

Henri pushes ahead, out the door, and toward the waiting taxi.

Despite the early hour, the bazaar is teeming with people.

Normally, the crowds would irritate him, but today Henri finds himself grateful for the presence of so many bodies, so many spaces in which they might disappear. The taxi driver has taken them on a circuitous route through the city, dropping them on Çadircilar Caddesi, nearest the Beyazit entrance. As they step out of the taxi, Henri guides them toward the opening of the bazaar, anxious to be inside. He glances around them—there is no sign of the man, no other taxi pulling up to let a passenger out. He had looked when they departed the restaurant, but hadn't seen the man—knew that didn't mean he hadn't been there, somewhere in the shadows, watching them.

Inside the bazaar, Henri blinks, trying to adjust to the dim lighting, trying to get his bearings, trying to ignore the chaotic scene of vendors and customers before them. He glances up, sees they are on Kalpakçilar Caddesi, the main street in the bazaar. This is good, he decides, recalling the map he had asked the concierge to draw while he waited for the taxi, a contingency plan in case something like this happened. He knows where they are, where they need to head from here.

He grabs her hand, pulls her forward. They rush past stalls selling jewelry, the gold catching in the light. The smell of frankincense and myrrh fills the air, thick and cloying. He feels momentarily overwhelmed but pushes ahead, searching for the heart of the bazaar. It's the best plan he has been able to come up with—to hide in plain sight.

At the heart of the bazaar, surrounded by dozens of others, they should be able to keep themselves safe. They will be in the open, yes, but hidden as well—by the people, by the stalls, by the chaotic atmosphere that defines the place. The man would not, Henri has since decided, be so brazen as to take out a weapon and threaten them here. And then there is the matter of an exit. At the heart of the bazaar any such escape will be far off, but Henri doesn't see this as a problem, thinks it will work to their advantage because again, the man won't be willing to risk the chance of being noticed, which will be impossible while walking two hostages through labyrinthine twists and turns, a pistol at their back. At least, he hopes.

They walk up Sipahi Caddesi at a clipped pace, not quite a run. Henri doesn't want to attract attention, but nothing so slow as a leisurely walk, either. The vendors don't bother them; he doesn't give them enough time.

He glances over. She is wearing those damn sunglasses again, and that same coat, but while the latter doesn't jump out, it's easily recognizable to someone who has been watching her now for several days. He pauses at one of the stalls, silk scarves stacked from floor to ceiling. "Here," he says, motioning her to come closer. He picks a scarf at random, something dark blue—silk, by the feel of it. He asks the price, hands over the money, not bothering to haggle.

Louise accepts it obligingly, draping it over her coat, her hair. It hides the blond, anyway, he thinks, which stands out among the crowd. "And take off those sunglasses."

"Why?"

"Because they're impossible to ignore."

She takes them off, places them in her purse.

"And I wouldn't advise wearing them again," he warns her, "unless you're looking to be found."

"All right, point taken." She glances around. "So will you tell me the plan now?"

He nods. "We stay here, in the bazaar, until enough time has passed, until we're certain he is no longer following, and then we head to the docks. There is a ferry that leaves for Bursa at noon."

She smiles, weakly. "And we sail away, across the Bosphorus."

"Something like that."

"But why here?" she asks, looking around them, unease evident on her face.

"We're surrounded by people. There isn't much he can do with an audience watching."

And yet even as he says the words, he already sees him, already knows that he is wrong.

The man is standing just behind Louise now, though she hasn't noticed him yet. Henri feels his heart sink, feels his stomach churn, as he tries to figure out what to do, whether they should run or stand still—knowing all the while that there is no way out of their current situation.

"What is it?" Louise asks, her face filled with fear. He hasn't seen it before—she's always so defiant in her expressions, turning angry when she should be afraid—but it's there now, fear turning her features into something that makes his stomach ache. Her eyes widen then, and she gives a small gasp. Henri knows the man has placed the pistol in her back. She raises her eyes to Henri. He does his best not to look as hopeless as he feels.

"Straight ahead, toward the shop just there," the man says. He waits until Louise begins to turn, keeps close to her, his pistol hidden. "The three of us need to have a chat."

Together, they sit outside the café on Yağlikçilar Caddesi, at one of the wooden tables covered with an Anatolian cloth. Henri glances inside and sees a room with no exit—apart from the cavern-ous ceiling, chipped and peeling, at the top of which a bit of light shines through from a window above. Useless, then.

The three of them sit in silence until the waiter appears. When he does, Henri speaks first, in Arabic, hoping he understands. "Tha-laatha Qahwa bi-Duuna Sukkar," he says. "IttaSil bi-ShshurTati, min FaDlika. Haadha ar-Rajulu yuhaddidunaa."

The waiter frowns slightly, before giving a short bow.

"What was that?" the man asks, in Spanish, once the waiter has left. "What did you say to him?"

"I ordered coffee," Henri replies.

The man nods, smiles. "You speak Arabic now as well?"

Henri shrugs.

The man narrows his eyes. "That was a lot of words for just an order for coffee."

"I told him not to put in any sugar." He pauses, watches the man. "I remember that you don't like it too sweet."

The man nods at this. "If this is true, you are fine, but if it is not—" He gives a small shrug and they fall into silence, Louise watching both of them with a deepening frown.

The waiter returns a short while later, placing three cups before them, a piece of lokum sitting on the saucer of each. The man picks up his sweet with his right hand—his left has remained firmly beneath the table—and places it onto Louise's saucer. "It makes my teeth ache," he says by way of explanation.

"How did you find her?" Henri asks. He knows how the man followed her to the restaurant, but he means before that, even. He's curious to know how the man found the hotel she was staying at when he had been so careful not to mention it before.

"The porter from the train." He levels his gaze at Henri. "Do you really think I would let her slip away, let you slip away, if I didn't know where you both were going?" He looks between them. "Where is it?"

Neither of them responds.

"The wire transfer, have you done it yet?" he presses.

Louise lifts her chin. "There is no wire transfer," she says in English.

The man frowns, looks to Henri. "What is she saying?"

Henri looks down at his coffee, though he wants to look at her, to examine her face, to try and ascertain what it is that she is doing, whether she is saving both of them or only herself. He doesn't know, can't decide, but there isn't time to learn. "She said there is no wire transfer."

"There never was a wire transfer," she says, switching to French. "I only put the receipt in my bag as a way to throw off anyone who might come looking."

The man shakes his head, turns to Henri. "Tell me."

Henri doesn't know how much the man can understand. He suspects enough, but he translates the words into Spanish, knowing that this is the point, that he wants to hear it from Henri himself. "There never was, she said. It was only to stall."

The man lets out a noise of disbelief. "What did she promise you?" he asks Henri. "A cut of the money? Something else?"

Before Henri can respond, Louise turns to the man, asks in French, "Vous pouvez me comprendre, n'est-ce pas?" He hesitates, then nods. "Good. Then I will tell you myself. No need for him to translate," she continues, indicating to Henri with a nod of her head. "There isn't any money to promise."

"What does that mean?" he demands.

She speaks slowly. "It means the money is gone."

The man bangs the table, curses. A group of men to their left look over and frown. When he recovers, he demands, "Where exactly has it gone to?"

"There was an accident," Louise says. "In Belgrade. The money was lost then."

It is a moment before the man speaks. "An accident?" he asks, frowning, as though he has misheard, or perhaps mistranslated.

"Yes."

"What type of accident?"

"In the Sava River. I fell into the water. It was late, and I had been drinking." She reaches for her coffee, and Henri can see that her hand is trembling. "I had taken some pills."

Another curse. The man lifts his hands, sets his head between them.

Henri looks to Louise, knows they are both thinking the same thing—the pistol. The one that has since disappeared but that Henri suspects he has kept a hand on, just underneath the table, perhaps resting on his knee, perhaps hidden away in his pocket. Now, for the first time, he has released it from his grip.

"Why would you have had the money on you?"

"I wasn't going to leave it in my hotel room—not when I was being watched. I put it in my purse."

"All of it?" The look on his face indicates that he does not believe her.

"I rolled it into bundles." She shifts. "If you want the money, that's where you'll have to look, I'm afraid. At the bottom of the Sava."

The man shakes his head. "And is that where I should put you, as well?"

She shrugs, places the piece of *lokum* that he set on her saucer into her mouth.

It happens suddenly then, all at once. A flurry of sound, of movement—the call of prayer filling the air—startling them all from their conversation. It causes the man to start in surprise, as one by one, the people around them begin to move, to lower themselves to the ground. It's a small moment, lasting no more than a few seconds, but it shakes them all from the intensity of their conversation, gives Louise and Henri time to look to each other, to decide. The rest unfolds quickly.

Henri stands—jumps, really—taking the table and its contents with him. Louise throws her leather satchel, which manages to connect with the man's face. Chaos erupts. Louise is gone, running up Yağlikçilar Caddesi, rounding the corner. Henri runs, following her lead. Behind him, he can hear the tumult he has just caused—angry words thrown in the air, followed by shouting. He pushes on, turning on Halicilar Caddesi, just as she has. He passes a stall selling Turkish lamps, the glow from the glass mosaics throwing patterns against the plaster walls. He passes vendor after vendor selling carpets, some hanging, pinned on the wall, others stacked from floor to ceiling. An idea begins to form in his mind. He slows, glances over his shoulder. There is no sign of the man yet.

"Louise," he calls ahead to her. She is only steps away now and she turns, panting, her face covered in a sheen of sweat. He motions to one of the shops. "In here," he says, doing his best to lower his voice, glancing over his shoulder once again to make sure they have not yet been discovered. "Quickly."

The man inside the shop says something in Turkish, Henri shakes his head, not understanding. He points to Louise. "*Yukhfiiha*," he says in Arabic. When the man hesitates, Henri takes a number of Turkish liras from his pocket, presses them into the man's hands. "*Hiya Barii'atun.*"

The man nods.

"What is it, what's happening?" Louise demands. "We shouldn't stop, should we? We should keep moving, or else he'll be here soon—he'll find us."

The old man turns to one of the rugs hanging on the wall, in the corner of the shop. He motions to Louise.

"He's agreed to hide you," Henri explains.

Louise glances toward the man and frowns. "What about you?"

"I'm going to run."

"Run where?"

Henri looks behind him. It was a good question—one he couldn't answer. "Just stay here and wait."

Louise makes a face, but allows Henri to lead her over to the carpets hanging from the wall. The old man and Henri work quickly, making sure that no part of her can be seen, setting a stack of carpets that rises to her knees in front of her. It might work, he thinks. Like the other shops in the bazaar, this, too, appears cavernous in its design, one carpet leading to another carpet, with row upon row, stack upon stack of varying designs and colors filling the otherwise small space. It is disorientating, he thinks. If Louise remains here long enough, if he can, in the meantime, lead the man away from the bazaar, there is a good chance this plan will work, that she will remain safe.

"You in there?" he asks, trying to keep his tone light.

"I can smell whatever they killed to make this," she says, her voice muffled now.

"Ah, that would be sheep. It looks like you're behind a kilim." He pauses. "They don't kill it, by the way. It's only sheared."

"Either way, I feel like Cleopatra."

He smiles. "Stay here. Don't leave until it's safe."

"And when will that be, exactly?"

He doesn't answer, begins to back away. She says his name, but he does not respond.

Outside the shop, Henri begins to run. He needs an exit but

doesn't know which way will lead him there. He turns, runs, finds himself in a vaulted hall, the Cevahir Bedesten, the very heart of the bazaar. All around him are priceless antiques—candlesticks, clocks, even weapons made of copper, brass, silver—so that he comes to an abrupt halt, fearful that he might destroy the things around him. A vendor approaches him, but Henri shakes his head, calls out, "*Cikis?*" The vendor points down one of the many streets in response.

Henri is thanking him, preparing to leave, when he hears a voice behind him, still at some distance. "Stay where you are!" the man shouts. Henri doesn't listen, only starts running once again. He can't believe that the man would really use his pistol here, with so many looking on. If he can just outrun him, find his way out, maybe he will stand a chance. He runs, his chest pounding, his breath coming in short gasps—and then suddenly, he feels the weight of the man crash into him, feels himself fall to the ground. He hears, rather than feels, the shattering of a mirror as they collide, the sounds of other objects knocked to the ground—broken, no doubt, beyond repair. He hears, too, the shouts of the vendor, the accusations, the curses, the demands. Both men are on their feet then. The man grabs Henri by the arm, pulls him close.

"There's nowhere to go now," the man says to Henri, and Henri thinks he sounds almost weary, rather than angry.

"No," Henri agrees.

"We're going to find the exit."

The vendor, still shouting, begins to approach them. Fulano waves his hand in warning and the vendor backs away, turning to survey the wreckage of his shop.

"Someone told me it was this way," Henri says, pointing, anxious to get the man away from the irate vendor, worried for his safety as well as his own. And then, because there is nowhere left to go, nowhere left to run, Henri tries the only plan he has left: "I can pay you the money. Not all of it, not right away. I could pay it back, eventually, through work."

The man shakes his head. "The money doesn't matter anymore."

Henri nods, knowing that it is true, knowing as well that this was always the conclusion. The man in front of him had never been tasked with just bringing back the money, doing away with the girl—no, Henri had been added to the list the moment he left Granada.

"We'll leave together now, no tricks."

Henri agrees. "No tricks."

The man motions for them to step away from the shop, where even now the seller is standing, wide-eyed, as the two men prepare to make their way down the street. Henri walks just slightly in front, the man at his back. He tries to think, but he has nothing left.

"And the girl. Where will I find her?" the man asks as they begin to walk.

"I don't know. She ran ahead and I couldn't keep up."

A laugh from behind. "Not so trustworthy a partner, was she?"

"No, I suppose not." He thinks of Louise then, hopes she is still hidden behind the kilim, that she will remain there, that the man will not return in search of her. Perhaps she will make the ferry after all.

"Slowly," the man behind him says. "Remember, no tricks."

"No."

"Just walk normally, and I promise it will be quick." The man pauses. "If not, I make no promises."

Henri thinks he is telling the truth. Something tells him that while the man behind him is not good—but then, neither is he—he is honorable, will keep his word if promised. That is something.

And to not suffer at the end, that is also something. Henri nods, but even as he does so, he knows that something is amiss—the pistol, he realizes. He can no longer feel the sharp bite of it in his side. He thinks of the scuffle before, when they fell against the vendor's shop, tries to remember whether he has seen the man in possession of the pistol since. No, it had not been there. He must have lost it, must have let it fall from his grip when they crashed into one another. Which means that Henri still has a chance. He stops walking, hears the man begin to protest.

Henri turns toward him, fists raised—when a shot rings out.

SIXTEEN

LOUISE

Louise hears the gunshot, muffled, from behind the carpet. She jumps, as though the pistol is aimed at her, the shot fired in her direction. She squeezes her eyes shut, waits for another to sound—but there is nothing, only silence. Then the distant sound of a shrill whistle.

She untangles herself from behind the carpet. Her skin is flushed from the heat of the wool; she can feel it, her hands like ice when she raises them to her cheek. "Thank you," she murmurs to the shopkeeper, who is looking off in the direction of the gunshot. "*Merci*," she says again.

The man nods, visibly shaken, but does not smile.

She leaves his shop quickly.

Back on one of the souk's many streets, she searches for an exit, wonders how she will ever be able to find one. She doesn't know what she had imagined earlier, when Henri first mentioned the Grand Bazaar—a few lanes filled with shops, similar to the passages in Paris. She had been mistaken. This is nothing like that. The bazaar is labyrinthine, an entire city unto itself. She cannot even imagine how far it must stretch, cannot imagine how many arms and legs it possesses in its offshoots.

She chooses one way, at random, begins to walk, trying not to hurry, trying not to look out of place. She gathers her new scarf around her, hiding part of her face within the folds of the fabric, while doing her best to take in her surroundings.

Ahead, she can see a crowd has begun to gather. She stops, feels someone knock against her shoulder, hears them curse, but she doesn't respond, doesn't bother to offer her apologies. She's not sure she would be able to speak, even if she wanted to. Because she can see it now. Through the crowd—when someone shifts, placing their weight from one foot to the other, when they lean this way and that—an opening forms, and there it is, right before her. A body. *His* body or the man's body, she doesn't know, can't tell. She tries to get closer, but her legs are leaden, protesting against each and every step. She is only several feet away and yet still, she cannot see—does not want to see, she admits.

The glint of something catches her eye. It is just to the right, on the floor, in the thick of the crowd. She weaves herself through the mass of people, around one person and then another, averting her eyes from the scene unfolding before her, deciding as she does so that she doesn't want to know, doesn't want to see, what has happened, whose body lies before her. She only wants to investigate this glinting object, because she thinks she knows what it is, and then she wants to be gone, disappeared from this place before anyone notices her.

She hears the whistle of the police and grimaces. She needs to be fast.

She tells herself that there is no time, that he is beyond her help—perhaps even beyond time, though she doesn't let herself dwell too long on this possibility. This is who she is, after all. Someone who leaves the ones closest to her dead or dying. But no, Henri is not her father, is nothing like him, and what is happening now isn't at all the same. The realization makes her start, makes her look, up and toward the two slumped figures only several paces from where she hides.

She sees him—Henri—watches as he begins to stand, arms held high, and she feels the breath catch in her throat. He is alive, then. Not dead, not dying, not even injured, she realizes, her eyes scanning over his body, her gaze greedy now for what it has been denied. She notices blood then, and the man who has been following them, slumped on the ground, clutching his leg. Good, she thinks.

The police are growing closer now. There is nothing she can do to save him—he is beyond her help, but not, she knows now, beyond time. There is that, at least.

After, Louise wills herself to slow her breathing, which has become short and raspy. Walking in the opposite direction, she passes by bolts of fabric, one stacked on top of another, creating a cave made entirely of silk and wool and other blends she knows after years of working in a laundry, but that she cannot think of in that moment. She pretends to nod at the embroidery, reaching out a hand, touching here and there, trying her best to make it look as though her steps are unhurried, despite her desperation now to escape this place, desperate for light, for air. She thinks of the oubliette, of the light shining at the top—and she can see it, that same beacon of light, of hope, just before her, only steps away. It is as though she has conjured it, the exit, freedom, just steps from where she stands. She worries that it is a mirage, knows that it is not. She breathes, slowly, softly, begins to increase her gait. It is closer now, in mere seconds, she will be there—she will be free. She covers the last of the distance quickly, not caring who will notice, who will see. She pulls at her scarf, feels her blood pounding—and finally she is there, standing just outside the gate, the sun on her face, so that she feels as though she can breathe again. She takes a big, shuddering breath, lets the mill of people separate and re-form around her. She is out of the bazaar and she is alive.

She takes one step forward, and begins to run.

For the first ten minutes or so, Louise runs blindly. Somehow, she manages to find herself in another bazaar, and she worries for a moment that she has only gone in a circle, that she has ended up at exactly the same point at which she began. History repeating itself, she thinks. Slowing to a fast walk, not wanting to draw any un-wanted attention, she looks around. Mounds of spices, of paprika and sumac, conical shapes made up of deep reds and rich yellows, surround her on either side. A vendor spots her, calls out, indicates a row of tea leaves, dotted with rose petals, with dried oranges, with buds of flowers that she can't identify. She sees hibiscus, dried and bloodred, waiting to be scooped up and purchased. To all this, Louise shakes her head, does her best not to look as frantic as she feels, and pushes on.

This is something different, she tells herself, another bazaar, not the one from which she just escaped. She whispers it, over and over, softly to herself, worrying all the while that she is going mad. That she is already dead. It occurs to her that the shot she heard before was for her, that she has already died, hidden in that stinking carpet. That now, here, does not actually exist, that it is only some sort of purgatory she is forever locked within, destined to try and find her way out, to fail, for the remainder of time and beyond. For surely, there is no time when it comes to purgatory, only a nothingness, an emptiness that stretches on and on.

Louise pushes the thought from her mind, tells herself to stop being so ridiculous—she doesn't believe in destiny, after all. Only herself.

Eventually, she finds her way to the port. The city is fully awake now—carts of steaming *simit*, trolleys with tea and coffee line the streets. She glances at them all, feels her stomach ache with hunger.

She ignores the feeling, only pushes forward.

At the Sirkeci docks, she purchases a ticket that will take her to Bursa. It's not as far as she had hoped, but it's something. It will take her out of this city, away from the man who is looking for her—the *men*, she corrects herself. She shakes her head. If she allows herself to think about it now, about *him*—no, she cannot afford such sentiment. Not now. Not when she has only fifteen minutes left before the boat departs, fifteen minutes between her and the start of her life.

Louise stands anxiously, her palms sweating. She cannot stop herself from glancing over her shoulder every few minutes, doesn't know who she expects to see. To distract herself, she wanders over to a stall that has been erected by the docks. An older woman, her hair wrapped in a colorful handkerchief of green, pink, and blue, stands behind it, selling fruit. Louise hands her a few Turkish liras and is rewarded with a large bag of apricots.

She leans forward, can smell the sweetness of the orange-and-red dimpled fruit inside. The old woman says something then, but Louise cannot understand. She reaches for Louise's hand, places something cold and ceramic there. Louise looks down, sees a charm of some sort, in the shape of a palm. She doesn't know if the woman is offering or selling, but she presses a few more liras into her hand and places the charm in the pocket of her coat.

Back at the dock, the boat is boarding. Louise takes a deep breath, prepares for the journey across the Sea of Marmara. She turns toward the ferry but is stopped by the pressure of a hand, grabbing her lightly by the arm. She glances over her shoulder, half expecting to find the old woman standing behind her, asking for more money.

"How?" she demands, looking into his face.

SEVENTEEN

HENRI

When Henri hears the shot ring out, he is certain he has come to the end at last.

He drops to the ground, instinct taking over. A moment passes, then another. His ears ring, blocking out all noise, all explanation. But then gradually, his senses come back. He is not bleeding, not dead. He is still alive. And the man—he, too, is on the ground, but turned away from Henri, his arms wrapped around his leg, his pants stained dark with blood. Fulano, Henri realizes, is not the one who has fired.

He can see them now, the Turkish police, pistols pointed in their direction.

Henri is still on the ground, his body half-hidden by the man who lies in front of him. He decides quickly. Reaching out, he grabs at the nearest item to him, a brass pocket watch, one of the many items still scattered from their earlier fall. He starts to stand—at the instructions of the police, who are drawing nearer—shuffling closer to Fulano, his left side obscured by the man's right. Carefully, he takes the pocket watch and drops it into the man's coat pocket, which hangs now, slightly away from his body. Henri waits, certain Fulano will feel it—but there is nothing, no movement, nothing at all that indicates he has noticed the change in weight. The man is too busy assessing the damage to his leg.

Henri's eyes catch on the vendor then, who is staring directly at him—at what he has done.

He curses quietly, the police are nearly there now. He lifts his left arm to his coat pocket, extracts the bills there, and drops them to the floor. As he stands, his foot sweeps them in the direction of the man, though he is careful to never lift his leg from the floor. The amount, he knows, is far greater than the piece the vendor was no doubt trying to pass off as an Ottoman antique, greater than any damage they might have caused earlier.

Fulano must have felt this last gesture, for he turns toward Henri now, the motion causing the police to shout louder. They both lift their hands, and Henri takes this moment to step slightly away, to shout in Arabic—loudly, with the hope that someone will understand him—"*Saariqun!*" He indicates to the man before him, shouting again, "Thief!"

"What are you telling them?" the man demands, not turning, still clasping his leg. But Henri does not respond, only shouts louder until at last, one of the policemen frowns, calls out something to the others, and they pause before shifting their attention to the man in front of him. The same policeman shouts something to the vendor, a question, and the vendor looks only a moment at Henri before nodding his head, his words coming then, fast and urgent.

One of the policemen approaches, places his hands in both pockets of the man's coat—despite his vehement protests, despite his groans of pain—and produces a pocket watch. The man stares in disbelief. "That isn't mine," he shouts in Spanish—but they ignore him, lifting him to his feet. They begin to move him away, toward an exit, when the man turns his head back to Henri, his hands behind his back now. Henri tries to read his face, feels something like guilt, but knows, too, that it is the only way.

Afterward, there are many questions. It takes time, switching between one language and then another, until they can all understand. Henri takes out his identification card, the one that shows he is gendarmerie, just like them. It's a risk, a gamble, but he knows that the probability of them being able to read the script, of paying that close attention, is small, and his need to disappear from the bazaar is, in that moment, far greater.

Henri stutters, does his best to explain as they stand there, an imposing block of blue, in halting Arabic, exactly what has happened. How the man they now hold had been following him, making threats. How he had done his best to get away, but then he had seen what the man had done, the item he had stolen from the stall. The shopkeepers standing around support his story, agreeing that the man had been following him, making threats, although they can't locate the gun that some claim to have seen. The owner of the shop from which the pocket watch was stolen turns out to be especially helpful.

By the time everything is explained, Henri's passport handed back to him, a word of caution thrown his way about trusting strangers, about being a stranger in a foreign country, he is all but convinced that she will be gone. That by the time he makes his way to the docks—if that is even where she is, thinking of the restaurant earlier, all the notices tacked up on the board—the ferry to Bursa is sure to have departed. But then, somehow, he manages to get there in time, manages to push his way through the crowd of embarking passengers and finds her, standing in her black wool coat, about to board.

"How?" she repeats again.

"The Turkish police," Henri responds.

Understanding crosses her face. "The coffee shop, when you ordered. You told him to call."

"Yes."

"But they might have—"

"Yes." He had considered it, thought it worth the risk, thought if it came down to it, they would tell the police the money belonged to the man—which wasn't a lie—and that he was trying to force them to cross borders with it, knowing it was tied to illegal activities.

"And where is he, the man? Where is he now?"

"Gone." Henri smiles, though they both know that this respite is only temporary.

The ferry is still boarding, the crowd growing less.

She takes a step nearer to him, closing the gap, so that they are only inches from each other. "I can't give you the money," she says, pulling her coat closer to her body.

"I know." He expects nothing less. She cannot give the money back and he cannot let her take it—it is the thing he has known since the very beginning, that they have both known, the dilemma that they have been hurtling toward ever since that day in Granada, however much he had lied and told himself it would be resolved before this moment. He has always known otherwise, has known that she will try to leave, that he cannot let her. That something else would have to happen for such an impasse to be breached.

And then he feels it—this thing needed to end their current deadlock—cold and hard, pressed against his abdomen, just below his rib cage. A quick glance down confirms his suspicion. He meets her eyes, wondering whether it is the same one and knowing that of course it is, because it's the only thing that makes sense. He wonders where she found it, at what point. It shouldn't matter, but it does.

The intention behind it. Now, it is his turn to look at her and ask, "How?"

"I came running, after the shot. I saw a body on the ground and the pistol not far off."

He nods, doesn't need her to explain the rest—how she had taken the gun, decided to save herself. He doesn't blame her. There was nothing she could have done in that moment to help him, and even if she could have, well, he doesn't think he would fault her for that either. He knows her now, knows that nothing she does is by chance or accident. He is the only part that she has not decided upon, not entirely.

He thinks then of the things that she told him the night before, those things that could only be said, whispered, in the dead of night, face half-hidden, obscuring the whole truth. Those things that she thought made her a monster, that meant her ending was written, a conclusion necessary in response to her crime. He does not know what the end will be, not for either of them, but he decides in that moment that it will not be here, that it will not be this. If she is to be caught and punished for her crimes, he will not be the one to do it.

Her hand is trembling as he steps back.

He feels the pressure against his abdomen ease as he says: "This is not the end." And then, he says more softly, *"Haadhihi laysat na-haayatanaa yaa Habiibati."* He knows the words will be unfamiliar to her, but he hopes that she might understand them, all the same.

Louise appears startled, uncertain, even, as if she cannot figure out how to respond, and before she can, before he learns what she might have been about to say, a dock attendant comes up from behind and she hides the pistol quickly within the folds of her coat. "Ticket?" he asks, to which she responds by holding up a shaking piece of paper. He takes the ticket from her hand, pointing her toward the boat.

Still, she does not move, only watches Henri, expectant. The dock attendant is speaking again, just behind her, his voice terse, his tone imploring. "Yes," she calls, over her shoulder. "Yes, I'm coming." Louise moves quickly then, coat clutched tightly between her hands. She settles one final glance upon him. She does not turn around again.

From the dock, Henri watches the ferry as it sets off across the Bosphorus. He tries to imagine where she will go next—the souks of Cairo, the bazaars of Aleppo, perhaps even the *yokochos* of Japan. He thinks he could imagine her in any of them, all of them. It occurs to him, as he stands there, that it is the second time in his life he has stood on the docks, watching someone he cares for sail away. This feels different; but then, he is different, the implacable stubbornness of youth and all that is born from it gone. And for the first time in a long time, he can see the possibility of the future and what it might hold.

He will go back to Spain, first, to face what he has done, and then after—if there is to be an after—somewhere he can begin again. He knows that the nightmares might never stop, might continue to haunt him until the very end—whether that be days or years from now—but he thinks, if allowed, he might learn to live with them, with the choices he has made and the regret he holds for those he has not. He thinks that one day, perhaps, they may even lead him back to Oran, to confront the past.

One day—but not tomorrow.

He can see her now, leaning against the balcony. He feels the breeze as it flits across the water, carrying with it the smells of the city, a trace of jasmine just on the edge. The sun pierces through the clouds, obscuring his vision, the dazzling light reflecting off the waters of the Bosphorus so that for a moment he can no longer see the figure on the boat, or anything at all; his vision filled with nothing but that bright light. He feels full of something he has not felt for many years now, if ever, and he sees it, the start of something ahead.

By the time his vision returns, she is no longer there.

EPILOGUE

Oran, Algeria

A woman with pink sunglasses pushes through the door of the restaurant.

"Table for one," she tells the host. "On the balcony, please."

She wears a black kaftan, her blond hair swept back into a chignon. There have not been many like her in recent years, she knows, though more have begun to return now. Still, she knows that no one will mistake her for one of these—someone who belonged to this place before—for while her French is nearly perfect in its accent, there is still something in it that marks her as foreign.

The man nods and she follows him, carefully lifting her kaftan so as not to stumble on the stone steps beneath. Outside the sun is blazing. She places a hat on her head, then takes it off, the wide rim obscuring her vision as she pauses to admire the view from the balcony. The mountains lie to the right, and surrounding that, surrounding everything, there is the sea, startling in its clarity.

She had admired the view on the drive from the city, in the car she has hired for the day, darting quick glances at the rugged coastline, the Mediterranean just beyond, her knuckles turning white as she completed yet another hairpin turn that took her closer, too close, to the water's edge. This is different somehow, she thinks, standing on the patio, her hands clasping the wrought iron balcony. Here, it appears as if there is no barrier between her and the sea below. She brings her hand to her neck, where a Hand of Fatima lies between her collarbones.

At the table, she points at the menu, tells the waiter, "I'll have this one," before amending to, "*Je vais prendre ceci.*" She is certain the waiter understood her the first time, but she makes the switch to French anyway. It's been months since she last had the opportunity to use it, and it feels good, her muscle memory flexing, returning her to a former version of herself that she has almost managed to forget. "*Et un verre de vin aussi, s'il vous plaît.*"

Her gaze sweeps the balcony. There are a number of other patrons at this hour. Couples, families, two children who have either finished eating or refuse to start, and who are now running back and forth across the space, daring one another to the edge. Their mother yells and they calm down, retreating to a corner. Both of their noses are already burnt from the sun.

"*Cette place, est-elle libre?*" a man asks, standing before her, his hand clasped on the back of the only other chair at her table.

She reaches forward, her touch gentle but firm. "*Non, désolée, monsieur,* this seat is taken."

Her meal arrives shortly after. Grilled fish on a plate of couscous. A salad of tomato and cheese. She eats quickly, famished by the day's earlier excursion, then lights a cigarette. She had spent the morning walking the corniche, gazing out at the port. In the early afternoon, she had hired the car that now waits outside for her, had taken it to the fortress on the top of the mountain, peered out at the town below, at the mountains, at the sky and sea—she tries to remember what it is called, that type of startlingly clear blue. The type that looks as though it has no ending point, but only goes on and on forever.

"*Vous desirez autre chose*, mademoiselle?"

"*Oui, un café.*" She pauses, trying to remember if she had seen it listed on the menu. "*Avez-vous du creponne?*"

He smiles. "*Oui, mademoiselle.*"

When it arrives, she pauses for a moment, taking in the white-colored confection, the iced sorbet that appears almost as though it is cream. She has found herself dreaming of it lately. Closing her eyes, she takes a spoonful. It tastes of lemon, but something else as well—something sharp and sweet, so different from the offerings found in other *gelaterias* she has visited. Eventually, the waiter brings the bill, but she pays it little attention.

It has taken her time to reach Oran. Several years have passed since that day she set sail in Istanbul, when she had planned never to return, when she had thought to outrun her narrative, rather than write it anew. It has taken nearly as long to translate the words he had whispered that day, on the docks. The endearment, she had understood, had whispered to herself over the coming days, weeks—*my love*—but the rest had remained a mystery she refused to solve.

Instead, she kept them close, memorizing the words, tracing them into her palm, until eventually, along the road, she began to query one word and then another, until she had collected them all. She had placed them together then, had arranged them and held them up to the light and finally seen what it was that he had said—a promise, and an invitation, she knew, one without a beginning or end, without place or time. At first, she had not known how to begin, where to start her search. But then she remembered—what she had called him once, before he had a name, before they had been introduced, on that train to Istanbul.

The Man from Oran.

She glances at her watch now, tells herself there is no rush. From her bag, she retrieves a novel, the stamped image of a black homburg and mustache on its cover. There are still several hours with the car yet, and besides, she has come all this way. Something catches her eye then—a man, standing at the entrance of the balcony. She watches as he steps forward, into the sun, and swoops up one of the children in his embrace. His face—a stranger's, she can see now—breaks into a smile. No matter—she has time. She signals to the waiter, orders another *café*.

Louise tilts her face to the sun, adjusts her sunglasses, and waits to be found.

ACKNOWLEDGMENTS

To everyone who helped make this book possible, a huge thank-you is in order. To my agent, Elisabeth, for your constant words of encouragement and your patience with my tendency to finish a draft, toss it, and start again on something new, despite impending deadlines; to my editor, Zack, for your continued enthusiasm for the stories and characters that I bring you and your guidance in shaping these into a proper novel; and to everyone at Flatiron for their continued support, I am more appreciative than I can express.

This book spans a number of countries and languages, but because of the pandemic, I wrote every word from behind my desk in the United States. As such, I owe a huge thank-you to all my friends throughout the world for helping with all matters of inquiries. To Belinda for reaching out from Australia to her friends in South America for all my questions relating to Spanish; to Jessica for taking time out from visiting family in Lebanon to look at my Arabic; to Sarah for reminding me there are different dialects of Arabic and then generously reaching out to her colleague in Dubai (thank you, Dr. Kassem Wahba) for questions about North African Arabic; and finally to Jamie, thank you for working on the

Acknowledgments

French translations during your own work/holiday in Europe, as my own knowledge never managed to progress beyond secondary-school level. Thank you as well to Glen, for answering all my questions on matters of money in the UK during the 1960s. And to Belinda, Marta, Sarah, and Deb for all the messages and Zoom calls, for listening to my worries and doubts throughout the whole process. It's been ages since I've been to any of the places mentioned in this book, and longer still since I've seen some of you in person, thanks to the pandemic. I'm hopeful I'll have the opportunity to say thank you again soon, this time in person.

ABOUT THE AUTHOR

Christine Mangan is the author of the national bestseller *Tangerine* and *Palace of the Drowned*. She has her Ph.D. in English from University College Dublin, with a focus on eighteenth-century gothic literature, and an MFA in fiction writing from the University of Southern Maine.